Barry Arthur was born in London and lived in England until, at the age of twenty-two, he boarded a ship to Australia – just to see what it was like. For the next thirty years he travelled extensively, living in France, Spain, England and Australia, and working intermittently, when completely unavoidable, as a Chartered Loss Adjuster. He currently lives with his wife, Linda, on a six-acre property in the Swan Valley, a wine-making region near Perth, Western Australia.

RED BACKPACK PINK SARONG

Barry Arthur

Ashcroft Publishing

Red Backpack Pink Sarong

Copyright © Barry Arthur 2012

Ashcroft Publishing
41 Dalgety Road, Middle Swan,
Western Australia, 6056
ashcroftpublishing@gmail.com

National Library of Australia
Cataloguing-in-Publication entry:
Arthur, Barry
Red Backpack Pink Sarong / Barry Arthur

ISBN 978-0-9870678-3-8

Cover photograph Mark Arthur
Author photograph Michael Fuller

*To my wife, Linda, whose support
and belief in me made it happen.*

*To the sarong sellers and masseuses
of Padangbai*

*With special thanks to Kadek,
who befriended me.*

CHAPTER ONE

Wednesday

'Daddy, what's the difference between being lonely and being alone?' asked Debra.

I looked carefully at my two children. It was generally at breakfast that they ambushed me with these questions, just as I was about to leave for work. I replied cautiously, knowing that the wrong words would lead to an endless interrogation.

'Alone is being on your own when you want to be, and lonely is being on your own when you don't want to be.' I felt happy with my answer. It was clear, concise and didn't encourage further questions.

I exchanged a glance with Allison and could see she didn't expect me to get off so lightly. As usual, I was rushing and needed to leave straight away if I were to meet up with Tom. I pushed my chair back and picked up my briefcase.

'I have to go,' I said.

Joshua ignored this and entered the debate. 'Then why are there more lonely people in big cities than anywhere else? I mean, you hardly ever get the chance to be on your own, because wherever you go there are thousands of people, so you should never be lonely.'

Allison was smiling. I thought quickly. I needed a clincher, or at least something that would slow them down long enough for me to make my escape before they thought of the next question.

'It's because there are a lot more people in big cities, so there are more lonely people in total, but not necessarily per capita,' I said, edging towards the door.

I seized my chance while Joshua and Debra were working it out, and with practised coordination, I kissed my daughter's cheek, the top of my son's head and brushed my lips against Allison's, before calling from the hallway, 'Have a great day everyone. See you tonight. I shan't be late.'

Allison remarked loudly enough that I could hear, 'The only time we see Dad move fast is when he's leaving the house.'

Every weekday morning Tom and I met at the junction of Railway Parade and Oakover at quarter to eight. He was late today and I stood at the corner and watched him hurrying towards me, a tall, heavily-built, untidy man, his baggy trousers flapping like washing. Twenty years ago, long before I knew Tom, he had been a heavyweight boxer and later played first-class rugby. He was now out of condition, but still formidable and looked as though he would be happier on the playing field than in his city office. He appeared uncomfortable in his suit, like a tramp dressed up for a wedding.

'Sorry, Geoff, Marilyn's car wouldn't start and I had to push it. She's had it less than two weeks and this is the third time. I still owe Nightingale's a thousand quid, but I'm damned if I'm paying them until they fix it.'

'*Ode to a Nightingale*,' I murmured. '*My heart aches and a drowsy numbness pains my sense, as though of hemlock I had drunk.*'

'Ah, very clever, Geoff. Yeats, wasn't it?'

'Close,' I said, 'Keats. Right, Tom, let's get a move on.'

We walked on with more urgency than usual, our steps punctuated with the companionable bump of briefcases. Tom paused in his stride and pointed to the defeated back of a fellow commuter up ahead. 'There's Harry Watson. His wife walked out on him last week.'

'Why did she do that?'

'According to Marilyn, she couldn't stand the monotony. Harry came home from work every night and plonked himself in front of the telly until bedtime, while she wanted to go to the cinema, or out dancing or something. At weekends he'd work around the house and garden, so they never did anything much.'

'Sounds pretty normal to me. If all the wives round here walked out on husbands who were too knackered to do anything during the week and spent their weekends doing chores there wouldn't be any marriages left.'

'You're probably right,' said Tom, 'but *their* only entertainment was the monthly meeting of the Woking Tripe Society, of which Harry is the president.'

'*Tripe Society?* Do they eat it or talk it?'

'They eat it,' said Tom. 'Mind you, knowing Harry Watson, they probably talk it as well, but the main object is to keep alive the grand old tradition of tripe eating.'

'That's like speaking Cornish or Esperanto. Completely useless, but some people insist on doing it. I'm starting to sympathise with his wife, though. Not many marriages would survive a monthly dose of tripe.'

Tom and I turned the corner and the station building was in front of us. The red brickwork was cracked and the once-white paint was grey from traffic fumes and dust. Work was due to start on a new train and bus complex next year, and the stately old building had been allowed to fall into disrepair. By the time the bulldozers arrived it would have collapsed on its own.

'An undignified end,' I said.

Tom didn't hear me. With an unexpected burst of energy he bounded up the station steps two at a time, and at the summit he pivoted and surveyed the scene below. I joined him in a more leisurely manner and at the top of the steps I looked back. A listless group of commuters was approaching the station. There was very little joy on display and their pace was slowing noticeably, as though in the illogical belief that if they dawdled long enough the train would leave without them and they could turn round and go home.

'Poor buggers,' said Tom.

The glum faces reminded me of football supporters leaving the ground after a home defeat.

'And that includes us,' he added.

'Come on, Tom, it could be a lot worse. Let's face it, we could be living in Afghanistan or Luton. Anyway, cheer up, it's Wednesday and only three more days to the weekend.'

'I know,' Tom said gloomily. 'I spend my whole week wishing the days away so that the weekend comes round. Then that goes so fast, before I know it, it's Monday and it starts all over again. Sundays are ruined for me just thinking about going to work the next day. So, really, I have a one-day weekend.'

I looked at Tom sympathetically. 'You need to change your job.'

'That's easy for you to say, but who's going to employ a middle-aged insurance clerk? No, I'm stuck there, Geoff. Nowadays, everyone wants these whiz kids out of university who can take a computer apart in their tea break.'

'Yes, but their trouble is they can never put it back together again,' I pointed out. The train was in and the station clock showed three minutes to eight. 'Come on, let's buy our papers and get on, otherwise we're going to miss it.'

Debra and Josh had left for school amid the last minute dramas of forgotten homework and lost lunch money, and now the house was quiet. For Allison, the first minutes were blissful, but soon the house became stifling. Her world had shrunk so much she felt that if she stretched out her hands she could touch its sides. But today was different; today, she and Marilyn were having an adventure. She looked down and saw that her fingers were trembling, and she tried to remember when she had last felt like this.

Allison dressed slowly while she studied herself in the mirror. Her figure was good, despite her two children and nearing forty. The grey dress was better suited for an interview than lunch at the Regent, but she looked cool and elegant, and it was important that she did not create the wrong impression. She sat at the dressing table to put on her make-up and looked at her face critically. Even features, firm jaw and clear hazel eyes. Too many lines, but these give it character and worldliness, or at least that's what the magazines tell you. They also tell you that life begins at forty, but begins what? She grinned and stuck out her tongue. Begins to go downhill fast, that's what.

Allison and Marilyn's lives were intertwined. Their husbands travelled to work together on the train and their children went to the same school. Marilyn and Allison sweated at the gym and went shopping together, and now today they were playing truant together. She heard Marilyn's car pull into the drive and snapped the vanity case shut. She got up and walked to the front door, exaggerated the swing of her hips and laughed at herself.

Travelling to work on the train was usually a silent affair, with Tom and I absorbed in our papers. Sometimes, one of us would comment about an item of sport's news or the exploits of a celebrity, but rarely about anything serious. It was as though we were emptying our brains in readiness for the corporate world we were about to enter. This morning, though, Tom had something on his mind.

'Have you noticed the current preoccupation with gays?'

I looked sideways at him. 'I hope to God you're not about to make an announcement, Tom.'

'No, of course not. It just seems, though, that wherever you go people are ramming their homosexuality down your throat.'

I smiled at Tom's choice of words. 'Well, it *is* fashionable at the moment to be gay. These things come in cycles. I'm waiting for it to be fashionable to be middle-aged and overweight. Anyway, why are you mentioning it?'

Tom hesitated. 'Well, my cousin's son has just come out, as they say, and told the whole family that he's a poof. Well, I don't suppose those were his exact words, but the point is I, for one, would rather not know. I mean, I don't go round telling everyone I'm heterosexual, but gays feel they're obliged to let the world know, as though it's something wonderful, like they've discovered the meaning of life.'

I digested this revelation. 'It must be hard for his parents.'

'They're devastated. They were looking forward to having grandchildren and that's not going to happen now.'

'It might only be a phase,' I suggested. 'He's still young, and surely he's had girlfriends, hasn't he?'

'Yes, but he had boyfriends at the same time, although everyone thought they were just his mates.'

'He's had the best of both worlds then.' I thought for a moment. 'Perhaps he just needs a more masculine type of girlfriend. I could introduce him to Janice in accounts. She's a cross between Eva Braun and Margaret Thatcher and attractive in a butch sort of way. When I put my expenses in she interrogates me like the Gestapo. I'm convinced one day she'll whip out electrodes and clamp them on my testicles.'

'I don't think it would do any good, Geoff, not now he's come out. I'm afraid it's boys only from now on.'

We sat there immersed in thought. Tom's head sank lower into his jacket, as though he was burying it, ostrich-like, to hide from the cares of the world.

'Never been tempted yourself?' I asked.

'Good God, no. I can't think of anything more disgusting. What about you?'

'Well,' I said slowly, 'I've never actually tried it, but the opportunity has come along once or twice.'

'But you didn't find public toilets conducive to passion,' snorted Tom.

'No, I wasn't talking about those occasions. That happens to everyone, I suppose. Someone propositioning you, I mean. They need surveillance cameras in those places.'

'They couldn't do it, Geoff. It'd be an invasion of privacy. Pictures of Hugh Grant having a pee would end up splattered all over the gutter press.'

'Not a nice thought, although I can't imagine he uses public toilets very often.'

'Anyway,' prompted Tom, 'you were saying about opportunities.'

'Well, it was a long time ago. I met a girl called Wendy at a party and she invited me back to her flat in

Wembley. She was quite attractive and of course I accepted. You can imagine my surprise when we got there and she introduced me to her husband.' I paused, and I could feel Tom's interest quicken. 'He was a nondescript looking bloke and he greeted me in a friendly way, almost as though he was expecting me. I was thinking that somehow I'd got my wires crossed and I started to make excuses that I had to leave, but they asked me to sit down and have a drink. We chatted for a while and they kept pouring more drinks, and then Wendy mentioned, quite casually, that her husband was bisexual and he liked to watch her with other men.'

Tom cleared his throat noisily. 'Come off it, Geoff. Pull the other one.'

I turned sideways and looked at him. His face had gone red. 'Scout's honour, Tom,' I said. 'Well, by that time I'd had enough to drink to be game for anything, and Wendy suggested a game of strip Trivial Pursuit. I know it's hard to believe, Tom, but I swear this is all true. We played for a while and Wendy was soon down to just her skirt and bra. I remember being surprised at how busty she was. It hadn't been obvious when she was dressed. She was wearing a bra that was about two sizes too small and she was bursting out of the top of it.'

I felt Tom squirm in his seat next to me. 'Are you all right, Tom? Sitting comfortably? If so, I'll carry on. Well, I must tell you, there was an odd thing about their rules for playing strip Trivial Pursuit. I mean, I've always been good at general knowledge questions and I thought I'd probably keep most of my clothes on. But, the funny thing is, their rules were that you kept answering questions until you got one wrong, and then you removed a piece of clothing. So, it didn't matter how many questions you got right you were going to get one wrong eventually. So, each turn, you always had to take something off. It seemed quite logical at the time and, after all, I suppose the whole point of it was that we ended up without any clothes on. But, when you think about it, we might as well have not bothered playing Trivial Pursuit and simply taken it in turns to....'

'Christ, Geoff,' interrupted Tom, 'you're babbling. Get back on track. What happened then?'

'Oh, all right. Sorry, Tom. Well, her husband left the room and came back a few minutes later, stark naked, holding a great big, black dildo.'

Tom snorted in half disbelief. 'I wouldn't have thought you needed a dildo with two blokes there.'

I ignored him. 'But the thing was, Tom, I felt no desire for Wendy's husband. I mean, it was a novel situation and all that, but there was nothing there.'

'I'm pleased to hear it,' said Tom. 'By the way, does Allison know about this?'

'No, of course not. It isn't the sort of thing you talk to your wife about, is it?'

'Anyway,' grunted Tom, 'get on with it. What happened next?'

'Tom, I get off here.' I looked up and saw that the shield of newspapers had dropped and people close to us were unashamedly listening. One man simultaneously winked and nodded encouragement for me to continue.

'My station,' I announced firmly. 'I'm getting off.'

'Jesus, Geoff, you can't leave it there,' cried Tom.

I saw the disappointment on the faces around me and grabbed my briefcase. 'You'll just have to carry on without me,' I said. 'Use your imagination. I'm sure you'll think of a good ending.'

Allison opened the door. 'Holy shit!'

Marilyn was wearing a low-cut black cocktail dress and her honey-coloured breasts thrust out exuberantly.

The skirt stopped mid-thigh and her legs were bare and lightly tanned. She wore black high-heeled sandals and a gold ankle chain.

She looked coolly at Allison. 'Less of the religious expletives, Ally, even if you are dressed for church.'

'Well, at least I don't look as though I'm on the game.'

Marilyn laughed. 'The new bra is a bit special, isn't it?'

'You look like Jordan.'

'Not her, mine are genuine. They're just getting a bit of help. Anyway, how about a drink before we go?' Marilyn looked closely at Allison. 'Hey, you're not having second thoughts, are you?'

'Well, I wasn't until you arrived dressed like a tart, because I'd hate them to get the wrong idea.'

'The trouble with you, Ally, is that you don't go to these high-class places. Everyone dresses up like it's the Oscars and you see more flesh than on St Tropez beach. I tell you, people will think you've got some horrible skin disease, covered up like that.'

'Perhaps I'll just go in my bra and panties, then,' Allison muttered.

'I'm sorry, Al, seriously, you look great. I'm only joking. So, *are* you looking forward to it?'

'Yes, but suddenly I'm starting to feel a bit nervous.'

'That's a good reason for a drink. What about Geoff's Amontillado sherry he keeps for special occasions? I think this is one of them.'

CHAPTER TWO

Thursday

'Daddy, what's the difference between lost and mislaid?'

I glanced at Debra, who was looking intently at her cereal bowl, and I studied Joshua's face. He had an unusual look of innocence, which made me suspect that he had put Debra up to this. Allison was in the kitchen, and I could hear the clatter of crockery as she unloaded the dishwasher. We had hardly spoken this morning and yesterday evening she had been in a strange mood.

'Right,' I said, 'that's easy. Mislaid is when you can't find something because you've forgotten where you left it, and then it turns up later. Lost is when something is gone forever, like if you drop a ring over the side of a boat in the middle of the ocean.'

Joshua pounced. 'Then why does mum say she's lost her car keys every morning, and then finds them five minutes later in a coat pocket or somewhere. She should say she's mislaid them.' He was grinning broadly and Debra was giggling.

I laughed. 'Okay, you horrors, I'll give you that one. You set me up beautifully.'

Allison appeared at the dining room door. 'You two, start getting ready for school. Now! And I'm fed up with all your jokes about me losing my car keys.'

'Mislaying them,' corrected Joshua.

Allison glared at Joshua and he quickly got up from the table. I kissed the children goodbye and remarked mildly, 'Let's hope Mum hasn't lost her sense of humour and it's only mislaid.'

Allison turned her glare on me before I bolted for the door.

'Jesus, you look terrible!' There were dark circles around Tom's eyes and his face was the colour of unwashed laundry. He'd cut his neck shaving and the red line was like a failed suicide attempt. 'Go home. Take the day off.'

'Thanks a lot, Geoff, but I don't think so. For once, I was glad to leave the house this morning. Marilyn's been an absolute bitch.'

'That's odd, Allison's been a bit off too. You don't suppose they've fallen out do you?'

'I can't see why,' said Tom. 'They spend all day enjoying themselves while we're out at work. You wouldn't think they'd have anything to fall out about.'

'Well, I wouldn't change places with them. It must get pretty deadly living your life around children and housekeeping.'

Tom gave an apologetic flap of his hand. 'Sorry, I'm just feeling a bit down this morning. I've had a thought, though. It could be that Marilyn's in a foul mood because she's not looking forward to going with the kids to stay at her parents' place this weekend, when *I've* managed to get out of it.'

'How did you do that?'

'I told her I'm snowed under at work and need to spend time at home on the computer. It's partly true, but the main reason is I can't stand her old man and I'd rather do anything than go there. It could just be that Marilyn's annoyed because I'm not going.'

'Her parents are Scottish, aren't they?'

'More Scottish than Billy Connolly, but without a trace of his humour. Dour is the only word to describe them. And her cooking! Everything is full of oats and bran. The last time we went there I thought I'd been poisoned. Those gritty bits of neat roughage do appalling things to my insides.'

'Yes, I've heard that the Scots think *haute cuisine* is making porridge.'

He laughed. '*Oat cuisine.* That's very funny, Geoff. I'll tell them next time I see them. They'll be incensed by the slur on Scottish cooking. You know, I do believe I'm starting to feel a bit better.' He quickened his pace and began whistling *Mull of Kintyre.*

'I preferred it when you were miserable. At least I didn't have to listen to that noise.'

'There's nothing wrong with my whistling.'

'Tom, you're out of tune and you miss half the notes.'

'It sounds fine to me,' said Tom breezily.

'That's because you've got Van Gogh's ear for music.'

Tom continued with a dreadful rendition of *Isle of Skye* and I thought that I might have to listen to him whistling Scottish tunes all the way to the station, but I finally managed to distract him.

'You'll never guess what Joshua had to take to school yesterday ... a large carrot!'

Tom stopped whistling and looked interested. 'I thought they weren't teaching cookery, too demeaning or something. Anyway, when our kids grow up, all they'll eat is takeaways.'

'It was nothing like that, Tom. The carrot was for sex education.'

'Well, I don't want to hear what he did with it.'

'No, it was all quite harmless. A woman social worker was telling them about birth control.'

'I can't see what that's got to do with carrots.'

'They used them to practice putting on condoms,' I explained. 'I mean, you couldn't have half the class with their willies out, could you? But it did cause confusion and Josh said that one really dim boy actually thought that by putting the condom on a carrot it would stop a woman getting pregnant!'

Tom chuckled. 'I've heard that something similar happened in a tiny remote village in India. The social worker got them to practice using condoms by putting them on their fingers. I suppose they were out of carrots at the time. Anyway, about nine months later, they sent what was left of the condoms back, saying they were completely useless. It turned out that, during sex, the villagers had been putting the condoms on their fingers, both the men and the women – *and on all fingers*.'

I laughed. 'That's wonderful, but back to the carrots. It seems some of the boys were competing to see who could bring in the biggest carrot. You know that boy, Travis, whose mother does lingerie parties?' Tom nodded. 'Well, he managed to find a carrot the size of a cucumber and the woman didn't have a condom big enough. She kept trying to roll the largest condom over it, but when she got about half way down it would fly back up and plop on to the floor. The boys were in hysterics.'

'I bet they were,' grinned Tom, 'but I imagine it put half the girls off sex for life.'

'Yes and the other half are going to spend their lives searching, but disappointed.'

Wednesday

Marilyn weaved through the traffic and left in her wake a trail of surprised mid-morning motorists who were not used to someone disturbing their unhurried trips to the shops. The traffic became heavy as they neared the city and Marilyn was forced to slow to a crawl. She relaxed and turned to Allison.

'So, what do you think of the MG?'

'It's great, but there's not much room for the kids and the shopping, is there?'

'Ally, you never cease to amaze me. You're so ... *practical*. This car is meant to be fun. It's not designed for people with five kids and three trolley-loads of shopping. My two squeeze in, and if they start complaining I tell them to get out and walk.'

'Haven't you had some trouble with it, though?'

'Yes, but I got it fixed, although Tom doesn't know that. I told him this morning that it wouldn't start and he pushed me down the road. It does him good. He never gets enough exercise.' Marilyn laughed.

'You told Tom that the car wouldn't start when there was nothing wrong with it? What on earth did you do that for?'

'If I drink too much today, I'll leave the MG in the city and we'll get a cab home. I'll just tell Tom that the car wouldn't go. That's much better than saying I got ratted in the middle of the day.'

'Yes, I suppose it is.'

'And Kate and Gemma are going round to Cheryl's straight from school, and she'll drop them home about seven.'

'You've got this all worked out, haven't you?'

Marilyn grinned. 'Just using my initiative, Ally, which is something Tom says I don't have. Mind you, I'm sure he prefers me to be helpless and a bit dopey. It makes him feel needed, and not just for his salary cheque.'

'Marilyn, are you and Tom getting on all right? I know you joke about him being dull and not wanting to do anything, but I sometimes think you're really not happy. You can tell me if it's none of my business, but ...'

'That's okay, Ally, I don't mind you asking. Well, you know that Tom's a few years older than me and I was still at uni when we got married?' Allison nodded. 'Straight after uni I had Kate and soon afterwards Gemma. Since then my life's been looking after Tom and the girls. Sometimes, I feel that by getting married so young I missed out on a big part of my life ... *the fun part*. Just lately I've been thinking like that more often and it makes me depressed, although a few drinks usually fixes it. Anyway, let's get off the subject. I don't want one of my melancholy days today.'

Marilyn made an abrupt turn into the entrance of a multi-storey car park. 'We'll leave the MG here and walk,' she said. 'We've got twenty minutes, so we can have a drink while we're waiting.'

'Wouldn't it be better to be a few minutes late,' said Allison. 'They might think we're a bit keen if we're already there.'

'Look, Ally, they're paying us, so we're meant to be keen, and the least we can do is be on time.'

Thursday 8am

The station was gloomy this morning. There was no sun to brighten the platforms and I could see that Tom's spirits were sinking. The closer he got to work the more morose he became. He had a large mortgage on his house, Marilyn's new car hadn't helped their finances, and there was no obvious way he could escape from the job he loathed.

We had just sat down and were opening our papers, when Tom nudged me and whispered out of the side of his mouth, 'Geoff, look down the end of the carriage in the last seat. That's Roger Moore.'

'What, the film star?'

Tom grunted irritably. 'No, not the film star. Roger Moore, the film star, is about eighty and six foot three, whereas this Roger Moore is about thirty and five foot six. Apart from which, don't you think it's a bit unlikely that the film star is going to be travelling up on the eight o'clock commuter train?'

'All very good points, Tom. Anyway, what about him?'

'Well, he's just got out after twelve month's enforced vacation for burglary and assaulting a police officer.'

Tom seemed to know everything about everybody in the area, and it occurred to me that he would have made a good policeman or gossip columnist. He remembered tiny details of things that had happened years ago and had a scurrilous story about everyone. I sometimes wondered what he said about me.

I studied Roger Moore over the top of my paper. He was wearing a mustard-coloured suit and a fawn shirt. He had a pointed face with protruding eyes and his gingery hair was slicked back flat to his head. All in all, as unlovely an individual as you were likely to find on the train this morning.

'He looks like a weasel with a moustache,' I said unkindly. 'I wouldn't have thought you and he moved in the same circles.'

'We don't, but I remember the robbery because it was at the pub where Marilyn and I used to drink before we got married.'

'It's starting to ring a few vague bells, Tom, but you'll have to refresh my memory.'

'Well, he'd been in a bit of trouble before, but just petty things like pinching stuff out of cars, and then he got involved with a local gang. His first job with them was the Sail and Anchor robbery and he was keeping lookout at the back of the pub. The gang broke in through the side door and carried out the burglary without a hitch, but for some reason they forgot about Roger Moore. He heard them drive off, but assumed they'd be coming back for a second load. After about half an hour he got fed up hanging around outside and decided to go into the pub to see if any of the gang were still there. Well, they weren't and he decided he'd have a quick drink while he was waiting for them to come back.'

'He was in the right place.' I remembered the story now, but let Tom carry on.

'Yes,' said Tom, 'and that was his downfall. He worked his way through the bottles behind the bar, and at four-thirty in the morning a passer-by rang up the police and reported raucous singing coming from inside the pub.'

'Are you sure that it was raucous singing, Tom, and not raucous whistling?'

Tom looked at me suspiciously. 'It was definitely singing. Anyway, when the police arrived they found him behind the bar pouring himself a drink and they promptly tried to arrest him. He put up a violent struggle, for such a small bloke, before they finally 'cuffed him.'

'What, round the ear?'

'No, you fool, handcuffed him.' Tom saw me grinning. 'Oh, I see. You're taking the piss.' He gave a snort of disgust and opened his newspaper.

CHAPTER THREE

Friday

'Dad, what's the difference between making love and having sex?' asked Joshua.

I suspected another trap, but Joshua looked serious. Debra stared at her brother and then turned to me. The question seemed genuine and I realised that it had arisen from the sex-education talk at school, which would have caused a lot of fourteen-year-olds to air their knowledge on love, sex and parts of the anatomy. I wondered what had happened to all the carrots, and it occurred to me that they might have been collected up and taken to the canteen.

'Josh, did you have carrot cake at school yesterday?'

'No, we didn't and what's that got to do with what I asked you?'

'Nothing, sorry, I was thinking of something else.'

I wasn't sure whether Debra was old enough for the discussion that would inevitably follow if I answered Josh's question, and I was weighing matters up when Debra joined in.

'Perhaps Daddy doesn't know the answer, Josh.'

'Quite right,' I said. 'Mum's the best person to answer that one. I'll leave you three to thrash it out, while I go off to work.'

I looked at Allison and smiled, but she didn't respond. 'Are you all right?' I asked.

'Yes, of course I am. You go off to work and I'll get the children ready for school.'

The morning was still and a light mist was quickly disappearing. The sun was trying to break through and the day promised to be hot. The forecast for the weekend was good and our fellow commuters had a Friday happiness about them as they exchanged smiles and jokes.

I watched Tom striding towards me. He greeted me with a broad smile and a wave of the hand.

'Terrific morning, Geoff,' he called, '*and* it's Saturday tomorrow.'

'Are you all right?' I asked, and realised it was the second time this morning I'd asked that question.

'Of course I am. Why shouldn't I be?'

'Well, it's just that you were in a foul mood yesterday.'

'You mean that business with Marilyn? That's all over now. When I got home from work last night she surprised me with a candle-lit dinner. The kids were sleeping over at Cheryl's, so we had the house to ourselves, which doesn't happen very often. Marilyn was wearing a little black dress she'd bought and looked amazing. If she wore it out of the house she'd get arrested.'

'It was a night of unbridled passion then, Tom? There had to be a good reason why you're so depressingly happy.'

Tom laughed. 'It's certainly makes a difference to the way you look at the world. I was beginning to think I'd reached the age where I'd rather go to bed with a good book than a good woman.'

'While we're talking of such matters,' I said, 'Josh asked me this morning what the difference is between making love and having sex.'

'That's a tricky one, Geoff, and I'm not sure I know the answer. Although, last night, I'd say that Marilyn and I had sex. At least, that's how it felt to me. There didn't seem to be much love involved, just raging desire between two passionate people.'

'Do I know either of them? They don't sound like anyone around here.'

'You're just jealous,' said Tom. 'Anyway, how's Allison? Is everything back to normal?'

'I'm not sure. She was out at book club last night and I only saw her briefly, but this morning she was subdued ... almost sad.'

'Perhaps they've been reading a sad book.'

I smiled. 'Yes, maybe that's all it is.'

Wednesday 11.45 am

'Damn,' said Allison, 'that's Holy Foley over there. Of all the times to bump into someone you know.'

'Keep going,' Marilyn hissed, 'and don't look at him.'

They had reached the Regent Hotel and the Reverend Paul Foley was standing on the opposite side of the road talking to an elderly woman. Allison and Marilyn walked quickly up the steps and the uniformed doorman threw open the glass doors. Marilyn steered Allison through the foyer and into the cocktail lounge. Without asking Allison, she ordered two glasses of fino.

'I think he saw us,' said Allison.

'Don't worry. He doesn't know me, but I've heard about him from Tom. I didn't see him looking our way and with you all dressed up he probably wouldn't have recognised you anyway. Besides, what's the chance of him running into Geoff and saying, "Guess who I thought

I saw going into the Regent?" Come on, Ally, it's pretty unlikely.'

'You're right, but if Geoff's going to hear about this I'd rather it came from me.'

'You worry too much,' said Marilyn. 'Anyway, I was going to tell you that I saw Richard Morgan yesterday at squash and found out some more about these guys we're meeting. He rabbited on about client confidentiality, but I said we were doing him a favour and unless he gave me some more information we wouldn't turn up. He must have thought I was serious because he told me a bit about them, not that he knew much, or so he said.'

'They're Indonesian businessmen, aren't they?'

'Yes, and I've found out they own a string of hotels in exotic places like Bali and Malaysia. Apparently, the hotels are very posh and cater for the rich and famous. They're trying to set up a joint venture with some Japanese entrepreneurs to expand the chain. This lunch is a social meeting for them to get to know the Japanese better before the serious negotiations start. Having us around as their beautiful companions makes it all less formal.'

'Ah, the frivolous females to make small talk and look decorative,' Allison said.

'That's us,' said Marilyn, 'bimbos. But I learnt yesterday there's another reason why the Indonesians need us here. It's a face thing. The Japanese are going to turn up with a couple of models they've got from somewhere, and our guys will seriously lose face if they come on their own. So, all we have to do is play the perfect Stepford wives, smile a lot, don't say anything controversial and pretend to find the business talk fascinating. Then we go home, having been very well paid for lunching at the most expensive place in town.'

'Just so long as they don't expect us to be the desserts.'

'For God's sake, Ally, we've been over this fifty times. We're companions at a business lunch and, even if they did want anything more, there's hardly going to be much opportunity for groping in the dining room of the Regent.' She broke off. 'Don't look now, but I think the Japanese have arrived and, Jesus, you want to see what they've dragged in. It must be remnant week. Talk about rent a roughie.'

The Japanese and their companions were standing close to the entrance of the cocktail lounge. Allison followed Marilyn's gaze.

'More like hire a whore.'

Friday morning
'Funny things, book clubs,' Tom mused. 'Marilyn joined one once, but it wasn't her scene. I remember the night they had it round at our house. I'd been out and I got back in the middle of it. They were sitting on upright chairs, with their books on their laps, and it looked like a doctor's waiting room. I've never seen such an eerie lack of animation, before or since. I thought I'd walked in on a still life. Then one of them moved and it made me jump.'

I laughed. It was good to see Tom happy for a change. 'I've been a couple of times to Allison's book club. The people are okay, but they take it too seriously and they choose obscure books by supposedly up-and-coming authors, who no one ever hears of again. And they don't just read the books, they unravel them like they're unpicking a jumper. The worst thing, though, is that most of the books leave you feeling suicidal, or else they end in mid sentence and you have to guess what happens.'

'My mum reads Mills and Baboon,' said Tom. 'She goes through two a week and she's got a bookcase full of them. I don't know why she keeps buying new ones when the stories are all exactly the same. She could start on the top shelf, work her way down to the bottom, and then start at the top again and she'd never know the difference.'

'That's exactly why people do read them, because they've got predictable stories with happy endings. I think everyone is so fed up with all the gloom and depression in the world that the last thing they want to do is read something tragic and dismal. They want to escape from all that with stories of love and heroism where everything comes out all right in the end.'

'Talking of tragic and dismal,' said Tom, 'there's Holy Foley over there. I haven't seen him for months, not since he went off on a crusade after he got a call from God.'

'Well, it turned out to be the wrong number. I bumped into him last week and he told me that God had spoken to him in a dream and told him to set up a holy chapter, or something similar, in Swansea. No one was interested over there, so he decided he must have made a mistake and came home.'

'It's more Freudian than Christian,' said Tom, 'taking notice of dreams.'

'Dangerous, more like,' I said. 'If I acted on my dreams about Susie in reception, I'd either be in jail or the middle of divorce proceedings.'

Tom loathed Reverend Paul Foley. There had been rumours several years ago of a scandal involving Foley and some boys from the parish. The matter had been dealt with quietly by the church and no action taken, but Tom was convinced that he had committed unspeakable crimes and deserved to be publicly castrated.

'Bloody hell, he's spotted us,' said Tom, 'and he's waiting.'

'Take it easy, Tom, and watch your language.'

'Fuck.'

Holy Foley was short and thin, and in the final throes of middle age. His collar hung loosely around his neck, as though it belonged to a far sturdier cleric, and made him appear shrunken. For such an insignificant-looking man, he had a remarkably deep and powerful voice, which was the perfect tool for his trade and resulted in his sermons being theatrically uplifting. As he waited for us to catch him up, his face exuded benevolence and understanding. I felt certain he practised the expression and used it to welcome his parishioners at the church door.

'Boys,' he greeted us resonantly, 'it is good to see you. God be with you both.'

His arms were outstretched, as if in supplication, and he grasped our reluctant shoulders with his bony hands. In turn, Foley searched our eyes, as though he would discover the truth there.

'Hmmph,' replied Tom.

'How do you do?' I said politely.

At that point the conversation stalled. It was an extraordinary gift of Holy Foley's, and far exceeded his religious talents, that he was able to terminate any conversation almost instantly. The problem was that all his interests revolved around ecclesiastical matters and whatever the topic of conversation he would attempt to introduce religion into it. He had a unique ability to make people feel uncomfortable and Tom was already starting to fidget and was clearly anxious to escape. We had almost reached the station and I could see no way to avoid spending the journey with him.

We walked several more paces in silence before Holy boomed, 'God has blessed you with this lovely morning.'

He spoke as though we had been singled out for special treatment and waved a hand in the general direction of the heavens. I looked upwards, half expecting to see a benign God peering down at us through the clearing haze.

'It's not just us who are blessed though, is it?' demanded Tom. 'Everyone out there is getting the same morning. I mean, God hasn't picked out a few lucky winners and rewarded them with a sunny day, while all the miserable sinners are cowering under a blanket of rain and hail. It's just a random thing. It's a nice day because all the mist is blowing away. There's no religion about it. Jesus Christ, it's a nice summer day and that's all there is to it.' Tom paused and took breath.

Nothing perturbed Holy Foley. He had an implacable belief in his God and Tom's outburst was not going to shake it. 'You mustn't take the Lord's name in vain, Tom,' he bellowed.

'I'm not taking his name in vain. I'm just saying that God has got nothing to do with the weather, that's all. You might as well say it's God's fault when the train's late. I am simply pointing out to you that God will be concentrating on much weightier matters than whether or not the sun's shining. If God controls the weather, you'd have thought he'd have given me a decent day for my wedding, wouldn't you? It was at the parish church with all the usual rigmarole and trimmings, and sodding bagpipes at the insistence of Marilyn's parents. So, if God has the power to make the sun shine it would have been there and then, wouldn't it? But, oh no, it pissed down all day and Marilyn and I looked like drowned rats. When people see our wedding photos they can hardly contain themselves. Everyone thinks I'd been thrown into the river wearing a dinner jacket and Marilyn had entered a wet-tee-shirt competition. No one believes it was our fucking wedding.' Tom was getting into his stride. 'And another thing, the fact that I've said Jesus Christ without kneeling in prayer and crossing myself does not mean I am taking his name in vain. If God is all seeing, then he knows I don't mean any disrespect. I've noticed that you religious people never credit God with a sense of humour. It's all fear and damnation, with this stern figure waiting to strike you down if you say the wrong thing. Well, it's complete nonsense.'

'Mind that car,' I shouted.

Tom spun round. 'Very funny, Geoff.'

He stumped off to buy the papers, leaving me with Holy Foley. 'Look, Paul, maybe it would be better if we don't sit together on the train. You seem to rub Tom up the wrong way and I don't think I can take a whole journey of that.'

'I fully understand. One cannot be all things to all people, even when doing God's work,' Foley said sonorously. 'But don't worry, Geoff, I shan't be travelling with you; I'm going the other way to the end of the line, to visit some of our disadvantaged.'

I felt relieved and was about to rejoin Tom when Holy forestalled me. 'By the way, Geoff, I saw Allison going into the Regent Hotel on Wednesday.'

'Allison?'

'Yes, your wife.'

'Oh, that Allison. Well, I wouldn't have thought so,' I said. 'I can't imagine she'd go there, not with their prices.'

'I must have been mistaken then,' said Foley, his voice reverberating around the station walls, 'but it looked like her. She was with another woman who was wearing the smallest dress I've ever seen and that's what caught my eye. You're right though, Geoff, it couldn't have been Allison, not with someone like that.'

My head snapped up. 'What did you say she was wearing?'

'I didn't,' said Holy. 'But I believe it was a grey dress.'

'No, not the one you thought was Allison, but the other woman.'

'Oh, I see. Well, it was a black dress, very short and low cut.'

'And what was her hair like?'

'A sort of dark blond and shortish. You seem suddenly interested, Geoff,' resonated Foley.

I laughed it off. 'You know me, Paul. I'm always interested in that type of woman. Anyway, I must get the train. I'll see you around.'

I walked over to where Tom was waiting at our usual spot on the platform. He brightened when he saw that Holy Foley wasn't with me.

'You've got rid of that godless bastard, then.'

'Not my doing, Tom. He's not coming into the city. He's going the other way into darkest Africa, to convert a few heathens.'

'I hope they eat him.'

'Forget about Holy Foley. Tell me, have you or Marilyn been to the Regent lately?'

'Not bloody likely,' said Tom. 'We couldn't afford a beer in that place. I haven't been in the Regent for years and then it was only to pick my boss up from the foyer. Even so, it cost me a fiver tipping some bloke wearing an admiral's uniform who insisted on opening the door for me. He seemed to think I couldn't do it myself. Frankly, I wasn't sure whether I was supposed to give him a tip or a salute. And I wouldn't have thought Marilyn's been there recently. She's promised no more extravagances since she got the MG.'

'Apart from that sexy black dress,' I said carefully.

Tom grinned. 'I don't know when she bought that. The first time I saw it was last night, but whatever it cost it was worth it. Anyway, why are you asking about the Regent?'

'Oh, it's nothing really. It's just that I've got to take a client out next week and I was wondering if their prices are any more reasonable.'

'They're worse,' said Tom. 'My boss went there recently and complained for a week. I can't see your company letting you take someone there.'

'You're right. They're pretty stingy like that. I'll have to think of somewhere else. Perhaps they'll run to the Pizza Hut.'

While Tom read the paper, I thought about what Holy Foley had said. It didn't seem likely that Allison and Marilyn had been to the Regent; however it was odd that he thought he'd recognised Ally and, from his description, the other woman could have been Marilyn. But why would she have been wearing her sexy black dress? Ally hadn't said anything to me, so it seemed probable that Paul Foley was wrong. I toyed with the idea of mentioning it to Tom, but I didn't fancy starting him off again about Holy Foley and instead I decided to ask Allison when I got home. Looking back now, I wonder if things would have turned out differently if I had told Tom there and then and not several days later when it was too late.

CHAPTER FOUR

Wednesday 11.55 am

The Japanese were short-haired, short men, wearing dark suits. The taller and older was talking with obvious difficulty to the concierge, who was gesturing in the direction of the dining room.

Marilyn turned to Allison. 'It doesn't look as though they speak much English. That's going to make it hard for casual chit-chat and I don't think their escorts have been chosen for their conversational talents, so we might be in for a quiet lunch.'

Allison studied the two women. One of them was standing side on; she was nearly six feet tall, very slim, and was dressed in a silver halter-neck dress, slit to the top of her thigh. Her visible left breast jutted out spectacularly and the halter top struggled to contain it.

Marilyn watched Allison's scrutiny. 'She looks like a stick insect wearing a life jacket.'

'It'd be hard to drown with those,' agreed Allison.

'If she turns round quickly, she'll knock the little guy over.'

Allison smiled. 'I wonder if she pumps them up.'

Having temporarily exhausted the insults, they turned their attention to her companion. She was short and almost plump, with blond hair in loose curls. She was wearing a knee-length, pleated pink dress and a matching bow in her hair. Her face was round and doll-like, with wide-open blue eyes.

'Sugar and spice and not very nice,' said Allison.

'She looks like a Shirley Temple stripper-gram,' Marilyn said.

'And I bet you a fiver she lisps,' said Allison.

The unusual quartet passed out of their vision in the direction of the dining room.

'They look revolting,' said Marilyn, 'but then the Japs aren't exactly Samurais, are they?'

Two tall, fair-haired men, impeccably dressed in grey suits, had entered the cocktail lounge by the rear door and were standing behind them. 'So you don't approve of our Japanese friends' choice of companions?'

Allison spun round and went scarlet. 'I'm sorry. I didn't know anyone was listening.'

'No, we don't,' Marilyn replied, 'they look like whores.'

The two men laughed. 'That's because they probably are,' said the one who had spoken, 'but we must treat them as ladies. Isn't that what we're supposed to do?'

'That's what *men* are supposed to do,' said Marilyn, 'and I don't like the corollary to that.'

He smiled. 'I see that we are going to get on. I am Pieter Cruyff and this is my associate, Rudi Okker. You must be Marilyn and this is your friend Allison. You match the descriptions exactly.'

'Well, you don't,' said Marilyn. 'We were expecting two Indonesian businessmen.'

Rudi spoke for the first time. 'We are Dutch-Indonesians, leftovers from the colonial days.' He smiled. 'Now, if you have finished your drinks, we will join our companions on the terrace. The Japanese gentlemen speak very little English, so you won't be

31

required to do anything more than look charming and smile in the right places.'

'And bow,' suggested Marilyn.

'Yes, that *is* compulsory for Samurai warriors,' laughed Pieter as he took Marilyn's arm.

Allison followed awkwardly alongside Rudi, who stopped before they entered the dining room and smiled at her. 'Everything will be fine, Allison. Just relax and you will enjoy yourself.'

The waiter ushered them through the dining room to the terrace and diners glanced up as they passed. Allison saw several women's gaze linger over Pieter Cruyff and men stare admiringly at Marilyn. She was revelling in the attention and, not for the first time, Allison thought how little she understood her. The terrace overlooked the green lawn of the hotel and the brown water of the Thames, and was normally set with eight tables. Today, all but one had been removed and the spaces filled with silk screens and ferns. The Japanese businessmen and their companions were leaning against the rail looking across the river.

Pieter spoke in English. 'Osaki and Tosana, it's good to see you again.' He bowed slightly. 'You know my associate, Rudi Okker.' Rudi smiled and gave a short bow. 'And let me introduce our friends, Marilyn and Allison.'

Allison gave a token bow before Marilyn stepped forward and bowed extravagantly, a full ninety degrees. There were audible intakes of breath from Osaki and Tosana as they followed Marilyn's breasts to the limit of the bow and back again. Their companions watched Marilyn with narrowed eyes while Pieter looked sardonically at Osaki and Tosana. The Japanese returned the bows and beamed at Marilyn. Osaki said something to Tosana and both men laughed. He then introduced their companions as Monique and Chantelle.

Monique gave a bobbing curtsy that made her blond curls bounce like springs and she spoke in a little girl voice. 'Pleased to meet you.'

'You owe me a fiver,' Marilyn whispered to Allison.

Chantelle was almost as tall as Pieter and Rudi and she extended a limp hand to each of them in turn. She nodded to Marilyn and Allison. 'Hi, how you doing?' Her voice was hoarse and straining as if the membranes in her throat were raw.

Chantelle and Monique went over to the table and Marilyn turned to Pieter. 'What did Osaki say about me?'

'He said that you have the beauty of a lotus flower and the brilliance of a midnight sun rising over Tokyo. The Japanese are very poetic.'

Rudi corrected Pieter. 'What Osaki really said was that at least *your* breasts are real.'

Allison laughed, 'So much for Japanese poetry.' She whispered to Marilyn. 'Who do you think will get Chantelle?'

'I don't suppose it matters,' said Marilyn. 'I'm sure they'll swap over at half-time.'

The lunch passed slowly for Marilyn and Allison. They were excluded from most of the conversations, which were conducted between the men in Japanese, and Chantelle and Monique said virtually nothing and looked bored. Several times Pieter and Marilyn spoke together privately and their conversations ended in laughter, with Marilyn resting her hand on his arm. Allison watched them and was uneasy, but she felt remote from the events, as if she were merely a spectator to an unfolding drama.

The Japanese were captivated by Marilyn and Tosana asked Pieter to translate something. 'Tosana says that in ancient times in Japan, if a man wanted to meet a beautiful woman who had captured his heart, he would write her a tanka. Before the meal is over he will compose one for Marilyn and write it on his serviette. He says that it should be written in his blood, but in the circumstances he will use a red ballpoint pen.'

Marilyn stifled a laugh. 'What on earth is a tanka?'

Before Pieter could reply, Allison answered. 'It's a five line poem. The first two lines are about nature and the last two an emotion. The middle line links the themes.'

'Bravo, Allison,' said Rudi.

'Wow!' exclaimed Marilyn, 'perhaps you ought to be on the other side of the table with Osaki and Tosana. How on earth do you know that?'

'It's amazing what you learn at book club,' laughed Allison.

Not to be outdone, Osaki was determined to pay Marilyn a compliment, and for several moments he struggled with what he was trying to say. He finally said loudly, 'You ... are truly ... woman.'

'I'm glad he's realised that,' Allison muttered.

Rudi nudged her and Pieter said in English, 'I know what Osaki means and she certainly is.'

Marilyn stood up and bowed theatrically to Osaki and Tosana, treating them to another view of her breasts. They clapped their appreciation, as though she had just performed a difficult solo piece, and Rudi, Pieter and Allison laughed. Monique managed a half-smile, but Chantelle's eyes were hard and she looked at Marilyn sourly.

Allison was fascinated by Chantelle's breasts and throughout the meal her gaze was drawn to them. She found herself wondering what they felt like; whether they were solid like footballs, or pliable like stiff dough.

As if Chantelle had read Allison's mind, she turned to her and rasped, 'Do you see something you like, honey?'

'No, she was just looking at your plastic hooters,' said Marilyn.

'Maybe she'll get to see them properly later,' said Chantelle and winked.

'I don't think so,' said Allison. 'We won't be staying for the festivities.'

'I was wondering,' Marilyn asked sweetly, 'do you inflate them?'

Chantelle looked directly at Marilyn for the first time. 'What are you,' she gestured at their wedding rings, 'housewives out for thrills? Do your hubbies like to hear what happened?'

Monique was listening and her face was expressionless. The Japanese were unaware of what had been said, but Rudi had heard the exchange and he looked pointedly at Chantelle and Marilyn.

'Well, at least we're not a couple of hookers,' responded Marilyn.

'Ladies,' intervened Rudi, 'be nice to each other, please.'

The meal was over and there had been no further hostility between Marilyn and Chantelle. Osaki and Tosana were talking animatedly to Pieter, and Allison guessed that they were discussing the next phase of the afternoon. Rudi said something to Pieter in Indonesian and Pieter answered him sharply in the same language. Rudi looked annoyed, but then shrugged and said nothing further. Pieter stood up and addressed Marilyn and Allison.

'Ladies, we are going to our suite for coffee and liqueurs and we'd be honoured if you would join us.'

Allison answered before Marilyn could speak. 'Pieter, it's lovely of you to invite us, but unfortunately we have to leave now.'

Chantelle made a sucking noise through her teeth, and Monique gazed at Allison with her emotionless blue eyes. Marilyn started to say something, but Pieter prevented her.

'Yes, Allison, I know what was agreed, but Osaki and Tosana have particularly requested your charming company.'

'Marilyn's, you mean,' said Allison under her breath. 'Well, I'm sorry, Pieter, I have to be home by four.'

'That's an hour and a half yet,' smiled Pieter. 'Look, I will arrange for a taxi and you will be home in less than half an hour from here. That gives you plenty of time for a liqueur.'

'Come on, Ally,' said Marilyn. 'I've drunk too much to drive, so a taxi home will be great, and I'll come in tomorrow and pick up the car.'

Allison saw that there was no way out of the situation without being rude. 'All right,' she said reluctantly, 'but I must leave before three-thirty.'

In the elevator, Pieter stood close to Marilyn, while Osaki and Tosana spoke quietly. Rudi was listening to their conversation and at one point he smothered a laugh. Allison felt sure that they were discussing Monique and Chantelle and she wished she could understand what they were saying. At the fifteenth floor Pieter led them out of the elevator and into the apartment. There was soft music and a waiter stood by the table, on which there was an assortment of drinks.

'Will you please serve everyone and then you may leave,' said Pieter. 'I will ring if we need anything more.'

Marilyn stood with the four men in the centre of the room, talking and laughing. Allison took her drink and sat in an armchair, and Monique and Chantelle lounged at either end of a leather couch, sipping liqueurs and eating chocolates. After a few minutes, Tosana left the group and sat between Chantelle and Monique. He spoke to Monique and they got up and danced stiffly to the end of the room where they slowed to a halt. Then Osaki walked over to Chantelle and extended a hand. She stood up and they started dancing, with her huge right breast pillowed against the side of his head.

Allison stifled a laugh as Rudi came over. 'They should have chosen the other way round. At least Tosana's head would have cleared Chantelle's boobs.'

Rudi smiled. 'Yes, but Tosana is a bit disappointed with the remarkable Chantelle. He owns a silicone factory in Japan and her breasts remind him of work.'

Allison choked on her drink, 'My God, that is priceless.' She laughed and abruptly stopped. 'Oh Rudi, what am I doing here?'

'I was wondering the same thing,' said Rudi, 'but it has been a pleasure meeting you, and forgive me if I suggest you should stick to being a wife and mother. This,' he gestured behind him, 'is not your destiny.'

'No, it isn't, but I wasn't sure what to expect and it's been eye-opening. It's not something I'll ever do again.'

'Good,' smiled Rudi. 'Your taxi will be here soon and I'll take you and Marilyn downstairs before Osaki and Tosana start their fun in earnest.'

Marilyn and Pieter were still in the centre of the room and they were standing very close to each other. As Allison watched, Marilyn moved forward until her breasts touched Pieter's chest. She said something and he nodded. Marilyn left him and came over to Allison and Rudi.

'You go home in the taxi, Ally. Pieter and I are going down to the bar for another drink. We're leaving Osaki and Tosana with the hookers.'

'Marilyn, I'm not going without you. What do you think you're doing?'

'Ally, don't argue. I'm a big girl and I know what I'm doing.'

'I don't think you do. Look, I can't leave you here.'

'I've decided.' Marilyn's face was tight.

'Marilyn, you'll regret this.'

'Well, I'd rather regret doing it, than regret not doing it. Now go, or you won't be home when the kids get back from school.' She turned away and walked back to Pieter.

'Oh God, Marilyn, you fool, you bloody fool.'

Allison looked past Marilyn and saw that Chantelle was lying on her back on the couch with Osaki straddling her waist. He was leaning forward like a jockey, holding a halter strap in each hand. Suddenly, with a flourish, he pulled back the top of her dress and Chantelle's breasts were exposed in all their gravity-defying splendour. Osaki carefully wound the halter straps around her left breast, as though he was tying up a hostage who he suspected might try to escape. Chantelle looked directly at Allison and smiled for the first time that afternoon.

CHAPTER FIVE

On Friday, I didn't arrive home from work until after ten o'clock. The customary end of week drinks had extended to an Asian meal and several bottles of wine and, when I left, my younger colleagues were arguing over which club they were going to.

Allison pulled away from my slobbery kiss. 'Geoff, you've had that garlic stir fry again. You're sleeping in the spare room tonight.'

'It's all right, it'll go away after I've brushed my teeth.'

I poured two glasses of port and handed one to Allison. Her eyes were puffy and she looked tired. 'Are you feeling all right, Ally? You haven't been your normal happy self the last few days.'

'Geoff, I've got something to tell you and I don't know how to start. I've been a complete fool.'

I looked at her in surprise. Then I remembered the conversation with Holy Foley this morning and wondered if there was any connection. 'It can't be that bad. Let me guess. I know, you've finally gone out and ordered that leather lounge suite you've had your eye on for months.' She shook her head. 'Or else you've blown three-months' housekeeping having lunch at the Regent,' I added slyly.

'So, you know about that do you? Holy Foley must have told you. I knew he'd seen me.'

It was clear that there was more to this than an expensive girls' lunch and I felt the wine leave me. 'Okay, tell me all about it.'

I listened for nearly an hour while Allison told me the story. I refilled our glasses and interrupted once when she was describing the events in the hotel suite after lunch.

'And definitely nothing, you know ... happened?'

'No, of course not,' said Allison.

'What do you mean, "of course not"? You've gone out as a paid escort, which as you're well aware is a polite term for a prostitute, and you seem amazed that I ask you if anything happened. I think it's an entirely reasonable question and it's something I've got to know.'

'No, nothing happened, as you put it. I didn't have sex with anyone and, anyway, I was a companion, not an escort.' I snorted at Allison's semantics. 'Rudi Okker is married and he behaved absolutely correctly. I'd be happy to invite him and his wife round for dinner, anytime.'

I tried to envisage the evening. 'No, I don't think so,' I said. 'All right, I'm sorry, Ally, but I had to hear you say it. And next time you want an adventure just let me know and I'll arrange for something less risky, like skydiving or bungee jumping.'

She smiled. 'I love you, Geoff, I really do, but I was feeling desperate. You know, nearly forty, life passing me by and what am I doing with it, sort of thing?'

'I know,' I said, 'and I try not to think about it. But I'll tell you what you're doing with your life, Ally. You're bringing up two wonderful children. You're caring for them, loving them, and you're always here for them. You're my best friend and I love you.' We hugged each other and there was a lump in my throat.

'Ally, what do you think's going to happen with Marilyn and Tom?'

'I don't know, but you should have seen her with Pieter. There were sparks between them. It was as though Marilyn had taken leave of her senses and nothing else mattered. Since Wednesday, we've hardly spoken and I'm sure she's avoiding me. I've rung her, but I either get the answer machine or else she says she's too busy to talk, so I don't know what's going on.'

'Well, I think it's going to be all right,' I said. 'This morning Tom was the happiest I've seen him for ages. That is, until we bumped into Holy Foley. Anyway, he told me that last night Marilyn prepared a candle-lit dinner and she was wearing the famous black dress. Afterwards, they had a night of furious passion, the like of which they hadn't had for years.' Allison looked at me strangely, but didn't say anything. 'So, maybe it was just an afternoon of midsummer madness and now it's over. That is, if anything happened at all. Anyway, it's not really any of our business.'

'Well, I feel involved. I know that Marilyn organised it all, but I was there and I shouldn't have left her.'

'Look, Marilyn's an adult who made her own decision and, anyway, you didn't have much choice; you had to be home for Debra and Josh. Marilyn arranged for Kate and Gemma to be collected from school by Cheryl and then spend the evening at her house, so maybe she had something planned all along. Well, I'm not going to say anything to Tom and, if everything's back to normal, he's better off not knowing.'

'Let's hope it's that simple,' said Allison.

I didn't see Tom until Monday morning. I thought that he would have enjoyed being on his own while Marilyn and the girls spent the weekend at her parents' house, and I expected him to be relaxed and not his usual dejected Monday self. He was very late and I was about to leave when he pulled up alongside me in Marilyn's MG. I opened the passenger door. He was wearing jeans and a jumper and was unshaven. There was no welcoming smile.

'Geoff, something awful's happened and I need to talk to you and Allison.'

I couldn't help glancing at my watch. 'Okay, Tom, but talk as we drive.' I climbed in beside him. 'I'll have hell to pay if I miss the Monday meeting.'

'Bugger the meeting,' said Tom. 'This is serious. Marilyn's run off and taken the kids.'

'Oh Christ! All right, come back to my place.'

Allison had already left to take the children to school. She was going to the gym afterwards and wouldn't be back until mid morning. I rang the office and told them that a domestic crisis had occurred and I would be in after lunch. I made coffee and we sat at the dining table.

'You remember I told you that Marilyn and the girls were spending the weekend at her parents'?' I nodded. 'Well, they didn't. I got home late from work on Friday, after the usual drinks, and there was a note saying there was a meal in the fridge. It was signed Marilyn, but without any kisses, and if I'd had less to drink I might have thought that was a bit odd, but I didn't at the time. I assumed she'd given the children tea and gone off in a rush. I tried ringing a couple of times on Saturday, but got no reply. I thought they'd probably all gone out for the day and didn't think any more about it. I rang again Sunday afternoon to find out what time they'd be coming home, and Mrs McTavish answered the phone and wanted to know if Kate was feeling any better. I told her I didn't know what she was talking about and asked to speak to Marilyn. She then dropped the bombshell that

Marilyn had rung her on Friday morning and said that Kate was unwell and they wouldn't be coming for the weekend.'

'Jesus! Tom, I might know ...'

'Don't interrupt,' interrupted Tom. 'I'd like you to hear me out. Well, I drove straight round to her parents' place expecting Marilyn to be there and it was all an elaborate joke. But, of course, it wasn't and it turned out that Mr and Mrs McTavish had spent Saturday visiting an aunt, which was why no one answered the phone. Their first reaction was that Marilyn and I must have had an argument and she'd simply walked out with the girls. But that didn't explain why she'd lied to them about Kate being unwell.

'I tell you, Geoff, I've changed my opinion of Marilyn's parents; they were terrific. We all went down to the police station and I made a missing person's report. To start off with they weren't interested at all. To them it was just another domestic row and Marilyn would turn up with the kids in a couple of days. It didn't look as though we were going to get anywhere until Marilyn's dad gave them a ten minute lecture in broad Scottish. I didn't understand much of it and I doubt that they understood a word, but no one could doubt his sincerity. In the end, and I think it was more to shut him up than anything else, they agreed to do some routine searches. Well, we spent half the night there while they checked accident reports, hospitals, hotel registrations and police stations. It wasn't until they tried the airports that they came up with anything. They discovered that Marilyn, Kate and Gemma had got on a flight from Heathrow to Bali on Friday afternoon. Bali, Geoff, why Bali? Wives who walk out on their husbands go straight back to their parents, but not Marilyn, she cancels that arrangement and goes to Bali, for Christ's sake!'

'Tom,' I started to say again, 'I know something ...'

Tom glared at me. 'Will you let me finish? You'll get your turn in a minute. Anyway, I drove home to check the document drawer and her passport's gone, together with three suitcases and some of their clothing. I then got a cab to the airport and searched the car parks for Marilyn's car. I had a run in with an officious security guard, who actually turned out to be pretty helpful after I told him the facts. It seems his wife left him and took their BMW. He was more upset about losing the car than his wife, so he sympathised with me wanting to find the MG. He drove me around the car parks and after about half an hour we found it. I had the spare key, so I simply drove it home. I gave the security guy a tenner for his help, but really he didn't want to accept it. He said I was now part of the clan of jilted husbands and we should go around helping each other.' Tom paused for breath. 'Okay it's your turn now. What were you saying?'

I wondered how best to tell Tom what I'd heard from Allison and, to give myself time to think, I said inconsequently, 'So you didn't get a lot of sleep last night?'

'Jesus Christ, Geoff, is something fucking wrong with you? I can't believe you've been interrupting me just to ask that. Weren't you listening to what I've been saying? Marilyn's walked out and taken the kids to Bali and you ask me if I slept well. Of course I didn't fucking sleep well. I was up all night at the police station and Heathrow-bloody-Airport. Not only did I not sleep well, I didn't sleep at all!'

'Sorry, it was a stupid question. I'll get you another coffee, but there is something I want to tell you, if you can just be patient for a couple of minutes.'

I left Tom grumbling, and went into the kitchen to make him a strong coffee and to think. I quickly reached the decision that there was no alternative to telling him the whole story.

'Tom,' I began, 'I know quite a bit about all this.' Tom made a low noise in his throat and started to clench and unclench his hands. It had never struck me before just how enormous his fists are. 'Settle down, Tom, please and let me finish. Look, it's something that Allison told me on Friday night. I'll tell you the gist of it, but really it'd be better if you heard it from her.'

Tom listened attentively, with the occasional grunt of incredulity, and I watched his face grow redder until it was almost glowing. I was expecting him at any moment to shout and swear and smash furniture, but he remained quiet throughout and when I had finished he sat in thought for several minutes until finally he got up, walked over to the window and turned to face me. Silhouetted against the light he looked very large and menacing. He studied me for a few moments before he spoke.

'Geoff, how could they both have been so bloody stupid? And Marilyn running off with some bloke she's known for a couple of days? Right, I need to talk to Allison. When's she coming home?'

'She should be back in about ten minutes, but promise me one thing, Tom, that you won't take this out on her. She tried to persuade Marilyn to leave with her that afternoon and had no idea what she was planning. If you want to blame someone, then blame me for not letting you know what Holy Foley told me on Friday morning, but I didn't really believe he saw them going into the Regent and, even if he did, I still had no reason to think that anything was wrong. I wasn't going to say anything to you until I'd spoken to Ally.'

Tom was calm now. 'You're right, Geoff, of course it's not your fault or Ally's. It's just that I need someone right now to take this out on.'

I got up and stood beside Tom at the window. I was trying to think of something sympathetic to say when he suddenly turned to me. 'Do you know what that was on Thursday night?'

I didn't know what Tom meant and I shook my head. 'A goodbye bonk,' said Tom. 'That's what Marilyn gave me, a bloody going-away present.'

I groaned in embarrassment and then I remembered the look on Allison's face after I had told her about Tom and Marilyn's night of passion. She had suspected something.

Allison pulled into the drive behind the MG and I was saved from making a reply. She was wearing a bright yellow tracksuit; her face was flushed and her hair still wet from the shower. I forestalled her questions and Tom told her what had happened. Allison listened in horror and when Tom had finished she went over and hugged him.

'Oh, Tom, I'm so sorry. If I'd thought for one moment anything like this would happen I'd have told Geoff straight away, but I kept putting it off.'

Tom rested his big hands on the edge of the table and spoke gently. 'It's okay, Ally. I know there's nothing you could have done, but I want you to go over the whole business and tell me absolutely everything, right from the beginning.'

'Well, it started with Richard Morgan. He asked Marilyn if she was interested in being a paid companion at a lunch for some overseas businessmen. It was all perfectly respectable, Tom. No hanky-panky. They just wanted two females to lighten the mood so that it was more of a social meeting ...' Allison began hesitantly but, as she gained confidence, she spoke fluently and concisely. She told him what had happened during the meal and in the suite afterwards. She explained that since Wednesday Marilyn had hardly spoken to her and had clearly been avoiding her.

When Allison had finished, Tom patted her arm. 'Thanks, Ally. Can I ask you a few things?' She nodded and Tom continued. 'Firstly, this Richard Morgan, what do you know about him?'

'Not much, except that he plays squash with Marilyn on Tuesdays and he operates a dating agency.'

'Dating agency,' Tom snorted, 'an escort agency more like. Well, I should be able to track him down if he's a member of the squash club. Somewhere at home Marilyn's got a list of all the members. If I can't find it, then I'll have to take up squash.' He thought for a moment. 'Well, Marilyn and the girls have flown to Bali, so it's reasonable to assume they'll stay at Cruyff's hotel, at least temporarily. All I've got to do is find it. Did anyone mention its name, Ally?'

'I don't know; I wasn't really listening. They were talking in Japanese so I didn't pay much attention, but when Bali was mentioned they said "paradise" a lot, and it stood out because it's an English word, but I don't know what it referred to.'

'Well, we know it's going to be a big swish hotel and there will be a fair number of those in Bali, so it might not be easy to find. I think my best bet is to go and see this Richard Morgan character and beat the truth out of him.'

I thought that Tom was joking and smiled.

'I'm serious,' said Tom. 'I mean it. Right, I'm going home to look for Morgan's phone number. If I can't find it, I'll be borrowing Marilyn's squash racquet tomorrow.'

CHAPTER SIX

After Tom had left I rang the office and told them that the crisis had worsened and I wouldn't be in all day.

'Poor Tom,' I said.

'I can hardly believe it's happened and I feel so miserable for him. He must be completely devastated.' Allison paused. 'Geoff, what would you do in Tom's place?'

'I'd move heaven and earth to get my family back, and I think that's exactly what Tom's planning to do. And, Ally, I am very, very glad it's not you who's run off to Bali with Debra and Josh.'

Allison hugged me. 'That couldn't happen to us, could it, Geoff?'

'No,' I said, 'never. Look, Ally, we've got to cheer up or we'll be in tears. I think Tom's going to need positive support from us and we can't just sit around here moping. Let's go out and have some lunch and a decent bottle of wine.'

'Why don't we skip lunch and just have the bottle of wine. Geoff, I need to hold you very close, right at this moment, and you might be interested to know I'm not wearing anything under my tracksuit.' Allison smiled. 'I can think of something else that will cheer us up and I'm sure Tom wouldn't mind.'

'I wasn't hungry, anyway,' I said, helping her with the zipper.

Tom rang me early in the afternoon. He had found the squash club membership list and had telephoned Richard Morgan on the pretext that he and a business colleague required two "companions" for an evening later in the week. He had made an appointment to see Morgan at three-thirty and would I come along?

'I'd love to,' I said drowsily and got out of bed.

Tom picked me up from the house at three o'clock. He had shaved, put on a suit and looked better than he had earlier, but his eyes were bloodshot and his expression was hard.

'Thanks, Geoff, I'm glad you could come. I might need you as a witness to deny that I tortured him.' I smiled and hoped that he wasn't serious. 'He asked me to come in so he could vet my details.' He grunted. 'To see if I'm a fit person to shag one of his hookers, or more likely to check if I'm married and see if there's any way he can blackmail me. He sounds a real sleaze, Geoff, and I have this feeling that he and I are not going to get on very well.'

'I didn't imagine you would, but if he doesn't know the address of the Bali hotel then you'll be well and truly stuck.'

'Yes, that had occurred to me,' said Tom, 'but he must have some contact details for them, and I'll get those and see where they lead.'

Morgan & Associates was situated in an anonymous building of serviced offices and at three-twenty-five we were standing in the reception on the ground floor. The girl behind the desk glanced up and continued typing. Tom grunted in irritation and I was searching for a bell to ring, when she stopped typing.

'We don't have one,' she said.

'Don't have one what?' I said.

'You were looking for a bell. We don't have one.'

Tom was in no mood for games. 'I'm David Smales,' he said loudly, 'and my colleague and I have a three-thirty appointment with Mr Morgan.'

'Yes, I know who you are, but you're early. However, I will find out if Mr Morgan is free to see you.'

She pressed a button on the switchboard and spoke briefly into the phone.

'Office five on the first floor,' she said without looking up at us, and continued typing.

'Bloody sour bitch,' Tom muttered.

We walked up the stairs into an empty, grey-carpeted corridor. The floor appeared unoccupied. Office number five was the first door on the left.

'Impersonal place,' I said, 'more like a tax office than a knocking shop.'

Tom rapped on the door and a man's voice answered, 'Come in, it's open.'

The office contained a desk, three chairs, a filing cabinet and an exercise bike. Richard Morgan got up from behind the desk as we entered. He was slightly-built, about thirty and was wearing a tight polo-neck shirt that emphasised his narrow frame. He produced a smile of welcome, but his eyes remained flat while he assessed us.

'Which one of you is Mr Smales?' His voice was cultured, but it wasn't quite right; it needed more practice.

Tom closed the door carefully and ignored Richard Morgan's hand. 'You must be little Dick.'

'Richard, actually,' corrected Morgan.

'I think I'll stick to little Dick, it suits you better and, while we're on the subject of names, is that "Morgan" with a big M and a small organ?'

Morgan's expression hardened. 'Who are you? If you've just come here to insult me, then you'd better leave right now before I call the police.'

'I've come to do a lot more than insult you, son,' Tom said, stretching out his oversized right hand and grabbing Morgan by the throat.

'Urrgghh,' gurgled Morgan.

He moved closer to Morgan, changed his grip slightly, and with a remarkable display of strength lifted him off the ground.

'Listen very carefully, Dick, because I'm only going to say this once. You arranged for my wife, Marilyn Skellam, to have a cosy meeting last Wednesday with two Dutch-Indonesians, Pieter Cruyff and Rudi Okker. On Friday, my wife and two daughters went missing and it seems likely they went off with Cruyff. She bought airline tickets to Bali and I assume they're staying at his hotel there. I want the name and address of this hotel and you're going to tell me. Is that clear? Just nod your head, otherwise I'm going to shake you around a bit.'

'Arrgghh ... Urrgghhh.'

'Oh sorry, you can't nod your head with me holding you by it. Well, in which case, I'll take that as a yes and let you down nice and gently.'

Morgan stood in the centre of the office, wheezing and rubbing his neck. His first attempt to say something came out badly and I wondered if Tom had caused him permanent damage.

Morgan tried again. 'You're fucking mad,' he croaked.

'Now, now,' said Tom, 'if there's one thing I can't stand it's bad language. And I'm more than mad, son, I'm totally fucking livid. Now, I need this information in a hurry and if you don't give it to me I'm going to break your neck.'

From Tom's expression it was clear that he would carry out his threat. He took a step towards Morgan, who leapt back and held out his hand. 'All right, all right, but you mustn't let Cruyff know I told you.'

'That's settled then,' said Tom, as if he'd just negotiated a tricky business deal. 'You don't tell me, but instead you accidentally leave the file open on your desk and I just happen to read it while you're out of the office visiting the little boys' room. By the way, if you feel tempted to go to the police, don't. I'm sure they'll be interested to know that you're living off immoral earnings, and also that you are involved in the abduction of minors, namely my children.'

Morgan looked at Tom balefully, but said nothing. He went to the filing cabinet and took out a file, from which he removed a single sheet of paper and placed it on the desk.

'I'll be down the corridor and I want you to be gone when I get back,' Morgan croaked.

'Yes, cheerio then, and I suggest you take something for that throat of yours; it doesn't sound too good to me. And I am warning you, Morgan, don't give me any reason to come back here, because I won't be so easy-going next time.'

Tom nodded to him in dismissal and Morgan left the office without speaking.

My mouth was hanging open in amazement. I had seen a side of Tom that I never knew existed, but I should have known that there was more to him than the stolid and worthy citizen being ground down by the drudgery of his job, and I pictured his cupboard full of boxing and rugby trophies. I blurred Tom's face by screwing up my eyes and tried to conjure up an image of him in his prime.

'Is something wrong with you?' Tom was bristling with aggression.

'Just something in my eye.'

'You look retarded.'

I changed the subject. 'Have we finished here, Tom?' I was anxious to leave, in case Morgan decided to call the police, or else came back with reinforcements.

'Don't worry about him,' said Tom. 'He's that scared he won't be back for a while. I've got the name of the hotel in Bali; it's called Paradise Padang, but I'm going to have a look at the file and see what else is there.'

He went to the cabinet and flipped through the file. 'Bloody cheek. Do you know what he's written about Marilyn? A gifted amateur, great body and could go a long way professionally.'

'Well, she has gone a long way, but not professionally.'

'What?'

'I mean she's gone a long way to Bali, but not in a professional capacity.'

Tom stared at me. 'What are you talking about?'

'All I'm trying to say, Tom, is that Marilyn went to that lunch to have an adventure. You know, for a bit of excitement, not to make a career out of it.'

Tom continued to look at me strangely and finally shook his head. 'All right, Geoff,' he said, still shaking his head. 'Well, at least I know it was her first time.' He put the folder back in the cabinet. 'I've got everything I need. I think it's time to go. I'm tempted to put a match to this place, but maybe that's going a bit far.'

Instead he picked up a marker pen and wrote PONCE on the wall. He turned to leave, and then suddenly spun round and kicked a hole in the side of Morgan's desk. 'I'll leave him that as a memento.'

The receptionist must have heard the noise because, as we reached the bottom of the stairs, she called out, 'Is everything all right?'

'Yes, thank you,' replied Tom. He stopped in front of the reception desk and leered at her unremarkable bosom. 'Are you free tonight?' he asked.

She shuddered and held up her left hand. 'I'm married.'

'So's my wife, but it didn't make any difference.'

'What are you going to do now?' I asked, as we walked back to the MG.

'I'm going to find them. That's what I'm going to do. I've got six weeks holiday owing and I'm taking it. I'll go over to Bali and try to get them back, and I'm selling this bloody MG to pay for it. And I'm going into training. Lifting that pathetic character was harder than it should've been.'

'Tom, can I help in any way? I mean, can Ally and I help in any way?'

'Well,' said Tom, 'how do you fancy a holiday in Bali?'

Tom dropped me at home but didn't come in. He hadn't slept for over thirty hours and was going to bed. Allison was eager to hear what had happened, but Joshua and Debra were home from school and we hadn't discussed what we were going to say to them. However, Josh already suspected that something was wrong.

'Kate and Gemma weren't at school today and they weren't there on Friday either. What's wrong with them?'

Allison glanced at me and pulled a wry face. 'Marilyn has taken them on holiday and they won't be at school for a while,' she said. 'It's all a bit of a secret, so we don't want you to tell anyone.'

'Why is it a secret?' asked Josh.

'If we tell you, it won't be a secret, will it?' I replied.

'We've both promised that we won't talk about it,' added Allison, 'and we want you to do the same. Debra, you first.'

'I promise,' said Debra.

'Thank you. Now you, Josh.'

'Has Tom gone with them?'

'No, but we can't talk about it. Now promise.'

'They're not getting divorced, are they?'

'Joshua!' Allison and I shouted together.

'Oh, all right, I promise,' said Josh.

After the children had gone to bed, I told Allison what had happened at Richard Morgan's office.

'I think you should go with Tom to Bali. He's bound to need some help.'

'I don't know about that. You should have been there this afternoon. It was like Die Hard. I've never seen anything like it. I just stood there and watched him half kill Richard Morgan.'

'I still think he's going to need your devious brain and boyish charm,' said Allison. 'He can thump the truth out of people and you can extract it with subtle persuasion.'

'I suppose I could go if he really wants me to, but I can't imagine I'd be much help. It's just a matter of him talking to Marilyn and trying to persuade her to come home. I mean, he can hardly knock her on the head and smuggle her back in his hand luggage. She's got to come willingly or not at all. But, whatever I decide to do, Ally, I definitely can't go until after my presentation to Stukely and Arnold next week. Incidentally,' I added, 'do you remember where we put the snorkels and masks from last summer?'

Allison smiled. 'So you will go then?'

'Well, I might, but you seem to be very keen that I go. I'm starting to think you've got another lunch at the Regent lined up.'

'No such luck, I'm afraid.'

Later, when we were in bed, a thought occurred to me. 'Allison, what happened about that tonka, or whatever it's called, you know, that Japanese love poem? Did Tosana write one for Marilyn? You never said.'

'Ah, the tanka,' Allison said sleepily. 'Yes he did, and he gave it to her after the meal. Of course, it was in Japanese, but Rudi translated it. It was some drivel about Marilyn's innocence and purity being like lambs prancing around in daisy-clad pastures, and his feelings for her being stronger than the hardest granite, or some such rubbish.'

I laughed. 'But not strong enough to stop him bonking Monique an hour later.'

'Exactly, and Marilyn had difficulty keeping a straight face, but she was very diplomatic. She said that she was deeply honoured by his poem, but made it clear that she wasn't interested in him, as she was promised to someone else.'

'It's just a shame it wasn't Tom,' I said.

CHAPTER SEVEN

Tom rang the following evening.

'I think I'm getting somewhere. This hotel, the Paradise Padang, is on the east coast of Bali near a place called Padangbai, which is a small port. The hotel sounds amazing and it costs two thousand dollars a night to stay there.'

'Does that include breakfast?'

'Geoff, it wouldn't matter if it included all meals, car hire and a butler. That's two thousand US dollars.'

'Jesus! I thought you were talking Indonesian dollars. You can't afford that. Anyway, Bali's supposed to be cheap.'

'Firstly,' said Tom, 'they don't have dollars in Indonesia, they have rupiah, but the prices of all the expensive hotels are in US dollars. Secondly, Bali is cheap, but this Paradise Padang is in a league of its own. After a day spent at travel agents and bookshops, I'm now something of an authority on Bali and I've got lots to show you. Why don't you come over for a beer?'

Tom's dining room table was covered with holiday brochures, travel books and flight details. He had a map of Bali pinned to the wall, and he had propped up one of his daughter's drawing boards and had written an action plan on it. It reminded me of the old war films that showed Montgomery's campaigns in Africa.

'Where's Rommel?' I said under my breath.

'What?'

'Nothing,' I said and sat down. 'From the look of all this, Tom, I'm going to need something stronger than a beer.'

'Right, I'll open a bottle of Australian red. That'll strengthen your resolve.' He handed me some papers. 'Have a look at this stuff I've downloaded from Paradise Padang's website.'

I quickly skimmed the pages. Paradise Padang is an enormous self-contained resort, perched above a series of sandy bays, with a backdrop of lush rainforest and terraced rice fields. The guest accommodation is set apart from the main complex and consists of individual two-storey buildings based on temple designs, each with a private garden, swimming pool and spa. The guests are brought to the hotel by helicopter from Denpasar airport.

I whistled. 'This place is unbelievable. I can see why it's two thousand dollars a night.'

'It's for the world's seriously rich and famous,' said Tom, 'and I wouldn't be allowed to stay there even if I could afford it. It is very, very exclusive. You didn't have time to read the section on security, but it's awesome. There are electrified fences around the perimeter, the access road has two permanently-manned gatehouses, and non-guests are not permitted on to the complex. It is not the sort of place where I can casually wander in, have a drink at the bar and bump into Marilyn.' Tom poured the wine. 'I've thought about sending an email to Marilyn at the hotel, but I'm sure it would never reach her. Cruyff is certain to have told his staff to intercept any emails, letters or phone calls, and I'm worried he'll simply whisk her and the girls away to another one of his hotels before I even get close. This guy is loaded, Geoff, and there's no way I can compete with him if he gets wind of what I'm planning. I'm convinced that the only way I'll get to see her is by stealth and cunning.'

From what I'd seen of Tom's tactics so far, it seemed more likely he'd try to punch his way in there. 'So, have you got a plan?'

'Not really, but I think I've got to stay in Padangbai. It's close and because it's a port it'll be a bustling place with lots of comings and goings and I'll be inconspicuous. Once I've sussed things out I'll find a way to see her.'

'Tom, if you'll forgive me for saying so, that isn't much of a plan and you don't even know if they're still in Bali. It's a very long way to go, and what happens if you do get to see her and she says she's not coming back?'

'Don't think that I haven't thought of all that,' said Tom. 'Look, I just know that they're still in Bali. Marilyn wouldn't put Kate and Gemma through a long flight like that and then go off on another flight a few days later. You're right, Geoff, I don't have a proper plan, but I'll work something out when I'm there.'

Tom emptied the bottle into our glasses. 'Look, Geoff, I love Marilyn and I always will. I love Kate and Gemma and I want to watch them growing up, not get postcards from them and see them once a year if I'm lucky. If I can't get them back, my life isn't worth living. So, if I waste some time and money going to Bali, it isn't important. I believe in my heart that Marilyn loves me and this whole business is some temporary insanity.'

Tom drank his wine, walked over to the sideboard and opened another bottle. He refilled our glasses and carried on. 'So, I'm going to Bali and when I find Marilyn I'll apologise for all the things I've done wrong. I've spent as long as I can remember bogged down in my own worries about work and money and not given a thought to her. I'm just so bloody annoyed that it's needed this to happen for me to see how woeful I've been.' I drank my wine. I didn't think Tom wanted me to say anything. 'I've given this Pieter Cruyff character a lot of thought. He's obviously a very big wheel and he could have just about any woman in the world he wants, but he's chosen Marilyn along with a couple of kids. I don't know much about really rich people, but I imagine they're used to getting their own way and controlling things, and I can't see that going down very well with Marilyn. Maybe she's been swept off her feet and thinks this is true romance that's going to last forever, but I have a feeling that, for Cruyff, this could be an amusing diversion for a few weeks. I wonder how Marilyn's going to handle things when it starts to go wrong. I think that there'll come a time when she's going to be very hurt and alone, and she'll need me as much as I need her. I just want to be there when it happens.'

Tom had been talking into his glass, but now he lifted his head and looked directly at me. I saw the pain in his eyes and couldn't hold his gaze.

'Don't you see, Geoff, I've got to believe this, otherwise I've lost them forever.'

I felt Tom's misery and full of emotion and Australian red I made the decision to go to Bali with him.

Tom came round on Wednesday evening and brought me up to date with the day's events. He had been to see Marilyn's parents and told them there was little doubt that Marilyn had become infatuated with Pieter Cruyff, a very wealthy Dutch-Indonesian, and had gone to Bali to be with him. It was probable that she and the girls were staying at Cruyff's hotel, but he felt sure that if he tried to contact her there he would not be allowed to talk to her. All it would do is alert Cruyff to the fact that Tom knew where she was, and then she and the children might be moved to another part of the world where he couldn't trace them. He was not prepared to take that chance, and he was going to Bali to find her and try to persuade her to come home. The earliest flight that Tom could get was on Sunday.

'Mr and Mrs McTavish are really worried about what might happen to Marilyn and the girls and Rory said that they'll finance my trip to Bali,' said Tom. 'He got very enthusiastic and it took all my powers of persuasion to deter him from coming with me. Anyway, it now means that I don't have to sell the MG. I'd been thinking about that and it occurred to me, if Marilyn came back and discovered I'd sold her car, she'd just as likely go off again.'

'That's a point,' I said, 'but you could always have sold your car. Anyway, I never knew his name was Rory. I've never heard you call him anything except "that old bastard McTavish".'

'Well, since Marilyn left, I've become closer to her parents than I ever was in the fifteen years she was here, but I'm still glad I managed to dissuade him from coming to Bali. Imagine trying to be inconspicuous with him wandering around in a kilt.'

'I don't know. The men over there wear sarongs, so maybe he could have passed it off as a tartan sarong.'

'Well he's not coming and that's that. Anyway, I went into work and told Simon what's happened and I'm taking some leave. I thought he'd say that I was breaching company rules by not giving him any notice, but he was surprisingly sympathetic and gave me the name of someone who runs a dive business in Bali. They used to work together years ago and are still great mates. He's going to let him know that I might contact him. Oh, and by the way,' Tom added, 'this bloke's gay.'

'What's that got to do with anything? Anyway, you'll be safe. He won't be attracted to large hairy men who go around attacking people.'

'I was only mentioning it, Geoff.'

Tom rang me at work on Thursday. Mr and Mrs McTavish had received a card from Marilyn, posted from Singapore airport the previous Saturday.

'It doesn't say much, Geoff, only that they're okay and she's doing something she had to, and she'll explain everything later.'

I thought for a few moments.

'Geoff, are you still there?'

'Yes, I'm thinking.'

'Well, can't you hum while you're thinking?'

'Marilyn's parents don't have a computer, do they?

'No.'

'You've checked *your* emails, haven't you, Tom?'

'Ten times a day and nothing.'

'Don't you think it's a bit strange she hasn't *rung* her parents? She must know they'll be worried sick.'

'Of course it's strange. The whole bloody business is strange.'

'Hmmm. Look, Tom, I've got to go now, but I'll give it some thought and I'll see you tonight.'

When I went to Tom's house that evening he was in low spirits.

'Listen, Tom, that postcard was written the day after she left. She hadn't even arrived in Bali at that stage. You can't read too much into it and there could be a dozen reasons why she hasn't been in touch since she got there. For God's sake, don't weaken now, or I'll be forced to open another bottle of red.'

'I know, Geoff, you're right, but the hanging around is getting to me. I want to be over there doing something, not wasting my time here.'

'Then let's do something positive now. I was using my not inconsiderable mental powers on the train coming home and I've jotted down a few thoughts.' I produced my notes and sat with Tom at the table. 'Let's assume for the moment that Marilyn and the girls *are* at Paradise Padang. Cruyff's not stupid and he'll anticipate that you'll be able to find that out. The airline tickets to Bali are a dead giveaway and Cruyff must have expected that you would learn a lot from Allison. He won't know how much she understood during the meal, but he'll be aware that she knows about his hotel in Bali. Also, once Richard Morgan got over the shock of your visit, he might have decided he would be better off telling Cruyff what happened, before you turn up on his doorstep.'

Tom nodded. 'Yes, I've already considered that.'

'Also, Cruyff must assume that you'll try to contact Marilyn and the fact that you haven't means one of three things. Firstly, you haven't found out yet where she is, and that's only if he hasn't already heard from Richard Morgan. Secondly, you aren't interested in pursuing your wife and children - which is pretty unlikely. Thirdly, you do know where they are, and by not emailing or phoning you intend turning up in person. I think they'll be waiting for you to arrive, and their security will be on the lookout for a large man with pale skin and untidy hair loitering around the hotel entrance.'

'You might be right, but I can't see it makes any difference. I'm still going over there and once I'm in Padangbai I'll figure out a way to see her. I might be able to hire a boat and land at a bay, or walk in on a trail through the rainforest.'

'Tom, I honestly can't see you getting through their security, especially if they're waiting for you, but there is a way you can contact Marilyn without breaking in.'

'How?'

'You find out from someone on the inside, like a waiter or a chambermaid, if Marilyn's there, and then you pay them to deliver a message to her.'

Tom gazed at me thoughtfully. 'That's a good idea, Geoff,' he said grudgingly. 'I knew there was a reason why I wanted you to come along.' I smiled modestly. 'It might not be easy to persuade Marilyn to come back, but if I can communicate with her, even if it's only by messages shoved under her door, at least it's a start.'

'Tom, the first thing you have to do is make sure that Marilyn and the girls are at Paradise Padang. I don't want to follow you out there to discover it's all a red herring and they're renting a house in Watford.'

CHAPTER EIGHT

I had a work function on Friday evening and didn't see Tom until Saturday morning. He had the things for his trip spread out on the floor in his lounge. He was doing a trial pack using the bathroom scales and, when I arrived, was trying to cram everything into a large backpack.

'Christ Tom, you're not going to need a sports jacket.' I had also been reading up on Bali. 'It's going to be hot and everywhere is pretty casual. In most places just wearing shoes is considered overdressed.' I poked through Tom's clothing, half expecting to find a safari suit and pith helmet. 'And everything's really cheap. You're better off taking less than you need and buying it over there.'

'All right. I'm not going to get this stuff in, anyway. I'll just take what's in fashion this season for the well-dressed jetsetter, like a couple of pairs of shorts and some tee shirts.'

Tom had laid out his wetsuit and one of those torches that you strap to your head. I prodded it with my foot. 'Thinking of going potholing while you're over there?'

'This, Geoff, is an underwater light which stops you bumping into sharks when you're swimming around in the dark. I might end up landing on one of those dear little bays in the middle of the night and it'll be nice to see where I'm going.'

I rolled my eyes. James Bond had a lot to answer for. 'I'm taking water wings and a beach ball,' I said.

There was a knock at the door and a stocky, ruddy-faced man in his late sixties walked in. Tom introduced him as Marilyn's father, Rory McTavish.

'How do you do, Mr McTavish,' I said, holding out my hand and smiling.

Rory McTavish didn't shake my hand, but instead attempted to compress it into something the size of a matchbox. I made a yipping noise, which I turned into a cough, and he released me. I thrust my hand in my pocket to prevent a further assault and saw that Tom was watching me with amusement.

Rory McTavish looked me straight in the eye and said, 'Whaur occledoo yer splitcrunge noo. Oo gang guid ochauld braw mon? Aye monie brither naw headlock dyke and scrotum.'

'I'm sorry,' I said mystified, 'I didn't quite catch that.'

He repeated what he'd said and added for good measure, 'Wee gang the gither occenstock puke bladder, laddie.'

I looked helplessly at Tom, who was absorbed in his travel documents and oblivious to my discomfort. I assumed that Rory had been expressing concern about his daughter and grandchildren and decided to reply with a harmless platitude.

'Don't worry, Mr McTavish, things might look bad now, but every cloud has a silver lining.'

He looked at me with sudden dislike. 'Nae buken stopcock en dickit longtit yer fukkan fule.'

McTavish turned abruptly and went over to Tom. He handed him an envelope and stood in front of him making a hideous sound as though he was gargling with gravel. After a few minutes, he shook Tom's hand briskly, gave me a bleak look that I tried to avoid and stomped out.

'What the hell was all that about?'

'He says you're a moron,' said Tom.

'Well, you were a fat lot of help. How was I to know he speaks some ancient form of highland peatbog? You might have warned me.' Tom was laughing. 'You did that deliberately.'

'He's got a fair handshake, hasn't he?' said Tom. 'He did that to me the first time I met him, but after the second time he never tried it again.'

I looked at Tom's giant hands and smiled. 'I wish I'd seen that.'

'You know he practises?' said Tom.

'What, by squeezing a tennis ball?'

'No, I don't mean the handshake, although he probably practises that, as well. What I meant was, speaking like Rob Roy. A few years ago we were staying at their house and I got up early to go for a walk. I thought that everyone was in bed, but as I passed the lounge I heard this amazing voice, deep, gruff and full of phlegm, as though it was oozing from sludge at the bottom of a loch. It was punctuated with lots of oots and ochs, and rolling Rs and guttural grunts. I stuck my head round the door and there was old McTavish standing in the middle of the room reciting from a book of Robbie Burns' poems. He must have sensed I was listening, because he swung round and stuffed the book under a cushion. I wished him good morning and left in a hurry.'

'Well, that's hardly conclusive he practises.'

'All right, what reason could he have for hiding the book? It's not as though I'd caught him with a dirty magazine. Well, I'm convinced he was practising his incomprehensible dialect and he didn't want me to find out his secret.'

'Come on, Tom, he's probably a closet stage performer and was embarrassed when you caught him in the act. Anyway, why would he want to talk like that, when no one can understand him?

'Probably to maintain his heritage like the tripe eaters, but funnily enough you get used to it after a while. Nowadays, I can make out one word in three, but when Marilyn and I were courting he thought she was going out with a simpleton.'

'How come the only words I understood sounded suspiciously like "fucking fool," and the rest of it was total gibberish?'

'Because he wanted you to understand that bit, which is precisely my point.'

'What else did he say to me?'

'Sorry, I can't help you there. I need to give him my full attention and I wasn't really listening. To stand any chance at all, I use a combination of audio and visual. I concentrate on every syllable and try to lip read, as well as watch for spittle and listen for the clacking of his false teeth. I've learnt that, if large dollops of spit are flying around and his teeth are going like castanets, he's either talking about the government or David Beckham.'

'I can see why you don't like going round there. I'd emigrate if I had him as my father-in-law.'

'Well, he's been brilliant over this business. He just gave me a cheque for three thousand pounds, and I'm nearly positive he said that if I need any more to let him know. I can't see how I misjudged him in the past.'

'Probably because you never understood what he said.'

Tom spent the afternoon doing last minute chores and in the evening he came over to eat with us. Josh and Debra were in the lounge watching television when Tom arrived. He was carrying a bottle of wine in one hand and a sheet of paper in the other.

'I'd like you to have a look at this and tell me what you think.' he said.

I took the bottle of wine and read the label. 'Coonawarra shiraz. It should be good, Tom.'

'Not the wine, you fool. *This.*'

It was an email from Marilyn that Tom had received half an hour earlier. I stood next to Allison and we read it together. It was addressed to her parents and was very brief. She said that she was doing what she wanted and needed time and space to think things out. She said that Katherine and Gemma were well and having a good time. There was no need to worry and she would be in touch.

'This email address, sunburst@starmail.com, doesn't give us any clues where it's from,' said Allison.

Tom shook his head. 'No, it could have come from anywhere.'

I handed it back to Tom. 'Do Mr and Mrs McTavish know you've received this?'

'I rang them straight away. Obviously they're relieved that Marilyn and the girls are okay, but can't understand why she hasn't rung them or said what she's doing and where they are.' Tom paused. 'So, what do you think?'

'Well,' said Allison, 'it's good to know they're all right, but it doesn't say a lot. Not much more than the postcard from Singapore and the wording seems strange. It's too formal, but it could just be that Marilyn found it really hard to write.'

'I'm not sure,' I said, 'but I agree with Ally that there's something not quite right about it.'

'I'll tell you what it is,' said Tom, 'Marilyn has called Kate *Katherine*. She was christened Katherine after Marilyn's mother, but everyone, including Marilyn's parents, has always called her Kate. So, why would Marilyn put Katherine?'

'That's true, I've never heard Marilyn say anything other than Kate,' said Allison.

'And you're right about the tone of it,' continued Tom. 'It's like an old-fashioned postcard and just stops short of saying "having a lovely time, wish you were here". I know Marilyn is clueless on the computer, but I still can't see her writing anything like this.'

'What are you saying, Tom?'

'I'm not sure she wrote the email.'

'If she couldn't use their computer, then maybe she asked someone to send it for her,' said Allison.

'Yes, but she would still have written it out. So, it doesn't explain why she put Katherine.'

I thought about what Tom had said. 'If you're right, then it means someone, presumably Cruyff, altered her original message. Perhaps she put where they are, or she said something else that he doesn't want you to know.' I paused. 'But it could be that the message *is* what Marilyn wrote and she deliberately used "Katherine" instead of Kate, which puts an entirely different light on things.'

'Why would she do that?' Allison asked.

'I don't know,' I said, 'but possibly to show Tom that she isn't free to say what she wants and her email was vetted before it was sent.'

'Seems a bit far fetched,' said Allison, 'although Marilyn can be pretty devious.'

'So I'm finding out,' said Tom dryly, 'but I think it's more likely that Cruyff has reworded her original message for the reason Geoff said.'

I was trying to work out the implications of Marilyn's email and I needed inspiration from the wine Tom had brought round. After the first mouthful I had a brainwave.

'If Marilyn was trying to tell you something by putting "Katherine", then you need to show her you've understood. You could put "Katherine" in your reply and she'll know that you spotted it.'

'Good idea,' said Tom, 'and to make sure I'll call Gemma, "Gem", which is something we never do. I'll reply as if it's from Marilyn's parents and ask where they are and what they're doing. Not that I expect to get a reply.'

'It's great to see that you two are getting into the swing of all this intrigue,' said Allison, 'but what will Marilyn think if Cruyff did alter her original message and she doesn't know that Kate was called "Katherine" in the revised version?'

'She'll think that Tom's gone bonkers and he's already forgotten the names of his children,' I said.

CHAPTER NINE

The following morning we drove Tom to the airport. I tried to make conversation, but Allison and Tom were unresponsive and I eventually gave up and we drove in silence. Outside the airport Allison hugged Tom and tearfully told him to take care. He promised to ring or email every day, and would let us know the moment he found out whether Marilyn and the girls were at Paradise Padang. I shook Tom's hand and wished him good luck, and said I was sorry that I wasn't going with him. He slung his backpack over one shoulder and we watched him stride away. He had lost weight since Marilyn left and he looked tough and determined. As he disappeared into the terminal Allison put her arm around me.

'Over the last week I've seen a totally different Tom to the one I've known for years, someone who is forceful and dynamic, and the type of person who would have attracted Marilyn in the first place, but it's taken something horrible like this to bring it out. I think that if he and Marilyn get back together again, and he *has* recaptured his old spirit, then there's a good chance it will work out.'

'I hope so,' I said, 'but isn't it strange that Tom never saw this coming? He knew things weren't right and he blamed his job and money worries, but he never thought there was anything fundamentally wrong with his marriage. He loves Marilyn and honestly believes that she still loves him, but if they *do* get back together he's got to change his job or the same thing is likely to happen again.'

'Perhaps you and Tom could go into business together.'

'Oh yes,' I said, 'doing what?'

'Finding missing people, marriage counselling, that sort of thing.'

'I think it'd be better if Tom and I stay at home looking after the children while you and Marilyn carry on working as paid companions at business lunches.'

Monday was the start of my two-day marketing presentation. For the last week I had not given it my full attention and I woke during the night worried that I was under-prepared. It was too late now and all I could do was try to focus on the day ahead and pray. At breakfast Debra and Josh were talking about the school holidays, which started in three weeks.

'Dad, can we go on holiday to a tropical island this year instead of France?' asked Josh.

I hadn't told them that I would probably be going to Bali on Sunday. 'No, it's France this year. Everything's booked, so we can't change our plans, but we'll go somewhere different next year.'

'Somewhere like Bali?'

I looked inquiringly at Allison, but she shook her head.

'Why Bali?' I asked.

'Isn't that where Tom's gone?'

'What makes you think that?'

'I heard you and Tom talking about Bali when he came round on Saturday.'

'Just because we were talking about it doesn't mean he's gone there.'

'Why else would you be talking about it? Anyway, *is* that where he's gone?'

I groaned. 'Mum and I will tell you all about it later in the week, as we promised. But right now, I've got a really important day at work and I can't be late.'

On the train I found it impossible to concentrate on the presentation to Stukely and Arnold. For the last few months I had been working on a series of initiatives to increase the retail giant's market share, but these now seemed trivial compared to Tom's domestic problems. However, despite my misgivings, the day went smoothly, and Derek, my boss, mistook my detachment for professional calm and afterwards complimented me. When I arrived home, Allison handed me an email from Tom.

Geoff, wear something warm on the plane and if I were you I'd take sandwiches. Lots of free booze though, so it wasn't all bad. Met two Aussie surfers and I'll tell you about them when I see you. You were right about clothes, we're not going to need a lot in Bali. It's bloody hot. Staying in Kuta tonight and I'll hire a car in the morning and drive to Padangbai. Checked my emails and nothing from Marilyn. Let me know if she rings home. Love to Ally and the kids. Tom.

I telephoned Marilyn's parents and, to my relief, her mother answered the phone. She had a mild Scottish accent, consistent with someone who had lived in England for the past thirty-five years, and I thought it was decidedly suspicious that Rory's had become stronger and more unintelligible. Perhaps Tom was right and he did practise it. I told her that Tom had arrived safely and I would keep in touch with any news of Marilyn. I then sent a reply to Tom.

Glad you didn't get lost. No news from Marilyn. Let me know ASAP if Marilyn's there and you still need me.

Stay off the booze and don't drink the water. Cheers Geoff.

I received an email from Tom before I went to work on Tuesday.

Geoff, if you think rush hour at Piccadilly is horrendous, don't drive here. They're all suicidal or insane or both. Most of the roads are the width of footpaths and there are no road signs. The two hour drive to Padangbai took four and it was sheer luck I survived. I've found out that the life expectancy of drivers over here is about the same as World War II pilots. Had a stroke of luck, though. Wayan, the owner of Juniata Beach Hotel where I'm staying, has a cousin called Kadek who works at Paradise Padang. But she lives on the complex and it's hard to see her. I've asked Wayan to help (for a large sum of money I might add) and he's going there this evening to try to talk to her and see if she knows anything about Marilyn. According to Wayan, just about everyone in Padangbai is related or at least they know each other, which is great for finding things out, but a problem if you want to keep anything secret. This is a VERY small place, Geoff. I've told Wayan that it is VITAL nobody finds out I'm trying to trace Marilyn. I'll ring or email after Wayan talks to Kadek. Cheers Tom

I showed Tom's email to Allison and straightaway sent a reply.

Tom, I'm increasing my life insurance. Does your car have air bags? Good news about Kadek in Paradise Padang. It sounds as though you're making progress and without punching anyone. Let me know what happens. Cheers Geoff.

Although my mind was in Bali, the last day of the presentation went well. I stayed for celebratory drinks after work and told Derek that I might need to take a couple of weeks off to help a friend who was having marital problems. Derek said that he thought I was the last person who'd be of any help, but somehow they'd struggle along without me.

Tom rang at seven o'clock the following morning. He was excited and very loud. 'Geoff, they're here. I knew it! It wasn't a wasted journey. Kadek has seen Marilyn and the girls and says they're important friends of the owner. Wayan only spoke to her for a few minutes at the security gate, so I don't know much more than that except that they don't live in the main complex.'

'Tom, that's fantastic! What are your chances of seeing her?'

'I'm not sure. Kadek has a day off on Sunday and she'll be with her family in Padangbai. Wayan's taking me to see her, so I'll find out more then and decide what to do. And for the next few days I shall do some sleuthing.

'Good, and stay out of trouble. I'll be on the Sunday flight, the same one as yours.'

'Thanks, Geoff, I really appreciate it. When something like this happens you find out who your friends are.'

'It's nothing to do with friendship, Tom. I just fancy a holiday in Bali.'

Tom laughed. 'Okay, I'll see you at the airport on Monday.'

'So, you're going,' said Allison.

'Yes, it looks like it. Although knowing my luck, Marilyn will fall into Tom's arms and they'll get on the first flight home. I'll be on the plane going out there as they're coming back and we'll pass over India.'

'Somehow, I don't think so. If she'd wanted to come back, all she had to do was ring Tom or her parents and say she's coming home.'

'Yes, but could you actually see Marilyn doing that? She's not the sort to eat humble pie.'

Allison nodded. 'Yes, once she made that decision to leave it'd be hard for her to reverse it.' She put her arm round my waist and squeezed a bit of excess flesh. 'Anyway, you must go to Bali if Tom needs you. Even if it's only to stop you getting old and dull, and it will give you something to talk about besides cricket.'

I assumed Ally was joking, although I would be sorry to miss the Lords' test, but I was glad I hadn't mentioned it.

I was now very eager to go out there. I rang Marilyn's parents to tell them the news and Rory McTavish answered the phone. I spoke quickly. 'Mr McTavish, Tom has found out where Marilyn and the girls are in Bali and he's working out a way to see them. I'm going over myself on Sunday and we'll keep you posted.'

'Spraur splatleg, laddie. Wee bonnie knobrust und stucklebonk,' he spat.

'Thankyou, Mr McTavish, I'll let Tom know,' I said and hung up immediately.

At dinner on Wednesday we told Debra and Josh that Marilyn and Tom had fallen out, and Marilyn had gone to Bali with Kate and Gemma. Tom had flown over there to find them, make up with Marilyn, and bring them all home. But it still had to be kept secret and not spread around the playground.

'And Dad's going over to Bali on Sunday to help Tom,' Allison said matter-of-factly.

'Wow!' exclaimed Josh triumphantly, 'I knew something was going on. I'll go with you, Dad. I'll help

Tom find them. I'm good at finding things. Look who always finds Mum's car keys.'

'Don't start on my car keys again,' said Allison. 'Anyway, it's too late. Tom's already found out where they are. Apart from which, you're too young and you've got to be at school.'

'Well, Kate and Gemma aren't at school. Not if they're in Bali.'

'How do you know that?' I asked. 'What makes you think that they don't have English-speaking schools in Bali? It's nice of you to offer, Josh, but this is for Tom to sort out, and I'm going because he's my best friend and he might need my help.'

'Well, can we go there next year?' asked Josh, 'and are you bringing us back presents?'

'Maybe and yes.' I smiled at Josh and then looked at Debra. I saw that she was close to tears. 'Darling, what's wrong?'

'I think it's horrible that Kate and Gemma's mum and dad have fallen out and we might never see any of them again. And I don't want Daddy to go, either. What if something happens to him?'

'Of course we'll see them again, and don't worry about Dad. Nothing's going to happen to him,' said Allison.

'I'll be all right, Debra,' I said. 'Bali's not a primitive place where people go around eating each other. It's a tourist island, a sort of Asian Ibiza.'

Allison stared at me. 'An Asian Ibiza? You've got me worried, now.'

CHAPTER TEN

Tom didn't contact us for two days, and we thought that he might have tried to force his way into Paradise Padang and been arrested, but he rang on Friday morning before I left for work.

'Where the hell have you been?'

'In bed,' groaned Tom. 'I'm dying. For two days I've been flat on my back with dysentery or worse. All I've done is crawl from the bed to the toilet and back again. This is the first time I've left the room. Christ, of all the times for it to happen. I must get better before Sunday.'

'So, you got the dreaded Bali belly. I told you not to drink the water.'

'Look, I'm not in the mood for your nauseating wisdom. I just wanted to let you know that I'm alive. These phone calls from Bali are bloody expensive and now I'm going back to bed.'

I started to say something, but Tom had hung up.

'Ally,' I called, 'that was Tom. He's been in bed for two days with Bali belly and he's in a foul mood.'

'Thank God he's all right. I had visions of him rotting in some Indonesian jail.'

'Who's in jail?' asked Josh. 'Is Tom in jail?'

'No, he's not in jail, he's just had a bad stomach and he's been in bed, that's all.'

'Well, why did Mum think he might be in jail?'

'It was a joke, Josh. No one's going to jail, but I'm going to work. I've got a lot to do today.'

At lunchtime I walked to the travel agent to collect my ticket. I had been reading about Indonesia and learnt that, although it has the largest Muslim population in the world, the Balinese practise a form of Hinduism and the travel book described them as friendly, peace-loving and spiritual. They sounded very different to the people living around our way.

'Don't you worry about those dreadful terrorist bombings in Bali,' said the travel agent. 'They got the people who did it and anyway they'll never do it again. It won't have any shock value, see?'

He talked as though he was an authority on terrorist tactics and I was eager to agree. 'That's good logic. So I should be safer in Bali than most other places?'

He looked at me pityingly. 'Bombs aren't the only thing to worry about. You are going to an area with all kinds of horrible tropical diseases, and they don't have the National Health Service over there, you know.'

'That's a relief.'

'This is not a joking matter,' he said sternly. 'I strongly recommend you take out travel insurance with the maximum medical cover, because just about anything could happen while you're there.'

I thought of Tom, who'd been in Bali for four days and spent two of them in bed, and agreed it was a sensible precaution. I gave him my credit card and asked him to cover me for everything.

Looking back, I wonder if the travel agent's comment was a premonition of what was to occur, but it didn't really matter because none of that was insurable.

No one at work knew that I was going to Bali, but the word had gone around that I was taking time off to help a friend whose marriage was going through a bad period. When I left on Friday afternoon, Susie, the receptionist, said I was doing a very noble thing and gave me a soft, moist kiss on the mouth. I was smiling as I walked to catch the train home and decided I'd be noble more often.

Tom rang on Saturday and he sounded better. 'This is a remarkable place, Geoff, really beautiful and everyone is so friendly. The only trouble is they're all trying to sell you something. I ended up buying five sarongs today.'

'I take it you've recovered then. When you rang yesterday you were dying, if you remember. Anyway, you're supposed to be sleuthing, not shopping.'

'I'm a lot better, Geoffrey, thank you for asking,' Tom said levelly, 'and I have been finding out things. I'll tell you when I see you.'

'Why do you need five sarongs?'

'I don't, but I feel sorry for the people here. They've got so little and since the bombings there aren't as many tourists, so they're really struggling. I bought two sarongs from this lady who's supporting three children on her own. She left her husband because he spent all his time cockfighting. He'd gamble and lose, and then take it out on her.'

'Cockfighting? That must be hard to do. It sounds a strange way to settle an argument and must play havoc with your love life. What are the rules?'

'What?'

'Is it anything like kickboxing? You were a boxer, weren't you, Tom. Perhaps you could take up cockfighting and teach them a thing or two.'

'Very funny, Geoff. You know exactly what I mean. It's a fight between a couple of chickens and people bet on them. And stop wasting my money; this call is costing me an arm and a leg. I could have bought another five sarongs for the price.'

'Sorry, Tom, I just thought you might be missing my light-hearted banter.'

'Well, I'm not,' grunted Tom. 'Now listen, I'll meet you outside Denpasar airport on Monday. You'll recognise me because I'm a foot taller than everyone else and I've got blond hair.'

'It used to be greyish.'

'Well, the sun's bleached it. And I'll give you a word of warning. After you get through customs don't, whatever you do, let a porter carry your bags or you'll spend the next hour arguing over the price. Just grab a trolley, or carry the damn things yourself.'

It was obvious that Tom had had an unpleasant experience, but now didn't seem the time to ask him about it. 'Right, Tom, no porter. Anything else?'

'Yes, don't forget your diarrhoea tablets. Bye, Geoff.'

'Good luck on Sunday.' But I was talking to a dead line.

I had bought a splendid new backpack for the trip. It was a dazzling shade of fluorescent red and came with a detachable daypack.

'Was pink the only colour they had?' Allison said, looking at it critically. 'You'll blind people with the reflection.'

'It's not pink, it's red, and I'm making sure the lethal drivers over there see me at night.'

'See you? They'll think you're a traffic light and stop.'

'Just so long as they don't run me over. Anyway, it's too late now, I'm not changing it.'

I was trying to keep the pack as light as possible, but Allison had emptied out half the medicine chest and was insisting that I take it.

'If they check this at the airport they'll think I'm the flying doctor.'

'Well, look what happened to Tom. You won't be any use if you get sick.'

I sighed and packed the medical kit, along with my short-wave radio, just in case the BBC broadcast some commentary of the test match.

'That's it, Ally. I won't have any room for Josh and Debra's presents if I take anything else.'

'And mine,' said Allison.

'And yours, of course, darling. If I've forgotten anything I'll buy it when I'm there. The only other thing is my mobile. Tom's forgotten his, but he says that the mobile phone revolution hasn't reached Bali yet and there's no signal in Padangbai, so I'm not sure if there's any point.'

'If Tom hasn't got his, then you must take yours. Even if there's no signal in Padangbai there's bound to be coverage in other parts of the island.'

The evening meal was the last that we would have together for a while and I had expected it to be subdued, but Josh and Debra were excited about the trip and they had prepared an impossibly long list of things they wanted me to bring back, including a monkey for Debra. I pocketed the list and said that I would try my best.

Allison was drinking more than usual, and kept telling me to look after Tom and stop him doing anything stupid. 'When you see Marilyn,' she said, 'tell her that Tom's still the man she married. She'll know what I mean. Tell her to come home and we'll do something together. I'm not sure what, but we'll do something.'

'How about an escort agency?' I suggested and immediately regretted it.

'Trust you, Geoff. You never take anything seriously. I really mean it. We'll show you.'

'Sorry love, I couldn't resist it. I'm sure you'll be great in business together.' I turned to the children. 'Okay, it's time for you to go to bed. Mum and I still have a few things to do and it's an early start in the morning.'

'What are these things we've got to do?' asked Allison after Josh and Debra had gone to bed.

'Well, I'm going away and I won't see you for a couple of weeks, so I was thinking ...'

'You'd better stop thinking, after your remark about the escort agency.'

'I did apologise and I really didn't mean it.'

'You'll have to grovel a lot more than that, Geoff Larkham.'

'I'm not very good at grovelling. Perhaps you could take it out on me physically, instead.'

'No chance. You'll be lucky not to spend your last night in the spare room.'

But I've always been lucky like that.

The following morning at the airport I hugged and kissed my family and we said a sombre goodbye. Joshua produced a miniature torch from his pocket and gave it to me.

'Just in case, Dad, you might need it.'

I thanked him solemnly and put it my pack.

Allison said, 'We won't wait, Geoff. I hate all the hanging around. It just makes it worse.'

Debra clung to my waist until at last I had to gently remove her hands. They turned once and waved, and then they were gone.

The British Airways' check-in clerk stared at my backpack before he studied me with a faint smile. I unzipped the daypack, put it over my shoulder and checked in the large pack. I heard him laugh as I walked away.

Heathrow is in a permanent state of terrorist alert and the customs and security officers were unsmiling and thorough. A few people were asked to remove their shoes, which were checked for concealed bombs. The customs officer passed my pack twice through the x-ray machine and then asked me to take everything out. She examined my mobile phone, camera, and short-wave radio, and when she had finished she took me to one side and handed me over to a senior security officer. He looked bored and had bad breath.

'Why are you visiting Bali, sir?'

'Just for a holiday.'

'On your own, sir?'

'Yes. That is allowed, I take it?'

'Of course, sir, but it's a bit unusual, isn't it?'

'I'm meeting a friend over there.'

'Male or female, sir?'

'I can't see that's any of your ...' His nose twitched and his eyebrows rose half an inch. 'Male,' I said.

'And you're married ... sir?'

'Yes, I'm married with two lovely children, all right?'

'And your wife knows about this?'

I noticed that he'd dropped the "sir". 'Christ, of course she does. He's a friend of the family.'

'Of course he is. And do you have any cabin baggage apart from that nice little pink backpack?'

'It's red,' I said. I was really beginning to regret I'd chosen this colour. 'And I don't, just a nice big red backpack that I've checked in.'

'Fine. Will you take off your shoes.'

I took off my shoes and handed them to him, one at a time. He tapped the heels and then felt inside them.

'Sole searching?' I said.

He finished looking inside the shoes and then stared at me unpleasantly. Perhaps someone had said it to him before.

'We also do cavity searches,' he said and pointed to a pair of rubber gloves on top of a cleaner's trolley. 'Well, isn't that a coincidence. They match your pack.' He found this amusing and shared the joke with a colleague. They both looked at me and laughed. I smiled to show that I appreciated his scalpel wit, but he hadn't finished.

'Normally, I wouldn't recommend an internal examination of body orifices, but in your case you'd probably enjoy it.'

'Jesus Christ! Look, I'm not gay and, even if I were, I wouldn't want someone with rubber gloves poking around up my bum.'

'Don't you enjoy safe sex?' His colleague was listening and they both laughed.

'That is not bloody funny.'

They continued to look at me. 'Over the years, I've found that when people don't cooperate it means they've got something to hide and a cavity search usually finds it, doesn't it, Ralph?' His colleague nodded in agreement.

I was suddenly sweating. 'I am cooperating. I've answered your questions. What else can I do?'

'It's very nice of him to cooperate, isn't it, Ralph?' Ralph smiled at me. 'So, shall we carry on then?' I nodded. 'Are you planning to visit any Muslim parts of Indonesia?'

'No, we're spending the whole time in Bali. Honestly, we're just there for a holiday.'

'And you're both staying at the same hotel?'

'Yes ... but in separate rooms.'

'If you say so, sir. Well, I hope you enjoy yourselves together.'

He turned to Ralph and they sniggered. I picked up the daypack and made my way to the departure lounge. I was glad to be leaving England. It was becoming more like a police state every day.

I resolved that as soon as I got to Bali I'd buy another pack.

CHAPTER ELEVEN

Immediately I stepped off the plane I knew that I was a long way from home. The air was like nothing I'd encountered before; it was hot and moist, and smelled of incense and clove-scented tobacco smoke.

My plane had arrived at Denpasar at the same time as a Garuda flight from Australia. The people who got off the two planes were mostly young and the baggage collection was littered with surfboards and backpacks. The queues to get through customs and immigration were long and moved slowly, and it was nearly an hour before I was clear. I remembered Tom's advice and, shouldering my pack, I waved away offers from the porters to carry it fifty yards to the exit.

Outside the airport it was pandemonium. There were scores of taxi drivers vying for trade, lines of hotel employees with placards bearing the names of guests, and hundreds of tourists milling about. I spotted Tom standing near the back of the throng and waved.

He weaved through the crowd smiling. 'This place is bedlam. Come on, let's get out of here.' Tom had hired a Suzuki 4x4 and he threw my pack in the back. 'Christ, Geoff, did you borrow this from Allison? We're trying to be inconspicuous.'

I sighed. 'I'll get rid of it and buy another one.'

Tom grunted and shot out into the traffic. There was a shriek of horns and he grinned at me. 'You soon get used to the driving over here. Hold on,' he yelled and turned right in front of an oncoming car. I opened my eyes and was surprised to find that we were still alive.

'Jesus, Tom, was that really necessary?'

'Merely proving a point. I work on the principle that no one wants an accident, so they always try to avoid you. If you just keep going, ninety per cent of drivers simply get out of your way.'

'What about the ten per cent who don't?'

He looked at me as though it was obvious. 'You get out of their way, of course.'

'Right,' I said, 'it sounds straightforward.'

Cars and trucks were whizzing around us and I was still trying to work out what side of the road we were supposed to be on.

'Marilyn will be in her element here,' said Tom. 'She drives like this all the time.'

I smiled. 'Perhaps she's got some Indonesian in her.'

'That's what I've come over to put a stop to,' Tom said.

'God, I'm sorry Tom; I didn't mean it like that.'

The heavy traffic that clogged the sprawling outskirts of Denpasar took all of Tom's attention and he drove for a while in silence. As I watched the Balinese thronging the pavements I was assaulted by acrid smoke from food being fried on roadside stalls which mingled with noxious fumes from decrepit lorries. Repetitive melodies of gamelan music drifted out of shop doorways, punctuated by sharp cries from the traders. We passed clusters of shops selling basketwork, sculpted stone and carved wood, their wares piled high on the footpaths. I smiled as we passed several with signs advertising antiques made to order. After twenty minutes, the traffic thinned and the clamour of Denpasar gave way to the tranquillity of rice fields and groves of coconut palms. I breathed deeply and let Bali wash over me.

Tom glanced at me, 'You can see why the first Europeans who came here called it paradise.'

He had recovered from Bali belly and looked leaner and fit. He read my mind and smiled. 'It's a very effective way to lose weight and would do you some good, Geoff.' he said, prodding my stomach with a large finger. 'They ought to advertise Bali for slimming holidays, but it's pretty drastic and I don't recommend it.'

'All right, Tom, let's leave my tummy out of this. Now tell me what's happened since I spoke to you on Saturday.'

'Right, well yesterday I went with Wayan to see Kadek. She works in the central complex at Paradise Padang and rarely sees Marilyn, who's staying in Cruyff's mansion behind the main bay. A friend of hers, Made, is a cleaner at the mansion and Kadek needs her help to contact Marilyn. Most of the senior staff are Europeans who live on the complex with their families and there's a small school for their children.' Tom paused while he braked and steered the Suzuki around a dog that was asleep in the centre of the road. As we drove past the dog it opened its eyes but didn't move from its position and Tom muttered something before continuing his narrative. 'There are three ways to get into Paradise Padang; by road, helicopter or boat, and each route is well protected. The road has two sets of gatehouses, which are manned by armed guards, and the helicopter pad has 24 hour security. They keep a permanent watch to make sure no unauthorised boats come into any of the bays and there are a couple of launches moored at the jetty to chase people off.' He paused. 'Oh yes, and all phone calls go through the switchboard and are monitored. It's like a tropical Alcatraz.'

'Well, we already knew from their website that the security was going to be good, and all it does is confirm that you can't just breeze in there and tap Marilyn on the shoulder.'

'Which is a pity, but you're right; it is what we expected. Anyway, I wrote Marilyn a letter and gave it to Kadek. She'll give it to Made to hand to her personally when Cruyff isn't around. She said that if they're caught helping me they'll lose their jobs, so you can imagine how much this has cost me. It's the most expensive letter I've ever sent and it was also the hardest to write. I was thinking this might be my one chance to get to see her and I could mess it up if I wrote the wrong thing. In the end I kept it really short and just said that when she left it made me see all the things that had gone wrong between us, most of which were my fault, and I said that I loved them all and missed them. I asked her to ring me at six in the evening at the hotel or else give a reply to Made.'

'When's the earliest Marilyn will get your letter?'

'Probably tomorrow morning.'

'Which means that she might ring tomorrow evening. But, if she doesn't, how will you know if she's given a reply to Made?'

'Kadek will ring Wayan at the hotel and arrange to meet him at the top security gate, but the guards will get suspicious if she keeps doing that. So, after this, we'll have to find another way to communicate.'

'Tom, do you know if mobile phones work inside Paradise Padang? The billionaires who stay there would be lost without their mobiles, so maybe it has its own tower. I've brought my mobile and, if you can get it to Marilyn, she can ring you without going through their switchboard.'

'I don't know, but I'll ask Wayan. Anyway, let's wait and see how Marilyn reacts to my letter. If I don't hear from her by Friday I'm going to hire a boat and try to get in at one of the bays. The worst that can happen is they catch me and throw me out, and at that stage I won't have anything to lose.'

'Of course she'll answer your letter. You've come halfway round the world to see her, and after fifteen years of marriage the least she'll do is ring you or write you a note.'

'Even if it's only to tell me to stop following her around?' Tom said.

As we drove through a small village we were forced to slow to walking pace when we encountered a long procession coming towards us. The men and the women were wearing brightly-coloured sarongs and tops, and most of the women were carrying large baskets, laden with fruit, on their heads.

'They have endless ceremonies over here, Geoff. You see them everywhere. All the people get dressed-up and march off to the temples, but I haven't discovered yet whether they eat all that food they're lugging about or if it's offerings to the gods.'

'Well, either way, those women are incredibly strong. The baskets must weigh a ton.'

'That's nothing,' said Tom. 'You wait until you see the women on the building sites. They carry baskets on their heads full of rocks and sand that weigh more than they do. I've decided that Balinese women are not naturally short; they've just been *compressed*.'

I laughed. 'But have you noticed how graceful the women are? They seem to sort of glide along without moving their legs.'

'It's because of the baskets,' said Tom. 'I remember that Marilyn wandered around for days with a dictionary balanced on her head because it was good for her posture. So you can assume that if you spend half your life with a bloody great basket up there it's going to make you graceful.'

'But short,' I pointed out.

'That is the down side.'

We rounded a bend and there was a massive rock on our side of the road. As Tom swerved to avoid it, I saw that it was in front of a deep pothole into which someone had stuck a bamboo pole with a red cloth tied to the top.

'Bloody Balinese road works,' muttered Tom. 'I suppose they'll fill in that hole eventually, but in the meantime they've thoughtfully stuck a rock there to warn motorists. Frankly, I'm not sure which'd be worse; to go down that hole or hit the sodding rock. Anyway, if you've finished sightseeing, Geoff, I'll carry on telling you what I've been doing. You remember that Simon, my boss, gave me the name of someone who lives out here?'

I nodded. 'He runs a diving business or something?'

'That's right. Well, I rang him yesterday. His name's Murray Rollinson and he lives in Amed, which is an hour or two up the coast from Padangbai. Simon had already spoken to Murray about me, and he told me to come and see him and he'd do what he could to help. He sounds a real character, Geoff, very public school and you wonder how he ended up in Bali. There was one strange thing, though, he asked me my age.'

'Well, didn't you say he's gay? He's probably checking you out.'

'No, it can't be that. He knows I'm here to get Marilyn and the girls back, so he's not likely to be sizing me up. It was a bit odd. Anyway, I've explored Padangbai, which doesn't take very long. The port's pretty busy with the ferries going to Lombok and there are a lot of outrigger boats used for fishing or taking tourists out diving and snorkelling around the reefs. There are quite a few restaurants and small hotels, but nothing posh, and the whole place is pretty low key. Also, there aren't many tourists at the moment. In fact, there are more hawkers than tourists and they drive you mad. You can't walk more than a few paces without someone sticking a tray of watches in your face. But after you've been around a few days a lot of them get to know you and leave you alone. Anyway, you'll see for yourself, because we're coming into Padangbai now.'

The harbour town of Padangbai huddles around a horseshoe bay, with a steep, rocky headland at each end and a backdrop of hills covered by rainforest. A line of small red and blue outriggers were pulled up on the yellow sand, with larger boats moored close to the shore. The port is at the southern end of the bay, and Juniata Beach Hotel, where we were staying, is at the north.

I checked in at the hotel, unpacked, and had a shower. Tom came into the room and handed me a bottle of cold beer.

'This is Bintang,' he said. 'Everyone drinks it here. The wine is expensive and tastes disgusting, so I suggest you stick to the beer.'

'Thanks, Tom,' I yawned. 'It's been a long day. I think I'll have an early night.'

'Now, listen, the best way to avoid jet lag is to go out the first night and drink a large number of Bintangs and straight away you're acclimatised. I'm speaking from personal experience, I might add. Anyway, it's only lunchtime in England, so you've got no excuse to be tired. Come on, I'll treat you to a meal at the best restaurant in town.'

No one molested us on our walk to the restaurant, apart from one man who followed us for a short distance calling out, 'Transport, transport,' as he made steering-wheel movements with his hands.

'Where are all the hawkers you've been complaining about?'

'They're around in droves during the day,' said Tom, 'but even they've had enough by evening, so you're pretty safe after about seven.'

We sat outside at the front of the restaurant and watched the lights of the ferries in the port. We were drinking our second Bintang and I was feeling blissfully relaxed.

'This is perfect, Tom, I don't think I'll ever want to leave.'

Tom decided it was the right moment to tell me about the two days he'd spent in bed.

'It was green and like water, Geoff, and the smell! I tell you, I've never felt so ill in all my life. I could have died in that room and no one would have known. When you've had a near-death experience with Bali belly it puts things into perspective. Now, I've decided to eat at only the best restaurants while I'm here and to hell with the expense, because I'm not risking another dose of that.'

I looked at the menu. 'Tom, the most expensive dish on this menu is 60,000 rupiah. It sounds a lot, but that's only about four pounds, so I'd hardly call it an extravagance.'

Tom ignored me and carried on. 'But the unfortunate thing is, once you've had Bali belly, you view *all* restaurants with suspicion, even the best one in town. I mean, look at this glass I'm drinking out of. It was probably washed in the urinal. And these crumpled, filthy, 1,000 rupiah notes that I've been given in change have passed through hundreds of pairs of hands, each of which has wiped someone's arse.'

'Probably their own,' I suggested.

'The point I am trying to make,' Tom continued doggedly, 'is that it's impossible to be safe. Each time you touch a door handle, shake someone's hand, or use a knife and fork, you are at risk. You get paranoid, like Howard Hughes, and wash your hands fifty times a day, prepare all your own food and avoid contact with people.'

'Come on, Tom, it's just that our systems haven't got used to the different bacteria. You can't come here and live in a capsule. You have to eat and drink and meet people.' A thought occurred to me. 'Mind you, I remember reading that Shane Warne took a suitcase full of canned food to India on an Australian tour. He refused to eat the meals because he'd suffered horribly on his last visit. They were the only runs he got, as I recall.'

Tom laughed. 'It's great to see you, Geoff. Here's to success.'

'To success,' I echoed.

I picked up the menu. 'I need to eat something before I have another beer. What's *carried barracuda?*'

'That should be *curried.*'

'And it says that all fish dishes are served with *rice or chops.*'

'That's *chips.* You'll soon get used to the spelling.'

I scanned the menu. '*Soap,* I presume, is *soup?*'

'Not hard, is it?'

'No, it's pretty easy now I know the system. By the way, can you understand the waitress?'

'Yes,' said Tom, 'after Marilyn's dad, she's dead easy.'

'Good. Then you'd better order. I'll have the *flied chucken.*'

CHAPTER TWELVE

The next morning I had a hangover, but no jet lag, so it appeared that Tom's method actually worked. After breakfast, Tom suggested that we take a walk over the headland to Blue Lagoon, but outside the hotel the sarong sellers were lying in wait and they greeted Tom like an old friend. The women carried neatly folded parcels of sarongs on their heads, and they put them down as soon as they saw us. Within a few minutes we had six women around us holding up sarongs.

I nudged him. 'Just how many do they think you need? Tell them you can't support the sarong industry single-handed and let's go.'

'They're expecting *you* to buy some.'

'Well, I don't want any.'

'Come on, Geoff. Allison and Debra would love a sarong. Look, that pink one is perfect for Debra.'

'Jesus, Tom, are you on a percentage?'

'No, of course not. It's just that you'll really help these women, plus you'll get some great presents.'

'Oh God, all right then, I'll buy one for Debra.'

But I'd underestimated them. They are consummate artists who are used to resistance. They were smiling and friendly, and they wanted to know all about me. Am I married? Do I have children? Is my family here? Is this my first visit to Bali? How long will I be in Padangbai? I fell under their spell, and before I knew it I was seated on the beach and they had formed a ring round me. The prey was in the centre of their web and there was no escape. Their brown arms and legs gleamed in the morning sun, and when their skin brushed mine it felt like velvet. Their hands moved gracefully and hypnotically as they folded and unfolded the sarongs, and their eyes flashed with irrepressible life. I was now their friend and after mispronunciations and laughter I managed to repeat their names. Putu unselfconsciously rested her hand on my thigh as she told me about her children, and after she had finished it remained there like a promise.

Tom leant over and whispered in my ear. 'Don't get excited. She doesn't fancy you; she just wants to sell you a sarong. And, remember, you have to bargain. You never pay what they ask.'

'Six sarongs, Tom! What am I going to do with six sarongs?'

'Well, you were in a difficult situation there. You could hardly buy from just one or two of them and not the rest. It's a learning curve for you, Geoff. You'll get better at it.'

'I can't believe you said that. You were the one who persuaded me to buy a sarong in the first place. Christ, Tom, I wasn't going to buy anything, in case you've forgotten.' I looked on the bright side. 'Anyway, I expect they'll leave me alone now.'

'No chance,' said Tom. 'Now they've all sold you a sarong they'll try to sell you a massage and pedicure. These open-sided huts that everyone lounges about in are used for massages, or else you can have a gritty one on the beach.'

'You've had one, then?'

'No, I've just seen tourists being massaged. They lay there like porpoises, get covered in oil and then they're pummelled about. It's all a bit pointless, but they seem to enjoy it. I haven't had a massage for years. In fact, the last time was in Birmingham after a game of rugby. The whole team got pissed and we went to a place that did theme massages. I found myself in a dungeon with a large woman who'd managed to squeeze herself into PVC hot pants and thigh-length boots, and was topless. She spanked me with a riding crop and gave me a wank at the end. These Balinese massages seem pretty tame after that.'

'I suppose they would,' I said.

We carried on to Blue Lagoon and climbed up a steep rutted track to the top of the headland. It ended at a grassy knoll and there were cattle grazing in the distance. I was out of breath, but Tom appeared unaffected.

'You sound like an asthmatic,' he commented. 'You need some exercise. I suggest an early morning jog, followed by a twenty minute swim, and in a few days you'll feel like a new man.'

'I don't want to feel like a new man. I'm quite happy with the old one.'

We climbed down the dusty path from the headland to Blue Lagoon. It is breathtaking. The yellow crescent of sand has black volcanic rocks at each end, and tropical trees and ferns grow down to the beach. The turquoise water sparkled, and at the back of the beach three waitresses sat in the shade of a rickety bar built from bamboo and palm leaves. Tom smiled and waved, and they chorused, 'Good morning, Tom.'

'Very handy for a lunch-time Bintang,' said Tom. 'Come on, last one in buys the beer.'

We ripped off our shirts and ran into sea yelling like schoolboys. The last time I'd seen Tom without his shirt was at the beginning of summer when he'd been pushing a mower around the back garden. He'd been out of shape, but now he was looking fit and tanned, and I saw several women glance at him as we walked back along the beach. Perhaps Tom was right and I did need to get fit. I sucked in my stomach and jogged through the shallows, but the effect was ruined by a submerged rock and Tom watched with amusement as I hobbled over to my towel.

'I've broken my toe.'

He poked it unsympathetically. 'God, you're soft. It's only a bruise. Frankly, I can't see you being much use if it comes to any rough stuff.'

'I'm supposed to be the tactician. You're the one who blunders about walloping people.'

The sarong sellers had followed us to Blue Lagoon and were now around a young couple who were vigorously shaking their heads. I looked across at Tom and we grinned. 'Those two stand no chance against that lot. They'll be lucky to get away with buying only six sarongs.' I laid back and closed my eyes. 'I could get used to it here, Tom. I can see why the early European sailors jumped ship and stayed in these places. Imagine lying on this beach while a couple of bare-breasted women come shimmering across the sand, with baskets of bananas on their heads. If you compare that with life on board those ships, or in eighteenth century Europe for that matter, it's amazing *any* of them went home.'

'Will you stop fantasising about bare-breasted women? It's made me realise I haven't seen Marilyn for a while, so perhaps you could talk about something else. In fact, I've got a better idea. Why don't you buy me the beer you owe me and, as you're paying, I'll have a large one.'

We sat at a table in the shade at Blue Lagoon bar and I put down my beer. 'I've been thinking, Tom. Rather than just sitting about, we should be doing something constructive, just in case you don't hear from Marilyn today.'

'Such as?'

'Well, we ought to make a list of our resources and we should go and see Murray in Amed to find out if he can be of any help. It might all be unnecessary if you get to see Marilyn without any problems, but it could save time down the track and it'll keep us occupied and our brains working.'

'Good idea,' agreed Tom. 'Otherwise we'll just be hanging around Padangbai waiting for Marilyn to contact me. And you're right about keeping our brains working. After a few days in Bali you become so relaxed you start to lose the power of speech.'

'Was that what happened to me last night?'

'No, that was the beer.'

'Thank God for that. I'm glad it's not a progressive condition. Right, let's do the list. Where shall we start?'

'Human resources,' said Tom.

'Well, apart from us, there's Murray in Amed, Wayan at the hotel, and Kadek and Made at Paradise Padang. Anyone else?'

'You remember the two Aussie surfers, Darren and Laurie, who I met on the plane?' I nodded. 'Well, I told them why I'm here and they offered to help. They're spending a couple of weeks in Kuta and at a surf beach down south. I've got their mobile numbers and an email address, so it's easy enough to contact them.'

I wrote down their names. 'Well, if you don't hear from Marilyn, I think you should ring Murray this evening and arrange to meet him tomorrow for lunch. I don't know why, but I've got a funny feeling we might need his help.'

Glancing up, I saw two Balinese men with flat cases making a direct course for our table. 'Look out, here comes a couple of hawkers.'

Tom turned round. 'No thanks,' he called before they reached us.

'How do you know that, when you don't know what we've got?' rejoined the younger of the two in excellent English.

'We don't want anything, that's why,' replied Tom.

'There must be something that you want. You can't have everything.'

'Well, I wouldn't mind a Ferrari, but I don't imagine you're selling those.'

They laughed at Tom's joke and took it as an invitation to sit at our table.

'Look,' said Tom, 'We're having a private conversation and we'd be grateful if you'd let us finish it.'

'Okay,' said the one who did the talking, 'we'll just sit here until you've finished and then show you what we're selling.'

'Shit,' muttered Tom and shrugged in resignation. 'All right, what have you got?'

Each man opened his case slowly, like someone about to reveal special treats to an eager audience. 'Watches and rings,' grunted Tom. 'Got those. Look, here's my watch and here's my ring. You're wasting your time.'

'These are very good watches and rings. You buy for your family.'

'At the moment,' said Tom, 'I seem to have mislaid my family and I've got no one else I want to buy presents for.'

'Then I feel sorry for you,' said the spokesman. He reached into the case and handed Tom a polished black shell.

Tom started to say that he didn't want the shell, but the man said, 'It is a present. It will bring you good luck.'

Tom looked embarrassed. 'Thank you,' he said genuinely. He glanced down at the open case of rings. 'Well, perhaps I could get a ring for Debra. Do you think she'd like one, Geoff?'

'Tom, I don't believe it. You paid more than his opening price. I know you said that you never pay their asking price, but surely the point is you pay less, not more. You must be the only person in Bali who's ever bargained upwards.'

'Rubbish, I wasn't bargaining. It's just that he was so nice giving me the shell I thought I'd better pay him a bit extra to allow for it.'

I groaned. 'Look, Tom, he gave you the shell as a marketing ploy. It's the sort of thing I do all the time.'

'Give people shells?'

'You make the client feel that you've done him a favour and then he's in your debt. It's the oldest trick in the book.'

'You're a cynical bugger, Geoff. I honestly believe he was being nice.'

I shook my head sadly. 'That's why you need me over here. Anyway, let's carry on with the list. Apart from human resources, what other assets do we have?' I held up my hand and started counting items off. 'We've got a car, we can hire a boat, we have money to bribe people and a mobile phone that doesn't work. Anything else?'

Tom thought. 'Nothing springs to mind and it doesn't sound a lot when you consider we're up against someone who's mega-rich.'

'It does seem a bit meagre,' I admitted, 'but we might add to our assets after we've seen Murray. Anyway, this mission was always going to rely on stealth and guile to succeed.'

We left Blue Lagoon and walked back to the hotel where I had my first meal of *nasi goreng*. It is the staple diet of Indonesia and consists of fried rice and chopped vegetables with a few pieces of meat or fish. It was delicious, but I had no idea just how tired I would be of *nasi goreng* before I left Bali.

After lunch I left Tom at the hotel and explored Padangbai. Despite its status as one of Bali's main ports, it is surprisingly sleepy and only a few minutes walk from end to end. The hawkers pounced as I walked along the beachfront and I was offered massages, transport, and goods ranging from carved coconut shells to fake Rolex watches. I had read that the best way to deal with the hawkers is to pretend that you are deaf and dumb, because if you enter into any dialogue with them you will spend hours trying to escape. The tactic worked, and I eventually left them behind and arrived at the port.

I found out that the ferries to Lombok leave every two hours around the clock, and as a consequence boats are permanently tied up at the dock, either loading or unloading. There were crowds of people around the ticket office and rows of hawkers were selling food and drink to the passengers for the next ferry. I bought a bottle of water and sat on the harbour wall to watch an incoming ferry dock and then disgorge its human cargo. Several passengers rode bicycles but the majority were on foot, and once they were clear of the wharf a stream of cars and trucks emerged from the bowels of the vessel and rumbled down the ramp.

A few of the foot passengers gave their bags to the throng of porters, but most shrugged them off and carried their own through the terminal to the coach stop or to the nearby rank of waiting taxis. A middle-aged couple turned in my direction and smiled at me as they approached. They wore walking boots, shorts, and khaki jerkins with bulging pockets. Both were carrying backpacks and they were slim and tanned.

The man spoke with a soft American accent. 'Hi, do you speak English?'

It occurred to me that this was the first time since I'd arrived in Bali that I'd been spoken to by a stranger who was not trying to sell me something. 'Sure, I am English. My name's Geoff. How can I help you?'

'Hi, Geoff,' said the woman, 'I'm Rhona and this is my husband, Ted. Do you know where we can rent a car in Padangbai?' She pronounced each syllable slowly, like three separate words. 'We plan to explore north of here and we don't want to take one of those taxis.'

I'd passed a car hire business on the way from the hotel, and I told them that I was going back now and I'd show them. As we walked, I asked them about Lombok and the ferry trip.

'Oh, the ferry takes around four hours or so and it can get pretty rough. There are some huge swells between the islands and the boat goes up and down like a carnival ride. A lot of people were sick on the way over but coming back it was not so bad.'

Rhona paused and Ted took over. 'Lombok is not as friendly as Bali. The people are Muslims and they're more reserved. We spent five days there and had a good time. No problems at all, but we didn't go around waving the American flag.'

Rhona agreed. 'That's right. Tourists from the States used to have a reputation for being loudmouths and standing out in a crowd. Now, the smart ones are super quiet and sneak about.'

I laughed. 'I'm not sure that British and Australian tourists are any more popular in a lot of places right now. Travelling's become a risky business. By the way, I noticed that there's no customs or security when you get off the ferry. Is it the same in Lombok?'

Ted answered. 'It sure is. Both islands are Indonesian and you don't cross any borders. It's no different to you travelling from mainland England to your Isle of Wight.'

I left them at Wayan's Car Hire, and sent an email to Allison from the internet café before going back to the hotel. It was five-thirty and Tom was sitting in the bar waiting for Marilyn's call. I bought two beers and joined him.

I told him about the American couple. 'I think we should add the Lombok ferries to our asset schedule, Tom. I'm not sure how they might help, but they're on our doorstep and there are no customs or security checks.'

'A slow escape to Lombok. Well, it could be useful, I suppose,' Tom said doubtfully.

'Another thing, Tom, have you noticed how many Balinese are called Wayan and it's not only the men?'

'Wayan here at the hotel told me it's the name they always give to their first child. And after that it's Made, Nyoman and Ketut, in some particular order that I can't remember. So every family has at least one Wayan.'

'Well, it means that you don't have to agonise over names for your kids,' I said 'but it must get a bit confusing at school if eighty per cent of the class is called Wayan.'

At six o'clock Tom got up and stood at the bar next to the telephone. At six-thirty he sat down again and at seven o'clock I said quietly, 'It doesn't look as though she's going to ring now, Tom. I think you should call Murray and see if he's free tomorrow.'

'Damn, I thought she'd call me, I really did.'

'Tom, I know you're really keen to talk to Marilyn, but I think this could be a good sign. Look, assuming she's got your letter, it means either that she doesn't want to talk to you, which I don't think is very likely, or alternatively she hasn't rung because her calls are monitored and she doesn't want Cruyff to know you're here. Therefore, it's reasonable to assume that she wants to talk to you without him finding out, which is really positive, if you follow my logic.'

'No news is good news, then.'

'Exactly, and if I'm right Kadek will ring Wayan to say she's got a letter from Marilyn. So, stop being so bloody miserable and ring Murray.'

Tom arranged to see Murray Rollinson at his dive business in Amed at 1 pm the following day. He told Wayan that Kadek might possibly ring tomorrow to say that she had a reply from Marilyn.

Wayan grinned. He was enjoying his role as intermediary. 'Okay, Tom. Kadek ring, I get letter.' He tapped the tip of his nose and winked. 'She tell security got present for sick mother. No problem.'

'What happens if security wants to see the present?' I asked.

Wayan's grin grew larger. 'Kadek make baskets. She bring one with letter.'

I looked at Wayan admiringly. 'That's clever, Wayan.' I turned to Tom. 'You know, we've got the makings of a crack commando team here.'

We had learnt from Wayan that there was a mobile-phone tower at Paradise Padang and I handed him my phone. 'Wayan, if you see Kadek, will you please give her this to pass on to Marilyn so that we won't have to go through this rigmarole of secret messages again.'

CHAPTER THIRTEEN

I was woken throughout the night by unfamiliar noises. The moans of the sirens that announced the incoming and outgoing ferries were answered by the shrill barking of dogs. Geckos squabbled amongst the roof beams above my bed and, as dawn approached, the crowing of roosters dragged me from sleep. Eventually, a grey light penetrated the room and with it the smell of burning rubbish.

I groaned. This was definitely *not* paradise. I abandoned further attempts at sleep and searched the short-wave band on my radio. I discovered that if I balanced it on top of my backpack under the window I got a crackly reception of the BBC World Service.

I met Tom at breakfast. 'I know the team for the first test, the latest stock market news, and all the disasters that have happened around the world.'

'And are you any better off for knowing these things?' asked Tom.

'That's not the point. I've been incommunicado for three days and I was feeling out of touch with reality. By the way, Surrey has officially been declared a drought area.'

'Surrey? God, it's pathetic. Ethiopia is a drought area where famine kills a million people when their crops fail. That is reality, Geoff. A drought in Surrey means that people can only water their lawns once a week. Reality is

Bali where people subsist on a couple of bowls of rice a day.' Tom breathed deeply. 'I've been incommunicado, as you put it, for ten days and I don't miss the media version of reality at all.'

'So I take it you don't want to know the test side?'

'That's different, Geoff, and you know it. And I must say you look a bit rough this morning. Did you sneak out for a night on the town after I went to bed?'

'No, but I might as well have. I got woken up every half-hour by a combination of barking dogs, ferries, chickens, and the stench of burning rubbish. It was okay the first night, so perhaps it's a Tuesday night ritual.'

'No it's the same every night,' said Tom. 'You didn't notice the first night because you were unconscious from all the beer you drank.'

'Then it looks as though I'll be getting pissed every night.'

'No, I'll give you some earplugs and if you shut your window and use the fan you won't breathe in carcinogens for half the night.'

'Christ, what exactly are they burning, Tom?'

'You've seen all the rubbish lying around everywhere. Well, at some point in the early hours it is mysteriously collected up and set fire to. There are a lot of plastic bottles and unmentionable things that even the scavenging dogs and those skinny chickens leave behind, so it's pretty toxic and unpleasant stuff.'

'Is there anything else I should know that you haven't told me about?'

'No, I don't think so, Geoff. You know about the hazardous nature of the roads and I believe I've mentioned the unsanitary conditions in restaurants.' He thought for a moment, 'Oh, poisonous fish and sea snakes are common around the reefs, but as long as you don't pick them up and play with them you'll probably be all right.'

'Anything else?' I said grimly. 'Radioactive seawater, perhaps?'

'No, that's about it, Geoff.'

Over breakfast we planned the day, 'We need to set off by eleven,' said Tom after he'd looked at the map. 'That gives us loads of time, and even if the traffic and roads are appalling we'll still get there by one. You'd better do some of the driving, Geoff, so that you get used to it.'

'I had an awful feeling that today would be my introduction to the insanity they call driving over here.'

'You'll be fine. After half an hour you'll be whizzing around like the Balinese. Just remember the basic techniques I told you about on the drive from the airport.'

We set off for Amed shortly before eleven. Tom drove for the first half-hour and I took over for the remainder of the journey. It turned out to be much easier than I'd expected. The rules on Bali's narrow roads are quite simple. Bicycles and motorcycles give way to everything, cars give way to trucks, and trucks do whatever they like. I decided that if I followed these rules there was a reasonable chance that we would survive and I didn't try Tom's techniques. The journey took us through rainforests, across brown rivers on rickety wooden bridges, and along twisting roads clinging to the hillsides above terraced rice fields. As we approached Amed a grey mountain dominated the horizon.

'That,' remarked Tom, consulting the guide book, 'is Gunung Agung, an extinct volcano that has great spiritual significance for the Balinese. It says that at dawn, if you sit on the beach at Amed, you can watch the sun rise over the sea at the same time as it lights up the summit of Gunung Agung. I wouldn't mind doing that sometime.'

We turned off the main road at Culik and drove a few miles into Amed. Tom checked the directions he'd been given by Murray. 'Look out for a low blue building just the other side of the village. There's a sign on the roof that says Jemeluk Pro Dive.'

The building stood out from the traditional bungalows and Murray was sitting at a table in the shade as we pulled into the courtyard. He watched us get out of the car before he stood up and walked over to Tom and shook his hand.

'Tom, good to meet you, and you must be Geoff.'

He was a slim, neat man approaching sixty, who spoke with an extravagant public school accent. He was wearing white slacks, a silk cravat and a red shirt with Jemeluk Pro Dive printed on it. I smiled and thought that there would not be too many like him in Bali.

'I'll get you a cold drink and you can start telling me about your problem.' He spoke rapidly to a Balinese boy who disappeared across the road. 'I've asked Made to order us some lunch from the restaurant. We'll eat over here.'

Tom started from the beginning and told him everything that had occurred. When he came to the part about Richard Morgan, Murray laughed.

'I'm not surprised he told you what you wanted to know. I would have in his place.'

When Tom had finished, Murray did not respond immediately, but instead he talked about Bali. 'One thing you learn about Bali is that nothing is what it seems. Behind the beautiful carved stone facade there is a tin shed, and then the carved stone turns out to be cast concrete mortared together in sections. The turquoise stone in your ring is blue-painted resin and the paint peels off in a month. Your "Rolex" watch stops on the plane going home. The tee shirt marked 100% cotton is polyester. Also, you will be charged two or three times the price for everything until you know your way around. It is a land of deception and petty fraud.'

I was intrigued. 'So, why do you live here?'

'Once you've come to terms with all that, there is a lot to love. The Balinese are peaceful and gentle, and respect your space in a crowded island. They are deeply religious, support their families and are loyal to their friends. The island has a spiritual essence and the scenery is magical. The climate here suits me. Nowadays I can't abide the cold and damp of England and even in summer I find it intolerable.

'Originally, the pretty young men were a consideration, but I'm past that now, although I still enjoy having them around. It's an appreciation of works of art, without the desire to possess them. Now, I'm at the age where I'd rather go to bed with a hot drink than a hot lover.' He smiled.

I looked at Tom. Where had I heard something like that recently? I shook my head.

He continued. 'The Balinese are truly lovely people, just so long as they are not trying to sell you something.'

'I'm sure they are,' I said, 'but so far I haven't met anyone who wasn't.'

Murray laughed. 'Yes, it does seem like that at first.' He looked across the road. 'Ah, I see that our lunch is coming.'

Made placed bowls containing a variety of Indonesian dishes on the table in front of us and Murray talked while we ate.

'The Amed area has only recently been discovered by the tourists and it is still quiet and unspoilt. Up until a

few years ago there were no telephones here, which kept
progress and development to a minimum, and it is far
enough away from the airport never to become another
Kuta. The water here is very clear and there are coral
reefs and wrecks, so it is a favourite spot for divers. Do
either of you dive?'

'Yes,' said Tom, 'I do. Geoff just sinks.' Murray and I
laughed. 'I've brought my wet suit, mask and fins, but no
other gear.'

'That's no problem. I'll give you whatever else you
need. You can leave it at your hotel when you leave.'
Murray paused and then addressed Tom's situation, as
though there had been no break in the topic of
conversation. 'So, your current predicament is that until
you hear from Marilyn you don't know where you stand
or what course of action to take. I've found that inactivity
and uncertainty are always the hardest. Well, depending
upon what you decide to do, I know two influential
people who may be able to help you. The British Vice
Consul, Graham Richardson is currently based in
Denpasar. We were at Harrow together and you form
strong ties when you've shared that type of experience.'
He laughed. 'The English public school system, there's
nothing in the world like it. Flogged every morning and
buggered senseless in the afternoons. Never did anyone
any harm and got me where I am today. Now, if you get
into trouble, I'm sure Graham will help you.

'The other person is Wayan Solahto. He holds a
senior position in Bali's internal security, and since the
bombings his department has been granted far greater
powers. He has close contacts with other government
agencies including the police and the military. He and I
have known each other for more than ten years and I
trust him absolutely. In the past I have done him a few
favours and I am sure that he would assist you if I ask

him. But, more importantly, he has a personal reason for helping you against Cruyff.'

'So, you know Pieter Cruyff?' said Tom.

'I haven't met him, but I know of him by reputation. He is very wealthy and wields a lot of power. Like all rich people in Indonesia he has considerable influence with politicians and bureaucrats. He is known to be manipulative and ruthless, and he would make a bad enemy. If you tangle with him, you should be very careful and make sure your getaway is well planned. Bali is a small island and he will find you.'

'Oh Christ,' I muttered.

'We'll worry about that if we have to,' Tom said indifferently. 'Now, Murray, you said that Wayan has a personal reason for helping. Can you tell us what it is?'

'Yes, it is not a secret,' replied Murray. 'It involved Wayan's brother, who owned the original resort at Paradise Padang. Cruyff lent him a large amount of money, which was secured by the resort. Wayan has told me that Cruyff deliberately bankrupted his brother, and after he obtained the title he developed the resort into a billionaires' retreat. Wayan's brother committed suicide. So, you see that Wayan has good reason to hate Cruyff.

'Personally, I can help you with a team of experienced divers and a fast boat, but unless you are planning a midnight raid to snatch your wife and children then I don't think that you will need that kind of assistance.'

'I really appreciate it, Murray,' said Tom. 'It's tremendous of you to offer to help.'

'Well, nothing much ever happens here and it will get me out of my routine being involved in this. Also,' he added mischievously, 'it's nice to help an old boxer, particularly one who looked like Adonis.'

I choked on a mouthful of food. 'Tom ... Adonis?' I spluttered.

'Oh yes,' said Murray, 'he was beautiful.'

Tom was bright red. 'That's why you wanted to know my age. Do I know you?'

'No, but I watched you fight as an amateur, and as a professional at Wembley. Tommy Skellam, the great white hope.'

I sat back. This was going to be interesting.

'Years ago I was very keen on boxing, or to be perfectly honest I was probably more interested in the boxers themselves. Anyway, Tom's name sounded familiar when Simon told me over the phone and later it came back to me. I dug around in my boxing memorabilia and even managed to find a picture of Tom in his prime.'

'Oh no,' groaned Tom, 'don't do this to me.'

Murray reached behind him and picked up a folder. He pulled out an old black and white studio photograph of Tom wearing boxer's shorts and boots. His body was oiled, highlighting his muscles, and he was in the classic pugilist's pose, with feet planted and gloved fists raised. His blond hair was cropped and he was snarling at the camera. All in all, he looked hard and menacing.

'Didn't you like the photographer?' I asked.

They ignored me and Tom looked closely at the photograph. 'It's been a long time since anyone remembered me as a boxer. That photo was taken more than twenty years ago, before my one-and-only pro fight.'

'I remember it,' said Murray, 'and you retired about six months later, didn't you?'

'Did you get badly hurt?' I asked. Tom rarely talked about boxing and I hadn't known that he'd turned professional.

Murray answered. 'No, he didn't get hurt at all, at least not from being hit. He just punched his opponent so hard it damaged his hand and stopped him boxing. Tom knocked him out with one of the best punches I've ever seen. It was terrible luck, because Tom was really good.'

'Why have you never told me about this?' I exclaimed.

Tom said nothing for a while and I thought he wasn't going to answer. Eventually he looked at me. 'Well, you see, Geoff, boxing was my love, and it's the only thing I've ever been really good at. The person I fought that day was next in line for a shot at the British heavyweight title and I was given no chance against him. But I outboxed him for five rounds and then knocked him out at the start of the sixth. After the fight the papers called me the "great white hope", as Murray said, and I believed that I was going right to the top. I took it very hard when I found out that my hand was smashed-up and I'd never fight again. It was so unfair, but I wasn't going to be like all the other boxers who never made it. I've met enough of them who talk to anyone who'll listen, and they all say that, but for the bad breaks, they'd have been world champion. I didn't want to end up like them, so I never spoke about it, and pretty soon no one remembered any more, at least not until today.'

'I'm sorry, Tom,' I said, 'I had no idea.'

'Well, after what's happened with Marilyn and the girls, it no longer seems so important. I only took up rugby because I couldn't box, but funnily enough I played in matches where I threw more punches than in some of the bouts I fought.'

CHAPTER FOURTEEN

We left Amed late in the afternoon. Tom had borrowed scuba equipment from Murray and promised to ring him after he heard from Marilyn. When we arrived back at the hotel in Padangbai, Wayan's wife, Ketut, was waiting for us.

'Wayan go see Kadek at Paradise Padang.'

'Did Kadek ring and say she's got a letter for me?' Tom asked urgently.

'Wayan no say.'

'She must have,' I said. 'There's no other reason why Wayan would go there.' I turned to Ketut. 'What time did Wayan leave to go to Paradise Padang?'

Ketut misunderstood me. 'Yes, Wayan go there.'

'What time?' Tom asked again.

'Little time,' she shrugged.

'Yes, but what time?' Tom demanded.

'Tom, she hasn't got a watch,' I said. 'She doesn't know.'

'Oh, sorry, Ketut.' Tom was instantly apologetic.

'Come on, Tom, there's nothing we can do. Let's sit in the bar and have a beer while we're waiting.'

Wayan arrived on his motorbike half an hour later. He was carrying a woven reed basket and he smiled as he handed Tom a small envelope.

'Brilliant, Wayan, well done. Thank you.' Tom shook Wayan's hand and tore open the envelope. He read for a few moments and then passed the single page to me. I was surprised at how little she had written.

Tom, am I glad to hear from you.

Meet me on the black rocks at the north end of Coral Bay at 11 am Thursday.

Stay out of sight of the shore.

Marilyn

PS Eat this after you've read it.

Tom suddenly grabbed my arms and forced me into a jig between the tables. 'We're on, Geoff, we're on!' he shouted.

His delight was infectious, and Wayan and Ketut laughed and clapped as Tom and I pranced around like fools.

'Stop it, Tom. For God's sake, stop it.' I said finally. 'Thursday's tomorrow. We've got to move fast if we're going to get things organised.'

Tom let go of me. 'It's all right, Geoff. All we need is an outrigger to take us a couple of hundred yards offshore from Coral Bay.'

'Just a second, Tom.' I turned to Wayan. 'Did you give my mobile phone to Kadek?'

Wayan nodded. 'I give.'

'Will Kadek pass it on to Made tonight?'

'No, she not see Made 'til afternoon 'morrow.'

'All right, Wayan, thank you. Sorry, Tom, that's not going to help. I thought that if she had the phone she might ring and it would save you getting wet tomorrow.'

'It doesn't matter,' said Tom, who at that point would have happily swum the channel. 'Now, let's get this organised. Wayan, can you ask your brother, Nyoman, if he can take us out tomorrow in his boat? We need to be offshore from Paradise Padang by about half-ten. If he can't do it, can you find someone who can?'

'No problem. I ask Nyoman,' said Wayan and got back on his motorbike.

Tom fetched the map of the Padangbai coast from his room and we studied it together. Coral Bay is the most northerly of Paradise Padang's bays and the closest to Padangbai. The map showed a line of rocks stretching into the sea at the northern end of the bay.

'She doesn't want me to be seen,' said Tom, 'so I think the best way for us to do this is to take the outrigger in fairly close to Coral Bay and then I'll jump overboard and swim to the rocks. You can take the boat back out a few hundred yards and pretend to be fishing. Stay in sight of the rocks and keep a lookout to make sure nothing goes wrong. If you see any other people on the rocks or a boat coming in my direction, tie that pink sarong you bought for Debra to a bamboo pole and wave it around. I should spot that okay and it will give me time to get back into the water. And I'll use the scuba gear, just in case there are any boats cruising about. If they see someone swimming they're bound to investigate.'

'What about sharks?'

'The mood I'm in,' said Tom, 'I'd feel sorry for any shark that happened to get in my way.'

We heard Wayan's motorbike and a few moments later he walked into the restaurant. 'Okay, Tom. Nyoman take you 'morrow. You leave from beach at nine.'

'Thanks, Wayan. How much do I pay Nyoman?'

Wayan shrugged. 'You talk Nyoman 'morrow.'

Tom took out his wallet and handed Wayan some folded notes. 'This is for you, Kadek and Made. I couldn't have got this far without you and I know the risks that Kadek and Made are taking. I'm very grateful.'

Wayan nodded and took the money. 'Tom, you watch out 'morrow. They bad people.'

'Thanks, Wayan, I'll be careful.'

I was glad to be staying on the boat, but Tom appeared unconcerned by both Murray and Wayan's warnings. He was like a lot of Englishmen who shuffle through life half asleep, but in moments of crisis perform unexpected heroics. It's the small, everyday things that defeat them.

Tom turned to me. 'I'll ring Murray after we've eaten and tell him what's happening.' He yawned. 'And then I'm going to bed. I'm getting up early tomorrow to play with the scuba gear off the beach. I don't want to spend ages fiddling around with it when we arrive at Coral Bay.'

We ate at the hotel. The menu was limited, but the food was freshly cooked by Ketut, and I'd checked out the kitchen and it was spotless. I'd decided that Tom's bout of Bali belly had soured his judgement and you didn't have to eat at the best restaurant in town to stay alive.

'Tom, I'm getting a bit tired of *nasi goreng*. You can eat only so much rice and vegetables.'

'Have *mie goreng* for a change,' suggested Tom.

'Good idea. What is it?'

'Well, it's exactly the same, except you get noodles instead of rice.'

'Does it taste any different?'

'No, not really, but the texture's different.'

'Jesus. Oh all right, I'll give it a try then.'

'Ketut, can we have two *mie gorengs,* please?'

The morning was cloudless and there was a faint breeze from the shore. The sea was flat and would remain calm until late afternoon when every day the wind swung round, strengthened, and came off the sea. Tom and I waited with Wayan on the beach in front of Nyoman's shack while he tinkered with the outboard motor. I was convinced that Nyoman was being ultra careful that he did not break down close to Coral Bay. When he was satisfied that it was running correctly he waved to us to come aboard. We waded out waist deep into the water, passed our packs to Nyoman and hauled ourselves into the boat. Wayan cast off from the beach and we chugged towards the channel through the reef. As soon as we were out of the bay, Nyoman increased speed and the outrigger skimmed across the water. When it had been pulled up on the sand, the curved framework and long wooden floats of Nyoman's outrigger had made it look like an ungainly giant insect, but once in the water it was graceful and sure.

'Did you agree the cost of the trip with Nyoman?' I shouted above the noise of the motor.

'Sort of,' replied Tom. 'He said it would be 300,000 rupiah if there are no problems at Paradise Padang, but if there are problems then it's double, because the people there will make trouble with the authorities. Everyone seems to be very wary of this place, Geoff.'

'Me included. Still, I'll be spending a happy hour or two fishing while you're out there wrestling with sharks and security guards. By the way, did you pack any beer?'

'No, I didn't, because I don't want you sitting around boozing. You've got an important job that you won't be able to do if you're getting pissed.'

After motoring hard for an hour, Nyoman slowed the boat. 'We close now,' he called out. 'See black rocks.' The coastline was rocky and the heavily-vegetated land behind rose steeply. About half a mile in front of us a line of jagged black rocks stretched three hundred yards into the sea. 'Coral Bay behind rocks. You not see from here.'

I focused my binoculars on the rocks. 'You're lucky it's calm. It would be impossible to climb on to those in a rough sea. You'd be smashed to a pulp.'

I handed Tom the binoculars and he studied the rocks. 'It's a bit hard to tell from here, Geoff, but it looks like there's an inlet about halfway along where no waves are breaking. Some big rocks stick out into the sea at either end and protect it. That's where I'll aim to land, but we'll see better when we get closer. We're hidden from Coral Bay, but anyone could be watching us from the shore right now and we'd never know. So, I don't think that we should get complacent just because everywhere looks deserted.'

Tom started to pull on his wetsuit and called to Nyoman, 'Do a few zigzags, as if you're looking for a good fishing spot, and finish up a couple of hundred yards this side of the rocks. I'll get into the water from the seaward side, and afterwards you turn the boat around and go back a little way and drop anchor. And while I'm on the rocks you can catch my lunch.'

As we got closer, I saw that there was a large sign at the end of the rocks. I tapped Nyoman on the shoulder and pointed. 'What does the sign say?'

'It say: *Keep Out. Danger.*' Nyoman scowled and drew his finger across his throat.

Tom had put on his scuba gear and he signalled to Nyoman to slow the boat. 'Right, I'll swim in from here.'

'Good luck, Tom. Give Marilyn our love.'

'I'll tell her. And remember, Geoff, keep a lookout for any trouble. Wave the sarong around if anything happens.'

'Don't worry. My eyes will be glued to the binoculars.'

'Good, and bring the boat closer when I start to swim back.'

After Tom dropped over the side, Nyoman turned the boat round and we motored slowly for a few minutes before anchoring. I trained the binoculars on the water and looked for signs of Tom's progress, but the breeze ruffled the water and masked all trace of the bubbles.

CHAPTER FIFTEEN

Beneath the surface the water was clear and Tom swam steadily. The seabed was rocky with occasional patches of sand, and shoals of colourful fish scattered as he swam above them. After five minutes Tom surfaced briefly to check his direction before continuing. He estimated that it would take him fifteen minutes to reach the central section of the rocks where there appeared to be a natural inlet. As he approached the rocks the water became shallower and there were strong currents. He struggled to stay on course, but thirty yards from the rocks the water was again calm and the seabed changed to coarse sand. He surfaced and checked his position. He was in a sheltered cove that had a thin strip of sand and slabs of black rock behind. High jagged rocks enclosed the miniature bay and curved into the sea at either end.

When Tom was a few yards out he removed his fins and waded ashore. The bay was deserted and there was no sign of life on the rocky shore a hundred and fifty yards away. He crossed the narrow beach and climbed onto the flat rocks where he was hidden from the shore by the encircling rocks and visible only from the sea. Tom faced the outrigger, which was anchored about three hundred and fifty yards away, and raised both arms above his head, with hands clenched and thumbs extended. He thought he saw a figure wave from the back of the boat.

Tom felt sure he was at the right spot. There was no other place he could realistically have come ashore. He peeled off his wetsuit and looked around the flat rocks. He spotted a short length of orange mooring rope that someone had tied into a bow. Tom smiled, and lay on his wetsuit and waited. After ten minutes he heard a noise and turned his head. A tanned Marilyn stood over him. She was wearing a turquoise bikini and her hair was wet. She carried a mask and fins in one hand, and a spear gun in the other. She looked down at him but didn't speak.

Tom nodded at the spear gun. 'Expecting trouble?'

'Well, I'm told that desperate men have been seen on these rocks. In fact, I've arranged to meet one here, an overweight pasty Englishman.' She looked at Tom's newly firm body. 'Have you seen anyone like that around here?'

'Yes,' replied Tom. 'His name's Geoff. He's on that boat over there.'

Marilyn smiled. 'So, you've brought the cavalry. Then you must be expecting trouble, too.' She sat on the flat rock several yards from Tom and studied him critically. 'Well, you look a lot better than the last time I saw you. Bachelor life obviously suits you.'

'And *you* don't look surprised that I'm here. Perhaps you thought I'd taken a holiday to celebrate you and the children leaving and I just happened to pick Bali out of a hat.'

'No,' replied Marilyn, 'I thought you'd come looking for us and there were enough clues to find us. When I got your email I was sure. But Pieter didn't believe you'd be able to track us here, and even if you did he was certain you wouldn't get past security. It was smart not to telephone. He was convinced you would, if only to check that we were here before you made the trip. I mean, it's a very long way to come on a hunch.'

'I'm glad you had it all worked out,' Tom said evenly.

'And it was clever to bribe the maids,' continued Marilyn, 'but have you any idea what will happen to them if they get caught?' She didn't wait for an answer. 'Now, before you ask me, Kate and Gemma are fine, although they miss you and want to know when they're going to see you.'

'And when are they?' interrupted Tom. 'And you ... how are you?'

'Oh, I'm great. I live a life of luxury, with everything that I want. I mingle with famous and fabulously wealthy people who spend two thousand dollars a night to stay at the resort. What more could I want?'

Marilyn paused, but Tom didn't respond. He saw that her face was thinner and under the tan she looked tired.

'No, I'm not great, Tom, as you've probably realised. I wouldn't be meeting you in secret on these rocks if it were so wonderful.' She again paused and said carefully, 'Tom, I assume you haven't come over here just to tell me that I forgot to turn the lights off when I left, or that I've got a parking ticket for the MG?'

'No, I've come to tell you I love you and I want you to come home.'

'In spite of what I did?'

'It's as much my fault as yours, and I feel responsible for how ... ordinary our marriage had become.'

Marilyn raised her hand. 'Don't say any more. It was both of us. What I did was completely insane. I don't love Pieter and I never did, but something happened that I couldn't control, and now it's over for good. I don't know if you and I can make it work, Tom, but maybe we can.'

'That's all I needed to know,' said Tom, 'that you don't love him.'

They looked at each other, uncertain how to proceed.

'I don't understand why you didn't ring me and tell me how you felt.'

'I couldn't do that, Tom. I knew within a few days I'd made a mistake, but I didn't know if you'd have me back. I'd been so irresponsible and stupid and I hated myself. I couldn't pick up the phone and say, "Sorry, Tom, I made a slight error of judgement and now I'm coming home." But, more than anything, I had to find out if you believed our marriage was important enough to come out here to save it. It wouldn't have worked if I'd just come crawling back to you. We'd have carried on exactly where we left off except that you would never have trusted me. I needed you to come and rescue me otherwise nothing would have changed. Don't you see that?'

'I think I do,' Tom said slowly, 'and that's why you put *Katherine* in your email?'

'I couldn't think of anything else that would make you realise I wasn't okay.'

'But what would you have done if I hadn't found you?'

'Sent you some more clues, maybe, but it doesn't matter because you did.'

'I was coming here anyway,' said Tom, 'whether you'd sent me any clues or not.'

'And another thing,' said Marilyn, 'the thought of coming back and facing my father was totally appalling. I couldn't even find the courage to ring my parents. By the way, how *are* they coping with all this?'

'Well, obviously they're worried, but they've been brilliant really, particularly Rory.'

'Rory? Since when have you called him Rory?'

'Oh, we're getting on amazingly. In fact, it took all my powers of persuasion to stop him coming over here.'

'Thank God you did.'

Tom got up and knelt beside her, and they embraced gently. Marilyn's body was taut. 'It's okay now,' he murmured. 'It's going to be all right.'

They sat with their arms around each other while Tom told her about his exploits of the last three weeks. As he talked, Marilyn relaxed and she chortled over the encounter with Richard Morgan.

'Oh Tom, I wish I'd been there to see you terrorise him. Somehow, I don't think we'll be playing squash together again.'

Tom grinned. 'No, I'd say that's pretty unlikely.'

'It's good of Geoff to come over and help. I never saw him as a man of action, more of an armchair-and-glass-of-port adventurer. Excitement for him was a close finish in a test match.'

Tom smiled. 'He's been great. In fact, everyone has.'

Marilyn stood up. 'There's something I have to do. I'll be back in a minute. Don't go away.'

She walked to the back of the cove and passed through a narrow opening in the rocks behind. A short while later Marilyn stood at the summit of the rocks with her back to Tom. She waved briefly before she turned and came back down.

'What were you doing?' Tom asked.

'Waving to my maid on Coral Bay beach to let her know I'm all right. She's used to me swimming and snorkelling around the rocks, and she knows that I come over this side to sunbathe. I get up and wave every half-hour to keep her happy, otherwise she'll get the rescue launch round here.'

'It sounds like you're well looked after.'

'Oh yes, I'm a valuable piece of property. I can't move more than a few paces without someone checking up on me. It drives me mad. The only time I've been out of the complex without Pieter was to do some shopping in

Sanur, and then I had a bodyguard who was virtually handcuffed to me. Pieter says that he's worried someone may kidnap me. It seems to be a popular pastime in Indonesia to snatch the wives or children of very wealthy people and then demand millions of dollars ransom. So, I'm stuck like a prisoner inside the resort.'

'How are Kate and Gemma coping?'

'They're fine. They have school lessons every morning with the other children and they usually go to the pool or the beach in the afternoon. Also, there's a gym, an amusement park and just about everything you can imagine. The place is designed for everyone to have a wonderful time. They miss their friends, but they think they're on holiday and they'll see them again soon.'

'What have you told them about me?' Tom corrected himself. 'About us, I mean.'

'That we've not been getting on very well and we're having a break from each other to sort things out.'

'Don't they think it's a bit strange you're sharing a house with Cruyff?'

'They think he's an old friend.'

'And how do they get on with Cruyff?'

'Quite honestly, they don't see much of him. He works every day, and in the evenings the girls go to bed pretty early or else they're looked after by the nanny.'

Marilyn looked at Tom speculatively. 'Have you finished asking me these questions? Wouldn't you rather know why I come here to sunbathe?'

'I hadn't really thought about it. To get away and have some peace and quiet, I suppose.'

'No, it's to get an all-over tan. I'll show you.'

Marilyn reached behind her and undid the top of her bikini. She shrugged out of it and her brown breasts rolled forward. She eased herself down on all fours and came slowly towards Tom. 'This is me crawling back to you,' she whispered, as Tom sat motionless.

With each movement, her breasts swayed gently together, like two wayward drunks returning home. Without breathing, he watched her unhurried progress. When Marilyn's face was almost touching Tom's she lifted one hand and poked a finger into his mouth. She wiggled it thoroughly around his gums, as though she were counting his teeth, and then solemnly withdrew it, wiping it dry on each of her nipples. It was too much for Tom. With a roar, he grabbed Marilyn and they rolled over on the flat rock, but almost immediately he broke away.

'Oh shit,' Tom shouted. He stood up and waved frantically at the outrigger.

Marilyn lay propped on one elbow and stared at Tom in amazement. 'Are you calling for reinforcements?'

'I don't need any bloody help, but Geoff's got his binoculars trained on this bit of rock. I told him to watch in case there was any trouble.'

Marilyn was unconcerned. 'Well, as your best friend, I'm sure he'll be gentlemanly enough to put the binoculars down, or look somewhere else.'

'I know that bastard. He'll have zoomed in and be taking notes.'

Marilyn resignedly put her bikini top back on and stood up. She gave a two-fingered salute in the direction of the boat and then grinned. 'Oh Tom, that wasn't a good beginning was it?'

Tom looked at her angrily and then slowly started to chuckle. He suddenly bellowed with laughter and they held on to each other and howled.

Eventually, Marilyn said weakly, 'God, that was funny. I haven't laughed like that for years.'

They sat together on Tom's wetsuit and he said, 'OK, so how are we going to handle this? You've got to tell Cruyff it's over and you're all coming back to England with me. How will he take it? Do you want me to be there?'

'He'll try to stop me.'

'Well, he can't do that. The three of you can walk out any time you want. I'll meet you outside the entrance gates.'

'It won't be as easy as that.'

'Of course it will. Have you got return tickets?'

'Yes, for next Thursday, the day after Gemma's birthday. You can't get in to Bali without them.'

'My flight's the following Tuesday and I'll change it to the same as yours. That'll be great. It means we can have a week's holiday in Bali. We can go to Amed where Murray is. It's really unspoilt, with fantastic beaches and diving. Get Kate and Gemma packed and I'll meet you at the entrance gates at four. We can all stay at the hotel in Padangbai tonight. Come on,' enthused Tom, 'what are you waiting for?'

'Unfortunately, it's not that straightforward,' said Marilyn. 'You see, Pieter and I got married two days after we arrived here.'

'You did what?' Tom roared. 'You can't have got married. You're married to me.'

'Tom,' said Marilyn gently, 'we had a Balinese wedding in the temple at Paradise Padang, and the divorce law here is very simple. You just denounce your previous marriage three times before the ceremonial chief and then you're free to marry someone else.'

'Well, they won't recognise that in England.'

'No, but they do here, and now that I'm his wife I'm subject to Indonesian law. I've no idea what legal rights he has over me and the girls, but this is predominantly a

Muslim country and their laws and customs are very different to ours, particularly relating to women.'

'Oh Christ, I can't believe you did anything so stupid. What on earth made you do it?'

'I don't know. I suppose part of it was the euphoria of being here, and also Pieter said it would be disastrous for his reputation and make his business life impossible if he was in a relationship with someone else's wife.'

'He still can't stop you leaving.'

'Pieter is not the sort of person to let me walk away, Tom. You don't know how he controls people. He has tremendous power and everyone does exactly what he says. In Paradise Padang he can do pretty much as he likes and, if people disobey him, he can be really nasty. I've found out that he's mixed up with some very bad people in Bali and, if he knew that I was going to leave him, he could take steps to stop me. I don't want anything to happen to any of us.'

'Like what?' demanded Tom.

'I don't know, but he's ruthless and capable of doing some horrible things. I heard that a maid who was caught stealing from the guests was beaten and disfigured.'

'Jesus.' Tom looked skyward for inspiration. 'Right, the first thing I'm going to do is check with Murray's friend, the British Vice Consul, to find out just how legal your Bali wedding is. But you, Kate and Gemma are still British subjects and you can't be held here against your will, regardless of whether you're married to an Indonesian. I'll drive to Denpasar tomorrow and talk to him.

'You should get Geoff's mobile phone from Made this afternoon or tomorrow morning. You can't leave it turned on, in case it rings when Cruyff or someone else is around to hear it, which means I can't ring you. I'll make a point of trying to be at the hotel at nine in the morning, midday and six in the evening, and you can ring me at those times.' Tom pulled a waterproof pouch out of the zip pocket of his wetsuit and gave it to Marilyn. 'I've written down Murray's number in Amed. If for some reason I'm not at the hotel, leave a message with Murray.'

'You're wasted in insurance, Tom. You should be in counter-espionage.'

'If this wasn't so bloody serious I'd be enjoying it.' He looked towards the outrigger. 'Christ, that's Geoff waving his pink sarong.'

'Pink?' said Marilyn.

'Yes, it's the signal to say something's wrong and it matches his backpack.'

Marilyn listened for a second. 'That sounds like the launch coming to rescue me. Damn, I forgot to wave again to Nyoman. Quick, get your stuff and hide in the opening in the rocks. I'll deal with them.'

Tom threw his wetsuit and scuba gear into the opening and squeezed in, but almost immediately he remembered that he had left his fins on the flat rocks. He stuck his head out as the launch entered the bay and saw that Marilyn had removed her bikini and was sunbathing naked on the thin strip of sand. A man in a white uniform called to Marilyn from the boat. She sat up quickly and covered her breasts with her hands.

As Tom moved further back into the crevice, he heard her shouting angrily and smiled. She really was quite amazing. Tom heard a brief, muffled conversation and a few minutes later the sound of the boat's engine receding. He waited another minute before he looked out. Apart from his fins, the bay was deserted.

CHAPTER SIXTEEN

I watched Tom put on his wetsuit and scuba gear. He faced the outrigger and waved before he waded into the water and started to swim. I told Nyoman to raise the anchor and motor slowly towards the rocks. Ten minutes later Tom heaved himself back into the boat.

'Jesus, Tom, that was close. Did they see you?'

'No, I hid between the rocks just as their boat arrived.'

'I'd been waving that sarong for about five minutes before you took any notice. I thought that the other boat would think we were in trouble and come over. I was going to pretend to be a stupid tourist just being friendly.'

'Sorry, Geoff, we were busy.'

'So I saw.'

'What do you mean by that?'

'Only that I saw you were busy talking.'

'So you didn't see anything you shouldn't have?'

'Well, I saw that boat come over.'

'No, I mean any other things?'

'What other things?'

'You know, personal things.'

'Personal things? No, I don't think so, but unless you're specific I'm not sure what you mean.'

'Well, did you see Marilyn when the launch arrived?'

'No I couldn't see her. When their boat got close it completely blocked the view. I saw her after she got on board, though. She was wearing a very nice blue bikini, if I recall. Why, is something the matter?'

'Hmmph.'

He didn't pursue what was bothering him and I changed the subject. 'Well, how did it go, and what's happening?'

'We got on great, but it's not straightforward.' Tom nodded at Nyoman's back as he steered the boat. 'I'll tell you all about it later. 'What about you, Nyoman, did you catch any fish?'

Nyoman turned round and shook his head.

'Nothing, Tom,' I said, 'not even a bite. Just like fishing in England, except the scenery here was a lot more interesting.'

Tom looked at me narrowly, but didn't say anything.

On the way back we sat at the front of the boat and Tom told me what had happened. I didn't interrupt and when he'd finished I thought for a while.

'It's fantastic that it's over between them and you two can get back together. And I agree with you, Tom, there's no way their marriage is legal. The wedding ceremony obviously has some religious significance, but if it were that easy to annul a marriage in Bali, then it would be the divorce capital of the world.'

Tom nodded. 'As soon as we get back I'll ring Murray and arrange to see the British Vice Consul. He'll know the law about Brits getting married here. If he's free, I'll go to Denpasar tomorrow to talk to him, and I also want his advice on how to get Marilyn and the girls away from Cruyff. And then I'm going to Kuta to look up the Aussie guys, Darren and Laurie. Do you want to come?'

'You couldn't stop me, Tom, now that victory is within reach.' I stood up and punched the air, and Tom grabbed me as the boat lurched.

'Sit down, Geoff. I don't want you getting eaten by sharks.'

'You saw some, then?'

'No, and I think the only shark I'm likely to come across on this visit to Bali is Cruyff.'

It was mid-afternoon when we arrived back in Padangbai. Tom spoke to Murray, who rang back half an hour later and confirmed that the British Vice Consul, Graham Richardson would see us at eleven o'clock tomorrow in Denpasar. Afterwards, Tom rang Darren and Laurie and arranged to meet them between three and four on Kuta Beach.

Tom was cautious when he spoke with Wayan at the hotel. He told him that it had gone well and there was a chance he and Marilyn would get back together, but there was a lot of work to be done. It was as though he wasn't going to tempt fate by being overly optimistic, but later that evening when we were sitting in the bar Tom was more positive.

'She still loves me, Geoff. I always knew it and all we have to do now is get them on the flight home next Thursday. As our self-proclaimed tactician, have you got any bright ideas how to do it?'

'Yes,' I said. 'I've given it some thought and it's really quite simple. We turn up at Paradise Padang with the British Vice Consul, wave union jacks and demand free passage for them in the name of the Queen.' I pulled out my passport. 'It says here, *Her Majesty requests and requires all those whom it may concern to allow the bearer to pass freely without let or hindrance.*'

'Brilliant,' breathed Tom, 'so all we have to do is show our passports. Everyone at Paradise Padang will be in mortal fear of the Queen's wrath and doors will magically open.'

'Exactly, and if that doesn't work we get the Vice Consul to organise a gunboat to rescue them off the beach.'

'Well, I shall certainly sleep easier tonight knowing that we have the full might of Britain behind us,' said Tom.

At nine on Friday morning we set off for Denpasar. Tom had been driving for about an hour when he remarked, 'Have you noticed how immaculate the Balinese keep their gardens?'

I nodded. 'Yes, they're works of art.'

'Ketut went outside this morning with a pair of scissors and cut one leaf off the frangipani tree. One bloody leaf, Geoff!'

'Yes, it probably spoilt the symmetry of the tree, which upset the harmony of the whole garden.'

Tom muttered something under his breath that I didn't hear. 'And sweeping,' he carried on. 'They spend half their lives sweeping up twigs and leaves and those little baskets of rice they leave on the floor for people to tread in.'

'Jesus, Tom, they put those out as offerings.'

'Yes, I know what they are. They're the ones I'm talking about. The Balinese, Geoff, are a race of compulsive sweepers and I tell you, if there was an Olympic event for sweeping, they'd clean up,' he said with unconscious humour.

Tom was unusually aggressive this morning and it occurred to me that he must have been like this in his boxing days as he psyched himself up before a fight.

'And their paranoia with shoes,' he continued. 'Simply because they take their shoes off before they go

137

indoors they want everyone else to do the same. Every time you go into a shop there's a bloody great pile of shoes outside for you to fall over. You know that damned internet place? Well, the other day, the girl in there made me leave my shoes outside on the steps. She wouldn't even let me put them on the floor inside the door. I expected to come out after I'd finished and find they'd been stolen.'

'No chance of that, Tom, not when you're the only person in Bali with size fourteen shoes. Mind you, it's possible that someone might have mistaken them for a couple of canoes and taken them.'

'If you'll just stop interrupting and listen, Geoff, I'll come to the point I'm trying to make. You'd think that with their obsession for order and tidiness, keeping their floors clean and sweeping up twenty times a day, the country would be sterile and spotless like Switzerland. But, oh no, instead there's filth and crap everywhere, because the moment they're not on their own property they throw rubbish and half-eaten bits of food around. I've even seen the remains of fighting cocks left to rot in the streets. The bottom line is, if it's not their own piece of real estate, they treat it as a rubbish dump.'

'Yes, I've noticed that. It's strange that people with such artistry and pride in their own property have a complete disregard for everything else. Psychologically, there's an interesting Foucauldian concept here, Tom, regarding the subject formation of the Balinese.'

'Bollocks,' said Tom.

CHAPTER SEVENTEEN

The British Vice Consul was based at the Australian Consulate in Denpasar. His secretary showed us into his office.

Graham Richardson was exceptionally tall and thin, and stooped as though he was embarrassed by his height. He wore a pale grey suit with what I imagine was a Harrow tie, but might have been Marks and Spencer's. We shook hands and sat in leather lounge chairs around a marble-topped coffee table. His secretary brought in tea and biscuits on a silver tray and left the room after she had poured.

'Chocolate digestives,' said the Vice Consul, with satisfaction, 'my favourites. Wherever I am posted I make sure that there's a good supply of British biscuits. Have you tried the local ones?'

Tom and I shook our heads.

'Well, I wouldn't bother. Frankly, they're terrible.' He looked smilingly at us. 'By the way, you can call me Graham. Now, you're probably wondering why I'm in the Australian Consulate. Well, the British Embassy is in Jakarta and it's only since the bombings that we've had any representation at all in Bali. The Australians have very kindly let us operate a sort of temporary sub-consulate out of their offices until we move into permanent premises in Sanur. I've been seconded to the post as a stop-gap measure, so it's quite fortunate for you that I'm here. Murray tells me you've got some things you want to ask me. Fire away and I'll see if I can help.'

After Tom had given Graham Richardson an abbreviated account of events, he said, 'What I need to know, Graham, is whether it's a legitimate marriage.'

The Vice Consul responded immediately, 'Tom, I can say categorically that the marriage is not legal. There is an oft-repeated myth about Balinese law that all a person needs to do to revoke a marriage is denounce their spouse three times in front of witnesses. Well, it is simply not true. But, having said that, a lot of Balinese still practise this custom, and the only reason that it has any validity is because those couples were never legally married in the first place. It's a bit like a defacto relationship where one party has had enough and says, "it's over" three times and then storms out.'

'Thank God for that,' said Tom.

'Bali was a popular destination several years ago as an exotic place for Brits to get married. At the ceremonies everyone dressed in sarongs, lots of flower petals were thrown about, and it was very pretty and quaint. Vows were taken in front of the temple chiefs and it all appeared to be legal and binding. *But,* and it is a big but, until all the correct documents were submitted to the administrative department of the province and ratified, the ceremonies had no legal validity. In the case of a person who has been married previously it is necessary to submit a certified copy of the divorce papers and without those the marriage is not legal. Your wife went through a picturesque but worthless ritual, which was possibly intended to make her believe that she had married the charming Mr Cruyff.'

'You know him?'

'Oh yes, I've met him a few times at various functions. Cruyff is well known among the high society of

Indonesia. He has business interests in a number of hotels throughout Asia, as well as Paradise Padang here in Bali. I don't know him well, but he appears to be witty and charming. However, there are rumours that he is connected with organised crime in Bali and Java, and that he can be a pretty rough customer.'

'Marilyn thinks that he may try to stop her and the children leaving Paradise Padang,' said Tom. 'If that should happen, what can the British Government do to help?'

Graham Richardson cupped his chin with his right hand and looked out of the window. After a few moments he said, 'Excuse me, please,' and picked up the phone from the coffee table. 'Turn off three will you please, Penny.' He turned back to us. 'All the conversations in this room are recorded. I've asked Penny to turn off the machine so that we can speak freely. Now, in answer to your question, if Cruyff tries for whatever reason to prevent your wife and children from leaving, we could make representation to the Indonesian authorities to have the matter investigated. But that could take months or even years to resolve. You have no idea how slowly diplomatic wheels turn, and with someone like Cruyff it is quite possible that important papers would go missing and the whole process grind to a halt.

'From what I've heard of the matter,' Graham forestalled Tom's question with a raised hand. 'Yes, Tom, I do know a little about this. You have to understand that one of our roles is to pass on rumour and gossip to the British Government, which is classed as gathering vital intelligence information, and incidentally is responsible for about half the diplomatic cock-ups that occur.

'Anyway, about two weeks ago Cruyff took Marilyn to a high-level function and introduced her as his wife. A lot of important government officials and business people were there, and I am told that Cruyff took great delight in showing her off.' Tom shifted in his chair but kept silent. Graham reached across and patted Tom's arm. 'Sorry, old chap, but I have to tell you this. So, you see, he would look ridiculous if she were to walk out on him and his world of wealth and privilege to return to a humdrum life in suburban England. Everywhere he went there would be innuendo and sniggering behind hands. Therefore, I can fully understand that he may try to stop her leaving and then finish the relationship at a later date on his terms, in order to save face. I believe that he could make things very difficult for Marilyn if he chose to.'

Tom snorted. 'So there's nothing you can do?'

'We were hoping you might have a spare gunboat that you could land on the beach and rescue them,' I said.

Graham Richardson laughed. 'We had a memo come round only last week telling us to stop doing that sort of thing. Unfortunately, about the only things that we can do officially is help financially, give protection in certain circumstances, and issue replacement passports.

'At the moment Cruyff doesn't know that your wife wants to leave him. My advice, for what it's worth, is to keep it that way and try to get your family on the flight next Thursday without his knowledge. Once they've left Indonesia there's very little he can do about it. There must be some way that your family can get out of Paradise Padang and simply take a taxi to the airport, even if they have to leave their luggage behind. If it's any help, I can have a consular representative at the airport to provide assistance should anything go wrong.

'Now, entirely off the record, I suggest that you contact Murray's friend Wayan Solahto. As you know, he has good reason to despise Cruyff and he may have some excellent ideas on how to handle this matter. You have to understand that in countries like Indonesia corruption exists throughout all levels of society. The police, military and government officials are so poorly paid that they supplement their wages by taking bribes. Everyone knows this and it is an accepted way of life. It is considered little different to a waiter who lives off his tips. Wayan Solahto knows who to bribe to get things done and could possibly oil some wheels for you. But you didn't hear that from the British Vice Consul.' He smiled. 'Well, good luck, keep me posted and try to stay out of trouble.' He handed us both a card. 'In an emergency, you can contact me on the bottom number at any hour.'

'Well, that wasn't very encouraging,' Tom said as we walked to the car. 'Apart from telling us the marriage isn't legal, it doesn't seem he's going to be much use. What did you make of him, Geoff?'

'Well, you have to look at it from his point of view. Marilyn's here voluntarily, there's been no attempt to detain her at this stage and she's made no formal complaint herself. So he's got nothing to act on, but I feel certain he would help if he could.'

'You might be right, but it was odd when he waffled on about chocolate biscuits. Still, it was nice of him to give us a packet.'

'It comes out of our taxes.'

'True,' agreed Tom. 'Look, there's a *wartel* across the road. I'll ring Murray and ask him to arrange a meeting with Wayan Solahto, and I'll also call the airline and see if I can change my flight to the same one as Marilyn's. Then we'd better set off for Kuta.'

'So much to do and so little time, and we haven't had lunch and I'm hungry.'

'Here you are, Geoff, have a chocolate digestive. They're British.'

Tom spoke to Murray, who said that he would try to organise a meeting with Wayan Solahto. The airline told Tom that Marilyn's flight was full and there were six people wait-listed.

'There's not much I can do about it,' said Tom. 'I'll spend the five days sightseeing. Perhaps I'll go back to Amed and watch the sunrise, after all.'

'My flight's the day after Marilyn's and, looking at the list of presents I've got to bring back, I'll be spending every minute of that time shopping.'

CHAPTER EIGHTEEN

We arrived at Kuta beach at half past two and sat next to the surf-board hire at the end of Poppies Lane. The beach was crowded and, although the waves were small, there was an unbroken line of surfers in the water.

'They all look the same bobbing around out there,' said Tom. 'Here, give me the binoculars and I'll see if I can spot them.'

He panned along the shoreline and paused where a group of girls were frolicking topless in the surf.

'Nice view?'

'Just checking,' said Tom and continued his search. 'Can't see them and most of the surfers are Japanese, and it's bloody dangerous. I've just seen some bloke nearly get the pointy end of a surfboard through the back of his head. I shan't be hiring one of those,' he said nodding at the stand of surfboards. 'I haven't survived the insane drivers over here and the chance of being eaten by sharks only to be impaled by a surfboard.'

I was happy to watch the bodies on the beach. 'Let's just sit and wait. They know where we are. They'll find us.'

Tom gazed at the people around us. 'That's odd,' he said and I glanced to where he was looking. A large, middle-aged woman was lying on her back on a bright-orange beach towel. She was tanned the colour of a cigar and was wearing a tiny pink bikini and a lime green sun hat. As though mortified by the vibrant clashing colours, her flattened breasts skulked disconsolately alongside her armpits. A pretty Balinese boy, with dyed ginger hair and an earring, was sitting next to the woman and she was resting her hand across his leg. 'Do you think she's adopted him?'

I laughed. 'In a manner of speaking, I suppose she has. He's a Kuta cowboy.'

'A what?'

'A gigolo. I've read about them. There's any number hanging around Kuta trying to latch on to rich tourists.'

As though on cue, they got up and walked hand in hand towards us. The woman stared boldly at the people she passed, as if daring anyone to challenge her right to be with a paid escort less than half her age.

'She must be desperate, mustn't she?' muttered Tom.

They walked past and Tom turned to watch. 'Fucking hell.'

I looked round and saw that the woman was wearing a g-string that completely revealed her wobbling bottom.

'I've seen many grotesque sights,' said Tom, 'but that beats the lot. That woman is close to fifty, she's running to fat and she's displaying a bum that would look better on a rhino. To cap it off, she's picked up some twenty-year-old gigolo, who looks gay but presumably isn't, and she's even happy to be seen with him in public. My God, what has civilisation come to?'

'Well, I just think it's a shame there aren't any beautiful Balinese girls trying to latch on to middle-aged men like us.' He glanced at me sharply. 'Only joking, Tom.'

Tom stared again at the retreating bottom, slumped back in disbelief and closed his eyes. I watched the surfers and the sunbathers, and the beach hawkers doing their relentless rounds. I was now experienced at dealing with them and, after several attempts to sell me sarongs and souvenirs, they left me alone. I smiled as I watched the woman and the Kuta cowboy stroll past, licking ice creams, and walk down to the water's edge.

Tom opened his eyes. 'Why are you holding up that piece of paper with four on it, Geoff?'

'I was scoring her bum out of ten.'

'That's extremely generous of you.'

'I included three for courage.'

'It's still generous.'

'Hi, Tom, how ya going?'

Darren and Laurie put down their boards and shook Tom's hand. 'Nearly didn't recognise you,' said Laurie, 'We were looking for the lily-white pom we met on the plane, but now you look like us.'

Tom laughed and introduced me to them, and we sat together on the sand. Both Darren and Laurie were around thirty and had long, sun-bleached hair. Their faces were smeared with white-zinc cream and they were wearing board shorts and Bintang tee shirts.

'I didn't see you out there,' said Tom.

'No,' said Darren, 'we surf on Kuta reef. It's about a mile offshore and we get an outrigger to take us there. You wouldn't get us surfing off this beach. The waves are crap, the water's like a sewer, and it's full of people who can't surf and fuck it up for anyone who can.'

I smiled. I could see why Tom got on well with them.

'So, you've found your wife?' Laurie prompted.

'Yes,' said Tom, 'and it's a long story, which is best told over a few beers.'

'Great,' said Darren. 'We're staying up Poppies Lane and there's a bar opposite. We'll dump off our boards and have a shower while you're getting them in.'

Tom recounted everything that had occurred since he arrived in Bali and, when he'd finished, Laurie got up and ordered four more beers. No one said anything until they arrived.

'So, he's a real hard bastard by the sound of it, then,' said Darren.

'And a rich one,' I added.

'Well, they're the worst sort,' muttered Darren.

'Have you worked out what you're going to do,' Laurie said, 'and do you reckon you'll need our help?'

'Are you still sure you want to?' asked Tom.

'Of course we do, don't we Laurie?' said Darren.

Laurie smiled at Tom and nodded. 'After two months in England we need a bit of excitement. We planned to go to Padangbai next week anyway to get the ferry to Lombok. We're going partying on the Gilis and then we're surfing the reefs down south. So, it's no problem spending a day or two in Padangbai on the way.'

'That's great,' said Tom, 'thanks. Well, all we have to do is get them on the Thursday flight without Cruyff being able to stop them. Right now we don't know how straightforward it's going to be. Maybe all we'll have to do is bribe the guards on the security gates.'

'Maybe,' I said, 'but it won't be easy to bribe four guards on two sets of security gates. All you need is one of them to say no and the plan's blown.'

Laurie nodded. 'What time's the flight on Thursday?'

'Twelve-thirty in the morning. They've got to be at the airport by ten-thirty on Wednesday, which incidentally is Gemma's birthday.'

I started to get the glimmer of an idea. 'Tom, they're bound to do something special for Gemma's birthday, aren't they? Something outside Paradise Padang, perhaps?'

Tom glanced at me. 'Yes, but Cruyff or a minder is bound to be with them the whole time.'

'Well, it might be possible to separate them, somehow.'

Tom looked thoughtful.

'That's a great idea,' said Laurie.

'Geoff like's to think he's the brains,' said Tom, 'but of course I'd already thought of that myself. I just let him take the credit.'

The three of us gave catcalls of derision and Tom grinned. 'All right, all right, I admit it. Sometimes he does have a good idea, but he's got such a big head you never want to tell him. Well, it's something to think about, but first I want to see Murray's friend and see if he's got any suggestions.'

'Okay, Tom,' said Laurie, 'unless you ring and tell us that everything's sorted out, we'll come up on the *Perama* bus on Tuesday. It gets in around lunchtime.'

'We'll meet the bus and take you to our hotel.'

'Tom,' I said, 'I think that Darren and Laurie should stay at a different hotel.'

'Just in case things go pear-shaped?' said Laurie.

'Exactly, and then there's nothing to connect us.'

'Good thinking,' said Tom. 'You see, Geoff's become very devious and by the time you arrive he'll have worked out a cunning escape plan.'

'Great,' said Darren unenthusiastically, 'but right now it's his shout.'

I ordered the beers and asked Darren and Laurie about their trip.

'It's been fantastic,' said Darren. 'We left Perth in March and spent a month surfing in Portugal, Spain and France. There's some big surf in the Atlantic, but the water's cold. Then we had two months in England visiting friends and rellies. We went to Torquay and tried to surf but, no exaggeration, I've seen bigger waves in my toilet.'

Laurie continued. 'We've got another couple of weeks in Indonesia and then we're going to the Philippines and Thailand before heading back in October.'

'How did you manage six months' holiday?' I asked.

'We're electricians and for the last few years we've been doing contract work up at the mines. The pay's great, but the conditions are pretty ordinary; so we work until we can't stick it any more and then head off somewhere. When we run out of money, we go back to work again.' Laurie smiled. 'We're taking our retirement in instalments while we're still young enough to enjoy it.'

'Sounds a great life,' I said, 'and you've been to Bali before?'

'Heaps of times,' said Laurie, 'and we always go to Bingin on the Bukit Peninsula. You climb down these incredibly steep steps cut into the cliff and sleep in shacks on the beach. It's a bit primitive, but it's a magic spot and the surf's great. You get monkeys on the beach and at low tide you can walk for miles along the reefs.'

'The only trouble is,' said Darren, 'there's bugger all to do and after a while you go crazy. So, every few days, we come to Kuta for a bit of culture.'

'In other words,' laughed Laurie, 'we drink too much, go clubbing and pick up chicks. Then we go back to Bingin and chill out. Which reminds me, we've arranged to meet a couple of chicks from Sydney on the beach just before sunset. It's a Kuta ritual to watch the sun setting over the sea. You two ought to come along.'

CHAPTER NINETEEN

Kuta beach was packed. People stood or sat patiently and groups talked quietly, as if they were waiting for the start of outdoor theatre. We found a space close to the shore and Darren and Laurie went off to look for the girls.

'This is incredible. There are thousands here just to see the sunset.'

'Yes,' said Tom, 'a free performance every night. It's the longest running show in Bali.'

To our right was a crowd of about forty young men and women. Many seemed to know each other, and they mingled and exchanged handshakes and kisses. Five men and three women stood apart from the main group as they practised on a mismatched assortment of instruments. The men were armed with four guitars and a tom-tom drum, which they played exuberantly, while the women practised sedately on two violins and a flute.

'Wonderful,' I said, 'we're going to have a concert.'

Tom turned and surveyed the group's honest, open faces. 'There's something unnatural about them,' he concluded. He tilted his head back and sniffed the air. 'I can smell religion at fifty paces and that lot are overpowering. Come on, let's move.'

'What does it matter if they're a church group? They're not doing us any harm. Anyway, we can't move, because Darren and Laurie are coming back here to find us.'

Tom studied them critically. 'They're Christians,' he pronounced finally, 'and the problem with Christians is that they want everyone else to be Christians. Don't say I didn't warn you and, if they come round with a collection plate after they've finished singing and praying, I'm not contributing.'

'Right, Tom, I'll let them know.'

The musicians had stopped practising and they now stood in a row with their backs to the sea and their instruments poised. The main group formed into a loose half-circle in front of them, with each person holding up a word sheet. After two false starts, the musicians started to play and the choir sang enthusiastically.

The breeze carried the music away from us and all we could hear were unrecognisable snatches. Transfixed, I watched the singers mouth the words of the unknown songs, their untroubled faces lit by the glow of the setting sun.

'Hi, my name's Sam. Would you like to join us?' invited an American voice. A boy about seventeen was holding out a sheet of paper. 'Here, take this. All the songs are written down.'

'No thanks,' replied Tom.

'Yes, I would like to,' I said, 'very much.'

The half-circle was now swollen with newcomers and I stood at the back and sang to music that I could barely hear. As the sky and the water turned crimson I felt an unaccustomed peace.

I watched the sun hesitate for effect before it vanished into the sea. At the moment it disappeared, the people on the beach burst into spontaneous applause. Tonight had been a stellar performance and tomorrow the sun would return for an encore.

The original group of singers moved purposefully among the newcomers and a beautiful dark-haired girl, wearing board shorts and a bikini top, came up to me and asked if I would like to take part in the baptism ceremony. While we talked, I watched as a long-haired, bearded preacher, dressed in a flowing white robe, baptised a young Balinese man. After the girl had left me to find new converts, I said goodbye to the people around me and strolled back to Tom.

'Got religion, have you?' he grunted discouragingly.

'No, but you should sign up, Tom. It wouldn't do you any harm to hedge your bets. Just think of it as a piece of free insurance.'

'Look, I don't need to go through any of those stunts. You must see what's going on with the exotic location, the setting sun, and the music and the singing. The whole thing's been stage-managed and then they hit you with the sting.' He imitated a fairground huckster. 'Roll up, roll up and become a Christian. Come on folks, don't delay - baptisms on special today.'

I laughed. 'Come on, it wasn't as bad as that.'

'Well, I saw that bunch, glowing with religious fervour, queuing up to get done, and I noticed that they quickly worked you out as a middle-aged man on his own. So what did they do? They got the most beautiful girl there, who most men would happily *give up* their faith for, to try to convert you. Christ, they didn't *do* you, did they?'

'No, I've already been baptised. Even so, she suggested that I might like to go through it again to reaffirm my vows. However, once was enough and I politely declined.'

'They're probably on commission,' said Tom. 'If they reach the target of fifty in a week they all get a bonus. Anyway, what did you sing, *Come All Ye Faithful* and that sort of stuff?'

'I honestly don't know. I never found the right place on the word sheet. It was getting a bit dark and I couldn't read it properly. The people around me were all singing something different and they drowned out the music, which didn't help, so I just made similar noises to everyone else.'

Tom began to laugh and then realised that a young Indonesian man had spoken to him. I recognised him as one of the original choir.

'I'm sorry,' said Tom, 'what did you say?'

'Gede is my name. Pliss, are you Christian?'

'My name's Tom, and I don't think it's any of your business, but as you've asked so nicely I'll answer your question.' He thought for a moment. 'Instead of calling myself a Christian or anything else, I'd rather just say that I believe in God.'

'Which God?'

'Are you saying there's more than one God?' Tom asked.

'No, but if you not Christian, you believe in wrong God.'

'Well, if there's only one God and I believe in him, how can it be the wrong God?'

'Christians believe in true God,' insisted Gede.

'Well, that doesn't make any sense,' said Tom. 'Let's go through this again slowly. There is only one God and you believe in him, right?' Gede nodded. 'I also believe in God so, therefore, we must both believe in the same God, agreed?'

This logic momentarily stalled Gede and Tom carried on. 'Look at it like languages,' he explained patiently. 'I'm English, so I point to a tree and call it a tree. The Spaniard says, rubbish, it is an *arbol*. The Frenchman says, you're all wrong, it is an *arbre*. So, we have a big argument, which is crazy because each of us is right. All we are doing is using different names for the same thing and I think the religions of the world are like that. Do you see my point?'

'If you trust in the Lord and do good, you will inherit the earth and be pissful,' said Gede stubbornly.

'Pissful?' queried Tom.

'Peaceful,' I said.

Gede had been flicking through a pocket Bible and he now held it close to his face in order to read in the fading light.

'Psalm 37,' he announced and read haltingly. *'Commit thy way to the Lord ...ciss from anger ... the meek shall inherit the earth; and shall delight in the abundance of piss.'*

'Sounds like the place for Darren, then,' remarked Laurie, who had come up behind us. 'He'd enjoy an abundance of piss. Sorry to interrupt you guys, but Darren's gone with the girls to their hotel. They're getting changed and then we're going clubbing; so we'll see you on Tuesday.'

When Laurie had left, Gede continued. 'There are false gods,' he explained, 'and they try trick you.'

'Right,' said Tom, 'thanks. I'll watch out for them. Look, it's great that you've got your faith and, in a different way, I've got mine. So it's best if we just accept our differences and part as friends.' Gede nodded and they shook hands, and Tom and I walked back to the car.

'I meant what I said on the beach about that Christian group baptising people in the emotion of the moment,' said Tom. 'Look, if you are going to take on a new religion, it should be after you've learnt all about it and not because of a few songs and a nice sunset and a preacher who looks like Jesus. I bet half those people who got baptised give more thought to buying a pair of shoes. Who are that lot, anyway?'

'Oh, some Christian surfers. They go to the top surf spots around the world and try to convert a few people while they're there. I guess it's a sort of working holiday.'

We bought two burgers at McDonald's on the beachfront and ate them as we walked. 'I didn't know that you believe in God, Tom,' I said. 'The way you always talk about religion I assumed you were an atheist.'

'Not at all, and since Marilyn left with the children I've prayed a lot. I suppose I'm the same as everyone else and ask God for help when I'm in trouble, but don't bother with him much the rest of the time. But I've never seen the need to waste a couple of hours every Sunday morning singing and praying and listening to some boring vicar, for God to know who I am. That stuff is just ritualistic rubbish. When my time comes, God will look me in the eye and say, "Thomas Skellam, you've been a dull and sometimes stupid man but, overall, you are not a bad person and you may enter heaven." Then he'll give me a minor job polishing halos.'

I smiled. 'Well, I'm glad you're not like Gede.'

'So am I,' said Tom, 'I've never met anyone so full of piss.'

'I hope God was listening,' I said. 'He would have enjoyed that and I know from now on I'll never read RIP on a gravestone without thinking ...'

'REST IN PISS!' we shouted together.

CHAPTER TWENTY

It was late when we arrived back in Padangbai and there was a message from Murray asking Tom to ring him in the morning.

I got up early on Saturday and left the hotel before breakfast. During the night I had woken several times with ideas jangling inside my head about how to get Marilyn and the girls on the Thursday morning flight. I needed to check a few things and I walked along the beach road in the direction of Blue Lagoon.

The road forks at the end of the bay. To the left, is the steep rough track over the headland to Blue Lagoon and, to the right, the narrow road rises sharply to the temple at the point of the headland. Close to the temple, Puri Sri Restaurant perches high above Padangbai.

I climbed the winding stone steps to the restaurant and sat at a table on the terrace that gave me a panoramic view over the bay. At night the illuminated ferries entering and leaving the port, together with the lights of Padangbai, would look spectacular. I ordered coffee and mulled over the plan. The location of the restaurant was perfect, but it depended upon whether Marilyn could persuade Cruyff to let her bring the girls here for Gemma's birthday on Wednesday evening.

When I walked back to the hotel the sarong sellers had arrived at the beach and I smiled and waved at them.

Putu left her bundle of sarongs on the sand and came over. 'Hi Jepp, you want massage?'

'Not now, Putu, I'm going in for breakfast.'

'Maybe later. I give you special massage. Very good price.'

'Maybe,' I said noncommittally, 'but I might be busy later.'

'Very good price,' she said again and began to knead my upper arm. 'For you, Jepp, 40,000 rupiah, very cheap.'

She moved her fingers to my chest and brushed them across my nipples. I felt an immediate constriction in my throat. Jesus Christ, get a grip, Geoff. It's just a massage and you don't even like them.

'Okay, Putu,' I agreed, 'some time later on.'

She held out a slim brown hand. 'Promise?'

I took her hand carefully. 'Promise,' I repeated and we smiled at each other.

'Bye Jepp.' She turned and walked away, her bare feet sinking into the sand. I stood and watched the roll of her buttocks under the pink sarong.

By the time I got back to the hotel Tom had already spoken to Murray, who had arranged for us to meet Wayan Solahto at three this afternoon.

'It's all a bit cloak and dagger. We're meeting him at Taman Ujung, an old water palace near Amlapura. It's off the beaten track and not many people go there. We can't go to his office in Denpasar, because he doesn't want any contact with us that could be traced. He's visiting his parents in Amlapura and he's bringing his father with him. I saw the sign to the water palace when we drove to Amed and it's closer than Denpasar, which is great, because I don't think I could have faced driving there two days in a row. Anyway, Marilyn should ring in a few minutes and I'll tell her what's happening.'

'Tom, I've been working on a plan to get Marilyn and the girls to the airport. It needs the three of them, and presumably Cruyff or a minder, to go out for a meal on Wednesday evening to Puri Sri Restaurant. I went there earlier and had a coffee.' Tom raised an eyebrow. 'Marilyn will have to make up a story that she's heard about its amazing views at night. She wants to go there to check it out and if it's okay she'll book a table.'

Tom looked doubtful. 'I think we should wait and see what Wayan Solahto comes up with.'

'Tom, the great thing is that they come to us. We can't get into Paradise Padang to rescue them, so they have to come out and then we can separate them from Cruyff or their minder. Plus, it's not going to ruin anything if Wayan Solahto has a better idea. All Marilyn has to say is that it's too much trouble going to the restaurant and she's changed her mind.' He looked at me without speaking. 'Listen, we only have a few days until their flight and we need something to work on, and it's vital they're out of Paradise Padang on Wednesday evening.'

'Okay, Geoff, I'll tell her.'

'You've made the right decision.'

'Which is exactly what the salesman said when I bought the MG and that kept breaking down.'

'Ask Marilyn if Cruyff uses a driver, or has a minder with him when he goes out. We need to know whether there could be two people we've got to deal with.' Tom looked at me speculatively. 'And another thing, tell her to ring the airline and reconfirm the tickets. We don't want to arrive at the airport and find they've lost their seats to the people who are wait-listed. Also, Marilyn *must* have their passports and tickets with her on Wednesday.'

'What about their luggage?'

'I'm afraid they'll be travelling light.'

'I can't see Marilyn being very happy about that.'

'Take her shopping when you get home. Now listen, she's got about four hours talk time on my phone, so keep the conversations short. I know what you're like.'

'You're the one who dribbles on all the time,' said Tom.

When Marilyn rang, Tom spoke with her for about twenty minutes and I was finishing breakfast when he came over and sat down.

'I told her that her marriage to Cruyff is invalid until the correct documentation is lodged with the authorities, and in her case it would need British divorce papers to be legal. Marilyn is incensed that Cruyff deliberately misled her. I also told her about Cruyff's rumoured links to organised crime, but Marilyn already knows about them and says they're not rumour but fact. I explained your plan to get the three of them out of Paradise Padang on Wednesday and, surprisingly, she thought it sounded quite good.'

'Why surprisingly? You haven't come up with anything better and, frankly, I can't imagine you will.'

'There, there, Geoff, it's all right,' hushed Tom. 'It's a very nice plan and, once you've figured out how to get Marilyn, Kate and Gemma away from Cruyff, it will be an even better plan. We both think you're terribly clever and handsome, as well.'

I grinned. 'Enough, enough, I can't stand it when you're being nice. Did you ask whether there's likely to be a driver or minder?'

'Marilyn said that, assuming Cruyff agrees to the three of them going out to the restaurant for Gemma's birthday, he's certain to go along and because he likes driving on the quiet roads round here she thinks it's unlikely he would use a driver for the fifteen-minute trip into Padangbai.'

'What about a minder?'

'She doesn't know. It's possible, but because it's so close he probably wouldn't bother.'

'Let's hope so. It'll be a lot easier if there's only one person to deal with.'

'I told her about Darren and Laurie's offer of help and that we're meeting Wayan Solahto this afternoon. I asked her if she thought there was any chance we could bribe the security guards. She laughed and said there are six guards, not four, and they're well paid and trustworthy.' He suddenly sounded dispirited.

'I thought it wouldn't be that easy. But don't worry, Wayan Solahto will have a brilliant idea, or else we'll use my plan. I promise we'll get them on that flight, or my name's not Jepp.'

'It's not Jepp.'

'It is here. Anyway, I'm off to have a massage.'

'Good God, why?'

'It's Putu, and I sort of ran out of excuses not to have one.'

'You don't need excuses. You just say you don't want one.'

'But I thought I might enjoy it and Putu is very attractive.'

'Now, now, Geoff, you'd better behave yourself. I have a feeling that the punishment for molesting the local women will be very severe. In fact, I think that I'd better come along and have a massage as well, just to keep an eye on you.'

I thought of Putu's fingers on my chest and decided it was probably a good idea. 'Okay, Tom, we'll both have a massage, but first I want to go to Blue Lagoon. There are a couple of things I need to look at.'

We reached the fork at the end of the beach road and I pointed to the weathered sign for the Puri Sri Restaurant. 'You can't see it from here, but you go up a lot of steps and it's right up there on the headland next to the temple.'

'And why is that location so important?'

'Firstly, it's only five minutes walk from our hotel. Secondly, it's away from the beachfront and there are almost no people around at night. Thirdly, the road is badly lit and not visible from the restaurant, which means we can ... liberate Marilyn and the girls with little risk of being seen.'

Tom studied me for a few moments. 'It sounds to me as though your plan is going to involve some violent and criminal acts. Not that I have any objection, mind you.'

'That is the problem,' I conceded, 'to find a way of separating them from Cruyff that doesn't entail garrotting him and throwing his body off the headland.'

We turned left and walked up the steep track to Blue Lagoon. It was wide enough for a car, but the surface was heavily rutted, with a lot of loose stones.

'Do you think we could drive a car up here, Tom?'

'I don't see why not. I've seen a couple of vehicles parked at the top. Why do you ask?'

'We need somewhere to hide Cruyff's car where it won't be found until after the plane's taken off. We can't leave it in the road by the steps, because if anyone came looking for them they'd straightaway see it, and if they weren't in the restaurant they'd assume they'd been kidnapped and raise the alarm. But if the car wasn't there they'd simply think that they'd gone for a drive somewhere. I can't imagine that anyone at Paradise Padang will worry if they're not back by midnight, and it won't be until later that they decide to do something about it. The first thing they'll do is ring his mobile, but because of the poor coverage here they won't be surprised if they can't get him. So, they'll ring the restaurant, which will have closed, and then they'll send someone to have a look. By the time they think of contacting the police and checking airports it will be much too late because the flight will have left.'

Despite his earlier pessimism, Tom was becoming interested. 'Are you thinking of tying Cruyff up and leaving him in his car?'

'I had thought about doing that,' I admitted, 'although if we're unlucky he could be discovered within five minutes and then we'll be in serious trouble.'

'Assault, kidnap and holding hostage. I'd say about fifteen years of serious trouble, Geoff.'

'Well, that's what I want to avoid, but we need some way of keeping Cruyff quiet for about four hours until the plane's taken off, and *crucially* he mustn't be able to identify us. If we were all on that plane, it wouldn't matter, but my flight's on Friday and yours isn't until Tuesday. If Cruyff knows we're involved, every cop on the island will be searching for us and we'll be arrested at the airport when we try to leave.'

'Geoff, this is starting to sound dangerous. I don't want you involved if there's any chance you'll get into trouble, either with Cruyff or the cops.'

'That's okay. Heroism never was my strong point. If there's even the slightest whiff of danger I'll be on the first plane home.'

Tom smiled. 'All right, but the alternative is that Marilyn tells Cruyff the truth and if he stops her leaving we get the British Consulate involved.'

'Yes, but based on what Graham Richardson said, that will be the last resort if we can't think of anything else.'

About twenty cattle were grazing on the pasture at the top of the track, directly between us and the path down to Blue Lagoon. It was the first time I'd been close to them. They were short and stocky with long horns, and at our approach they stopped grazing, stared at us suspiciously and started moving towards us. Two men were minding the cattle, and they got up from where they'd been sitting in the shade of a tree and began walking in our direction.

'Do you think they'll charge?'

'If they do,' Tom said grinning, 'it won't be much. I mean, all we want to do is cross their field to go down to Blue Lagoon.'

'Very amusing, but as you well know I was referring to the bulls.'

'Those are definitely not bulls, Geoff.'

'It must have escaped your notice, Tom, that they've got bloody great horns.'

'They've also got a thing like a large haggis hanging between their back legs. That's called an udder and it means they're cows.'

'I don't care if they're cows or bulls. Are they likely to attack us?'

'Wouldn't have thought so. They look pretty docile to me.'

He waved at the two men, who smiled and waved back. One of them called to the cattle and they turned and ambled slowly in his direction. 'There you are, Geoff, the nice men were just coming over to get the nasty cows out of our way.'

'Tom, that spot under the trees where the men were sitting is perfect for hiding Cruyff's car. No one will come up here at night and it won't be found until the morning.'

'The thing that worries me,' said Tom, 'is if someone sees the car being driven up here and comes to investigate. They'll definitely call the cops if they find Cruyff trussed up like a chicken on the back seat and we can hardly leave him to suffocate in the boot.'

'Well, regardless of what we decide to do with Cruyff, we've still got to move the car from outside the restaurant and hide it somewhere, and right here seems as good a place as any.'

CHAPTER TWENTY-ONE

I looked for Putu after we walked back from Blue Lagoon but she wasn't on the beach near the hotel.

'She won't have forgotten,' said Tom.

'No, but she's probably further along the beach selling sarongs. Anyway, it doesn't matter; she can give me a massage tomorrow. I'll email Allison now and let her know what's going on.'

I met Tom back at the hotel for lunch, and afterwards we set off for the meeting with Wayan Solahto. We arrived at Taman Ujung fifteen minutes early and strolled around the old water palace. There was an even mixture of about forty Balinese and tourists wandering around the grounds.

'How will we recognise Wayan Solahto?' I asked.

'I don't think we will, but I'm sure he'll recognise us.'

We gravitated to the main pool and sat on a stone wall to wait. At ten past three a short, wiry Balinese man in his mid fifties sat down beside us. I'd noticed him earlier, accompanied by an elderly man with a walking stick.

'It is good that the tourists visit our historical sights and learn something of our culture, rather than just lying on our beaches.' He spoke faultless English with a faint American accent. 'My father likes to come here, but he gets tired quickly and is sitting in the shade near the entrance. What is my name?'

The question took us by surprise and it was several moments before I replied.

'Wayan Solahto.'

'What are your names?'

'I'm Tom Skellam and this is Geoff Larkham.'

'Good. I think it is best if we sit here and talk. Murray has told me something of your problem. How can I help you?'

Tom gave a shortened account of the events that led up to the meeting on the rocks. He then recounted in detail his conversations with Marilyn and Graham Richardson.

'It should just be a matter of her telling Cruyff that she's going back to England with the children, but Marilyn and Graham both think that would be a very bad move.'

'The first thing to understand,' said Wayan Solahto, 'is that you are not dealing with a normal person. Murray has told you how Cruyff acquired Paradise Padang and what happened to my brother. That demonstrates the kind of man he is. Quite simply, he does not have any feelings or conscience. He is involved in organised crime in Indonesia and his businesses are used to launder drug money. He has also been connected to some very unpleasant and violent acts against people who have crossed him. Nothing has been proven and probably never will be, but I know these to be facts.'

I felt sick.

'Then it's about time someone stood up to him,' said Tom.

Wayan smiled at him. 'Just so long as you know what he's like.'

'Have you any suggestions how I can get my family away from Cruyff and on to the plane?'

'I have made some inquiries about Cruyff's ...' He hesitated as if he were being careful to choose the right word, '*intentions* towards your wife and it appears that he believes she is ... *suitable* for him. She is not like his previous women, who were stupid and greedy, and he quickly tired of them. It was always he who terminated these relationships, never the other way around. For a man like Cruyff, it would be an unbearable loss of face if Marilyn were to walk out on him, and I do not believe for one moment he would allow her to leave in that manner. I am sure that he would try to detain her and I agree with Graham Richardson that it would be ... *expedient* if your family were to catch the flight without Cruyff's knowledge.'

'Is there any chance of bribing the security guards to let them out?' Tom asked.

'None. They are ex-army where the penalty for disobeying an order is the firing squad. I imagine they would anticipate the same fate at Paradise Padang.'

I explained my scheme to get Marilyn and the children to the Puri Sri Restaurant in Padangbai on Wednesday evening. 'The good thing about the plan,' I said, 'is that they come out of Paradise Padang voluntarily and with plenty of time to get to the airport. The problem is how to separate them from Cruyff without using violence and without him knowing that we're involved. Also, there might be a driver or a minder to deal with.'

Wayan looked at his watch. 'I have to leave. I need to ... *ruminate* upon your plan and speak to some people. I will ring you either tomorrow or on Monday at midday.' He handed Tom a piece of paper. 'This is my sister, Komang's, number, except that the last four numbers, which are one seven double one, are missing. Do not write them down. Telephone her if you need me urgently; otherwise contact me through Murray.' Wayan nodded goodbye and walked off in the direction of the entrance.

'Tom, I need a drink.'

'Me too. I'm not sure if I should feel utterly depressed that we're taking on the Indonesian mafia, or optimistic because we have Wayan Solahto on our side and he's going to sort everything out.'

'You'll probably oscillate towards optimism after a couple of drinks, but Amlapura isn't the place for a night on the town. We might as well go back to Padangbai. It'll be happy hour at Jo Jo's.'

There were too many unresolved issues for us to plan coherently and on the drive back our conversation went round in circles. By the time we arrived in Padangbai neither of us felt like the music at Jo Jo's and we went straight to the hotel. Much later we sat on the beach and looked across the bay. The moon hadn't risen and the only lights were from the ferries and the stars. The water appeared black and oily, and we could hear the muffled slapping of waves against the moored outriggers. The wind off the water was cool and I was about to suggest that we go back to the hotel when Tom spoke.

'We should hear from Marilyn tomorrow whether or not Cruyff has condescended to let them go to the restaurant on Wednesday evening.' There was anger in his voice. 'If you knew how pissed off this makes me, Geoff, that she can't just leave and go back to England and she even has to get his permission to take Gemma out on a birthday treat. This is my wife and children I'm talking about, not his bloody servants. Everything I've heard about this bastard makes me think your idea of tossing him off the headland is what he deserves.'

Earlier in the afternoon, when Wayan Solahto had talked about Cruyff, I'd been afraid. Now, I was affected by Tom's rage, and I felt my anger build and give me new strength.

'Tom, we *will* get them away safely.' I said. 'We'll do whatever we have to, and we'll get them back to England. I came out here to help, without knowing that things would turn out like this, but I promise you I won't back out now.'

'I know you won't, Geoff.'

Tom and I sat there for several more minutes in silence before we got up and walked across the road to the hotel. We paused in front of our rooms and shook hands.

Before I got out of bed on Sunday, I tuned to the BBC to find out the score in the test match at Lords. Rain had disrupted play on both days and it seemed likely that the match would end in a draw. I told Tom at breakfast.

He laughed. 'We would have been there yesterday, Geoff, sitting under our umbrellas staring at wet grass. Rain stopped play at Lords. That seems a very long way from here and completely irrelevant, to be honest. I find that I couldn't care less whether England win lose or draw and, Geoff, stop shaking your head and muttering sacrilege.'

After breakfast Tom waited at the hotel for Marilyn to ring. I went to look for Putu and spotted her on the beach nearby. I waved and she came over slowly, her face sulky.

'Why you not have massage yesterday, Jepp. You promise.'

'I'm sorry, Putu. I looked for you after I came back from Blue Lagoon, but you weren't here.'

'Putu on beach all day.'

'Well, I didn't see you and then I was busy in the afternoon.'

'You promise.'

'I know and I'm sorry,' I put my arm around her shoulders. 'Look, how about you give me a massage this morning, in about half an hour. Please, Putu.'

'You know what they say about holiday romances, Geoff ... they never last.'

Marilyn's words were whispered so softly that at first I thought I'd imagined them. I turned and, to my astonishment, she was five yards away walking along the beach road in the direction of Puri Sri Restaurant. She didn't look back. Two yards in front of Marilyn was a solidly-built Indonesian man, who stopped and said something to her before pointing towards the headland. They carried on walking side by side.

'Putu, I must go now. I'll see you back here in half an hour.'

I almost fell over as I ran into the hotel. Tom was seated at the bar. 'She hasn't rung,' he said.

'I know, Tom,' I babbled. 'Jesus Christ, I've just seen her walking along the beach road in the direction of the restaurant. This means that Cruyff has agreed to them going there for Gemma's birthday.'

Tom jumped up. I evaded his hug and positioned a stool between us.

'Tom, listen. There's a minder with her. Now, before you decide that you're going to try to talk to her, stop and think. If anything happens to make him suspect that Marilyn knows you, then the whole plan will be ruined. He'll tell Cruyff, who'll immediately be suspicious and call the evening off. You've got to stay out of the way until they've left.'

Tom was about to argue, but then nodded. 'You're right. I'll go up to my room and watch them walk back. What's Marilyn wearing?'

'A pink sarong and a black tee shirt.'

'And you're positive it's her?'

'She *spoke* to me.'

'Christ, Geoff, what did she say?'

'At the time I was talking to Putu. Well, to be perfectly honest, I had my arm round her.'

'You had what?' interrupted Tom. 'I warned you, Geoff.'

I gave him a withering glance. 'I was simply apologising because I didn't have the massage yesterday after I'd promised I would. It was a conciliatory gesture, Tom, nothing more.'

He looked sceptical. 'All right, Geoff, if you say so. And what did Marilyn say?'

'Well, she walked by about two feet from where I was talking to Putu and spoke when she was level with us. I didn't see her approaching and when I turned round she was walking away. She whispered so quietly, at first I wasn't sure if anyone had spoken.'

'What did she say?' Tom repeated.

'It was nothing important.'

'Are you going to tell me what my wife said to you, or is it a secret?'

'Oh, all right. She said, "You know what they say about holiday romances, Geoff ... they never last." That was all she said, Tom.'

He hooted. 'Oh, Jesus, I wish I'd seen your face.'

I smiled weakly.

'So, what are you going to do while I'm locked in my room?' asked Tom.

'Have a massage.'

It was still early and there were few people on the beach. Putu was waiting for me and she had spread out a sarong in readiness. Her sulkiness had gone and she gave me a brilliant smile.

'Hi, Jepp,' she squeezed my arm happily, 'you take off clothes.'

'What, my shirt?'

'And shorts,' she said.

'But I've only got briefs on underneath.'

'That's okay, I've seen before.'

'Not mine, you haven't.'

'Damage shorts if leave on.'

'Well, all right, if I must.'

Illogically, I turned my back as I removed my shirt and shorts, and I heard Putu giggle.

'Give me clothes, Jepp.'

I stood uncomfortably in white Y-fronts while Putu folded my shirt and shorts and put them on top of her bundle of sarongs. She turned and examined the body she would shortly be massaging, and poked my stomach experimentally with her finger. She frowned briefly, as if disappointed with the result.

'You lie on face.'

She positioned my arms so that my forehead rested on the backs of my hands, and she moved my legs slightly apart. I felt the sun warm my body as Putu trickled oil onto the middle of my back.

'Coconut oil,' she said, 'very good.'

I relaxed as she rubbed the oil into my back.

'You like hard massage, Jepp?'

'No, a soft one please, Putu.'

She worked on the sinews around my neck and then gradually moved down the vertebrae to my lower back. I felt myself drifting towards sleep.

'Just now you in big hurry.'

'Yes,' I mumbled, 'I remembered something I had to do.'

Putu transferred her attention to my right leg. She poured more coconut oil and knelt beside me. 'Who your lady friend, Jepp?' she asked slyly.

'Which lady?' I said wide-awake.

She used her body weight to push down hard and worked the heels of her palms into my calf muscle. I gave an involuntary grunt of pain.

'I said a *soft* massage, Putu.'

'So sorry.'

She moved up my leg and used the flats of her hands to beat a stinging rhythm on my thigh.

'The one who talk to you, Jepp.'

'Putu, stop. You're hurting me. Nobody spoke to me. I don't know who you mean.'

She dug her knuckles spitefully into the soft inner flesh of my thigh and I stifled a yell. I rolled off the sarong to escape and sand immediately stuck to the oil on my body.

Putu put her hand to her mouth and laughed. 'Oh, Jepp, you so funny. You covered in sand.'

I glared at her and she was instantly remorseful.

'Come, I wash off.'

She took my hand and led me to the water's edge. I bent over, and Putu scooped up handfuls of seawater and threw them over me. The sand clung tenaciously, but finally most of it had gone. I started to thank her, when she began to laugh again and pointed to my Y-fronts. They were saturated, sagging and virtually transparent.

'Oh, Christ.'

'There your friend,' said Putu.

'Oh, no. Oh, shit.'

Twenty-five yards away Marilyn was walking back along the beach road. She was staring in my direction, trying to control her laughter. I turned away dismally.

'She's not my friend, Putu. She's just someone who thought she knew me. That's all.'

'Okay, Jepp.' She was no longer interested. She smiled sweetly and linked her arm through mine. 'Come, we finish massage.'

'No, I don't think so thanks, Putu. I'm not really sure I like massages.'

I saw Tom walk across the road and on to the beach. He spotted us and came over.

'Nice massage, Geoff?' He looked down at my sopping Y-fronts. 'Jesus, what on earth have you been doing?'

I mustered as much dignity as I could and strode over to Putu's bundle of sarongs to retrieve my clothes. A group of German tourists wolf-whistled as they strolled past. Smarting from the ignominy, I waved a curt goodbye to Putu and walked back to the hotel.

Tom caught me up as I got to the road. 'I saw Marilyn go past with her minder,' he said, 'and she was looking in your direction. You didn't wave or do anything stupid, did you?'

'I didn't need to. I was looking stupid enough as it was,' I said bitterly.

Tom laughed. 'It could have happened to anyone and you'll probably never see those Krauts again. I'd watch Putu, though,' he added. 'It's incomprehensible, I know, but I believe she fancies you.'

'Don't worry. I'm keeping out of her way from now on. Anyway, isn't she married? She was telling me about her children a few days ago.'

'She is definitely married,' said Tom. 'In fact, I've met her husband. He's unusually big for a Balinese and I'm told that he's got a vicious temper.'

I glanced sideways at Tom and saw that he was grinning.

CHAPTER TWENTY-TWO

Marilyn didn't ring at twelve, but Wayan Solahto did. He spoke briefly to Tom.

'Are you free this afternoon?'

'Yes, of course,' said Tom.

'Opposite the temple in Candidasa is a lagoon. At four o'clock I would like you to be sitting on the wall in front of the lagoon. I will be on my way back from Amlapura and I will stop the taxi. You are to get in the back. Is that clear?'

'Yes, I know the temple. It's not far from Padangbai. Okay, Wayan, we'll see you at four.'

Tom told me what he'd arranged. 'He's not exactly chatty is he, Geoff? He talks as though the entire world is some sort of listening device.'

'I suppose it goes with his job. Anyway, it's good that he wants a meeting. It must mean he's got a plan.'

At ten to four we were sitting on the stone wall of the lagoon in Candidasa. Lily pads choked the water and the occasional giant lotus flower rose up like a face surfacing for air. On the far side, a solitary optimist was fishing with a long bamboo pole. Almost immediately, a blue taxi with mirror-tinted windows pulled up alongside us.

I looked at my watch. 'He's early.'

The driver got out, glanced at us and nodded, before crossing the road to a food stall near the temple steps. He bought a plate of rice and sat in the shade to eat.

Tom waited a moment before he got up and opened the back door of the taxi. 'Good God! I'm terribly sorry,' he said immediately, and came back and sat on the wall, his face flushed.

'Wrong taxi?' I said.

'I sincerely bloody hope so. There's a couple having sex on the back seat.'

The driver walked back to the taxi, nodded to us again, climbed in and drove off.

'I wouldn't have thought they'd finished,' muttered Tom.

'Some strange things happen in the back of taxis,' I reflected. 'I remember a London cabbie telling me about women exposing themselves and couples fornicating, knowing that he could see them in his mirror.'

'Another Foucauldian concept, I suppose,' said Tom under his breath.

A second blue taxi stopped next to where we sat. The heavily tinted windows prevented us from seeing inside. 'You look this time, Geoff.'

I opened the back door and saw Wayan Solahto and a driver in the front. The back seat was empty and I beckoned to Tom and we got in. Wayan introduced the driver as his cousin Gede. 'This is my company car,' he explained with a smile. 'Taxis are the most common and ... *anonymous* vehicles in Bali. No one pays them any attention, which is very useful in my work.'

As Gede pulled out into the traffic, Tom told Wayan that we had seen Marilyn and a minder go to the restaurant in Padangbai, which could only mean that Cruyff had agreed they could go there on Wednesday evening.

'That is good news,' said Wayan Solahto, 'because now we can put the plan into operation.'

He spoke to Gede, who turned off the main road into a coconut plantation and stopped along a narrow track. The trees towered above us and clusters of coconuts clung to the tops of the trunks underneath the canopy of palm leaves.

'We will talk in the car,' Wayan said. 'It can be very dangerous if a coconut should fall. I have always wanted to perish heroically in action, or else pass away quietly in my sleep when I am very old. I would not like "killed by a coconut" as my epitaph. That is too comical a way to die.' He smiled. 'Now, I have given some thought to your problem and I believe that there are two ... *achievable* ways to separate your family from Cruyff on Wednesday evening. In the past I have successfully carried out similar operations by staging a road accident. However, this will work only if Cruyff is the driver and there is no minder with them. In order to carry out this exercise we need to know the time that they will leave Paradise Padang and have a description of their vehicle. The road to Padangbai is narrow with many bends, which is ideal for our purpose. We ... *orchestrate* a collision and the damage to Cruyff's vehicle is sufficiently serious to prevent it from being driven. There follows an ... *altercation* between Cruyff and our driver, who insists that the police are called. It can take anything from one to three hours for the police to arrive. Your wife and children complain of whiplash or similar injuries that need X-rays and urgent medical attention. At that moment a middle-aged couple in an expensive vehicle arrives. They stop to give assistance and offer to drive your family back to Paradise Padang or to the hospital in nearby Klungkung. Your wife and children get in the car and they are driven straight to the airport.

'However,' continued Wayan Solahto, 'there are weaknesses with the plan. It is not always easy to ...

effect the impact with the right degree of force and there is a remote possibility that the occupants of both vehicles could be hurt. In addition, the close proximity of Paradise Padang creates a problem. Cruyff might not be prepared to leave your family in the care of the helpful couple and he may ask them to drive to the security gate at Paradise Padang, tell the guards what happened and instruct them to send out another vehicle. There are other considerations, such as the expense of damaging two vehicles and paying three accomplices. Also, to involve the police in the motor accident could cause difficulties for our driver when it is suspected that the accident was rigged to ... *facilitate* the getaway. This would not matter with a legitimate security operation, but here there could be serious consequences for all concerned.

'Personally, I believe that the risk of failure is unacceptably high. In some operations that would not be important, because we would simply try something else at another time. But here we don't have that luxury. We have this one opportunity to get your family away from Cruyff and on to the flight. So, although the plan has some ... *meritorious* aspects, it does not fulfil all the criteria in this instance.' Wayan paused. 'Tell me what you think.'

'The thing I don't like,' said Tom 'is the chance of Marilyn, Kate and Gemma getting hurt if the accident goes wrong. Also, the whole thing seems a bit extreme, bearing in mind that we know they're going to Puri Sri Restaurant. It should be just as easy to find some way of separating them from Cruyff while they're at the restaurant, without running the risk of killing everyone.'

'I agree,' I said. 'Apart from all the other issues, it's too dangerous.'

'In that case,' continued Wayan, 'we come to the second option, but I must warn you that this necessitates committing a serious crime.' Tom and I looked at each other, but said nothing. 'I like your idea, Geoff, of getting Tom's family away from Cruyff outside the restaurant and I have thought of a way that it can be done without him being ... *cognisant* of how it was accomplished. Now, because we don't know if there will be a minder in the restaurant, or a driver who stays with the car, there are several possible scenarios. However, the essential element of the plan is that Cruyff is given Fozzine.'

'What's that?' asked Tom.

'Fozzine is a locally made drug that has similar qualities to the so-called date rape drugs, such as GHB or Rhohypnol. You have heard of them?' We nodded and Wayan carried on. 'The common non-medical use of Fozzine is by desperate men who spike women's drinks. But Fozzine has some interesting properties that could be very useful and I will explain these. It dissolves almost instantly in water and is tasteless and odourless, which means that it is virtually undetectable. The drug takes effect within half an hour and causes drowsiness, confusion, dizziness, and the recipient appears drunk. It greatly reduces the level of consciousness, and makes the person uninhibited and compliant. The effects of the drug can last up to eight hours and afterwards there is partial or total amnesia. When the victim recovers, he feels disoriented, hung over, and can't account for his time.'

'Christ,' said Tom, 'that's astonishing. How do we get hold of this drug?'

'I can obtain Fozzine very easily, and if you decide to proceed with this plan I will have it delivered to you on Tuesday. The simplest way to administer Fozzine will be to put it in Cruyff's drink when he is at the restaurant. If there is a minder, it will need to be given to him also. I strongly recommend that your Australian friends eat at the restaurant that evening. They pass the Fozzine to Marilyn to put in Cruyff's drink and they will also be on hand to ... *improvise* if things do not go according to plan. Shortly after being given the drug Cruyff will complain of feeling strange. Marilyn will tell the restaurant manager that he has not been well all day, say that they must go home, and pay the bill. The Australians will leave at the same time and assist Cruyff down the steps, which means that no one from the restaurant needs to help Cruyff to his car. Tom will be parked a little way up the road towards the temple. Marilyn and the girls get in Tom's car and he drives them straight to the airport.'

'That is truly brilliant,' exclaimed Tom.

'Pure genius,' I echoed.

Wayan Solahto smiled and nodded his acknowledgement of our admiration. 'It is my job to know how to accomplish these things,' he said. 'Also it is appropriate that we should use Fozzine to defeat Cruyff. In view of his involvement with the drug syndicates, you could say that he has been ... *hoist with his own petard.*' He laughed and repeated, '*hoist with his own petard.*'

Tom and I grinned at his obvious pleasure with the expression. 'Your English is wonderful,' I said. 'Where did you learn to speak it so well?'

'Thank you,' replied Wayan. 'I lived in America for several years a long time ago and since then I have been fascinated with the English language and am an avid student. Murray has been a tremendous help and we ... *converse* for hours. I take great delight in occasionally finding a word that Murray does not know and he has to ask me its meaning.'

'Well, you'd better keep the words simple for Tom and me,' I laughed. 'Anything longer than six letters and we need a dictionary.'

Wayan smiled and looked at his watch. He spoke in Indonesian to Gede before reverting to English. 'We have a meeting in Ubud and must leave now, but there is the small matter of what to do with Cruyff until Marilyn and your children are safely on the plane home. It would be risky to leave him in his car, in case he is discovered and a search for your family ... *instigated*. It would be difficult for Marilyn to explain matters if they were stopped at the airport. However, we have a few days to think of something.'

'What do we do if Cruyff's driver is sitting in the car while they're in the restaurant?'

Wayan Solahto laughed. 'Not even Cruyff's driver would wait in his employer's car for several hours. He will walk to the nearest *warung* and have a drink and talk. You must make sure that the driver also receives a dose of Fozzine, or alternatively he is mugged as he is getting back into the car. There are lots of possibilities.'

Wayan instructed Gede to drive. 'We will drop you back at the temple and I will ring you on Tuesday morning to let you know what time the messenger will deliver the Fozzine to your hotel. We can talk then about what to do with Cruyff.'

On the drive back to Padangbai we discussed the plan. 'All we have to do is work out the fine details and decide how to keep Cruyff quiet for a few hours.'

'I still think we should throw him in the sea and make it look like an accident,' said Tom.

'Well, I don't fancy standing in front of an Indonesian firing squad, so I'm going to lie on my bed and think of something else. I suggest you do the same and we can get together later on and compare notes.'

About fifteen minutes later I lay on the bed and started jotting down ideas. The next thing I knew Tom was knocking on the door and it was seven-thirty.

'Typical,' he grunted, 'we're supposed to be plotting and scheming and you go to sleep.'

'Sorry, Tom, it's all the excitement, or else Wayan slipped me some Fozzine. I'll plot and scheme after dinner and we can talk about it tomorrow.'

We ate at the hotel and afterwards I went up to my room. An hour later I decided that there were so many things that could go wrong it would be a miracle if the plan succeeded. I turned off the light, put in my earplugs and went to sleep.

CHAPTER TWENTY-THREE

'What does she think of the plan?'

Marilyn had rung at nine o'clock on Monday morning and had spoken to Tom for half an hour. 'Fantastic. She really believes it will work. She won't say anything to Kate and Gemma, so it'll come as a complete shock to them, and she's worried about how they'll handle being dragged from the restaurant and bundled on to the plane home.'

'Kids are pretty resilient and you'll have the drive to explain things.'

'The explanation is going to need a plan of its own,' said Tom. 'I honestly can't think of anything that sounds halfway plausible.'

'You should just be thankful you haven't got Josh to contend with. He's going to be MI6's chief interrogator when he grows up. You wouldn't even consider making up a story with him around. Now, there's a thought; you could actually try telling them the truth.'

'If all else fails tell the truth? It might work, I suppose,' mused Tom. 'By the way, Marilyn asked why you were wearing a nappy on the beach yesterday. I told her that you were under the impression it was the latest in swimwear fashion. Anyway, I'm going to take a walk to Little Beach to see if there's a good hiding place for a couple of bodies. See you later.'

I sat at a café on the beachfront and ordered a coffee. The likelihood of failure had diminished in the brilliant sunshine and an idea started to form. It was late morning when I saw Tom walking back along the beach road. I waved, and he came over and sat down.

'There are a lot of isolated spots not far from Little Beach,' he said, 'but access is the problem. The paths are bad and half the time I was scrambling on hands and knees. At night it would be impossible, so I think we'll have to forget that as an option.' He gazed around the café until he spotted the proprietor, who was sitting near the bar reading a newspaper. 'I've been studying the Balinese and do you realise that the owners of these establishments never actually do anything? Take the restaurants and hotels along the front. The bosses don't do a stroke of work. They just sit there while their helpers run around and do everything.'

'That's no different from my company,' I pointed out. 'Derek comes in at ten-thirty, has a cup of coffee, goes out to lunch, comes back and has another coffee, and then goes home. Anyway, if you've completed your analysis of Balinese work practice, I want to tell you about an idea I've had.'

'Okay, I'm listening.'

'Right, let's recap.' I read from my notes. 'Marilyn, Kate and Gemma have to be at the airport by ten-thirty on Wednesday evening. The drive is anything up to two hours, which means that you have to leave Padangbai around eight-thirty. Fozzine takes about half an hour to work, and we need to allow another fifteen minutes to get Marilyn and the girls out of the restaurant and into the car. So, Marilyn has to put the stuff in his drink before quarter to eight, but preferably closer to seven-thirty. Are you following this, Tom?'

'Of course I bloody am. It's hardly nuclear physics.'

'True,' I agreed. 'Well, Darren and Laurie need to have finished their meal and be ready to leave immediately Cruyff is affected by the Fozzine. They help him out of the restaurant and down to the road, and you set off for the airport straightaway with Marilyn and the girls. After that, we have four hours to keep Cruyff quiet until the plane takes off at twelve-thirty.' I paused dramatically. 'Now, what takes four hours?'

Tom looked at me blankly.

'The Lombok ferry,' I said grinning, 'that's what.'

'Are you mad? Do you seriously think he's going to take a trip to Lombok, even if we ask him nicely?'

'He will if Darren and Laurie take him on to the ferry. And they're going to Lombok anyway. Fozzine will make Cruyff seem like a happy drunk and if Darren and Laurie act a little bit drunk no one will think twice about him.'

'What if someone recognises him?'

'They'll travel second class with the locals, who get on the boat with sacks of vegetables and assorted livestock. It's unlikely anyone outside first class would've even heard of Cruyff, let alone recognise him.'

'Won't he be dressed wrong? An Armani suit and crocodile-skin shoes will look a bit odd in second class, particularly as he'll be with two guys carrying surf boards.'

'Simple. We change his clothes to shorts and a tee shirt.'

'And where exactly do you propose changing his clothes?'

'In the second rental car I'll be getting tomorrow. Look, Tom, all hell's going to break loose in Padangbai on Thursday when they start looking for Cruyff and it's the last place I want to be. So I'll drive to Kuta and meet you there in the early hours of Thursday morning. I'll also need a car to get Cruyff, Darren and Laurie, and their packs and surfboards, from the restaurant to the port.'

Tom thought over what I'd said. 'If something does go wrong on the Lombok ferry then Darren and Laurie will be in major trouble.'

'I think that the chance of something happening is very remote, but if it does then they tell the truth that they met him in the restaurant. He was with a woman and two girls and he seemed to be drunk. They helped him down the steps to the road where there was a big argument between him and the woman, and then she and the girls got into a car and drove off. They told him that they were catching the nine-thirty ferry to Lombok and someone they'd met was driving them to the port. He was obviously not in a fit state to drive his car and they offered him a lift. Cruyff appeared to think this was an invitation to come along with them to Lombok and they got on the ferry together.'

'It sounds weak,' said Tom.

'Well, Cruyff won't be able to contradict them because he'll be disoriented, confused and appear drunk, and when he wakes up the next day he'll be suffering from amnesia. Look at it from his point of view. He's gone out for a quiet meal in Padangbai, and he ends up in Lombok and can't remember anything about it. The whole episode will seem like a dream and he won't be able to separate fantasy from reality.'

'All right,' Tom conceded, 'but what are you going to do if Cruyff has a minder, or even worse a minder and a driver? You can't have a whole crowd of Fozzine-affected bogus surfers on the ferry.'

'That's true, and if that happens then we'll have to take a chance and leave them all in the car at Blue Lagoon. Alternatively, we could drive his car to Candidasa and park it on one of those tracks through the coconut plantation, and hope that the police don't stop us on the way.'

'That's much too risky.'

'Look, Tom, there are two types of people in this world, those who go around making problems and those who go around solving them.'

'Your point being?'

'Well, you're starting to sound like someone in the first category.'

'Christ, I'm just trying to stop the three of you ending up in jail.'

'Well, I'm prepared to take what I see is a very small risk.' I grinned and imitated Wayan Solahto's voice. 'However, Darren and Laurie have yet to ... *acquiesce* to the plan.'

Tom laughed. 'It's demoralising when a foreigner speaks better English than you and I combined.'

'That's what we do as a nation,' I said, 'invent things and then other countries come along and do them better. Football and cricket are classic examples. What else have we invented, Tom?'

'Railways?' he hazarded.

'Well, there you are. Look at the trains in Japan and France. We're still on steam compared to them.'

'Good point. Anyway, what were you saying?'

'I was saying that if you'd stop objecting all the time and ... *endeavoured* to contribute something ... *fundamentally constructive*, then we'd get on a whole lot better.'

'Well, I did try to warn you,' said Tom. I looked at my notes and he groaned. 'You've got all those lists, columns, and numbers, and at the same time you're proposing anarchy. You've turned into a clerical terrorist.'

'You can mock, but it's in the detail that these things go wrong. I was about to say that we have to buy some luggage for Marilyn, Kate and Gemma. It'll look highly suspicious if they turn up at the airport with only what they're wearing.'

We spent the afternoon in the hotel bar comparing ideas, plotting and arguing.

'I give in,' Tom said finally. 'You win. But I want a written disclaimer to the effect that you are doing this of your own free will and you in no way hold me responsible for any harm that may befall you as a result of your rash schemes.'

'Absolutely, Tom, whatever you say.'

I was suddenly drained and needed to be alone. I told Tom I was going for a walk and would see him later for dinner. I went past Blue Lagoon and along the paths that crisscross the headland. I saw nobody and half an hour later I arrived at a sheer cliff that gave a view across the water to Candidasa in the east and the island of Nusa Penida in the south. I lay on the grass at the top of the cliff, rested my head on my daypack and pondered.

When I got back Tom hadn't moved from his spot in the bar. I sat next to him and ordered a Bintang.

'Have you noticed,' he said, 'how the Balinese can sit for hours and do absolutely nothing? I've been sitting here for two hours since you left ... '

'Doing absolutely nothing,' I pointed out.

'Planning,' corrected Tom.

'I thought we'd finished planning and it was now time to do something.'

'And while I was planning,' continued Tom, 'I was also observing them. They don't seem to focus on anything. It's as though they've shut down and gone into a trance.'

'I've heard *you're* like that at work,' I said. 'Anyway, it's a form of meditation and takes years of practice. It's supposed to be good for the soul and recharges the batteries. I was doing something similar just now on the headland. It's beautiful up there, tranquil and somehow spiritual.'

'You're going to be one those people who spends a fortnight in Bali and then wears a sarong to the office, takes up Hinduism and builds a temple in the back garden,' said Tom.

'It's funny you say that, Tom, because while I was on the headland I was thinking how hard it *will* be to go back to our normal routine. I don't think our lives will be the same after this.'

'You're right, and mine is going to be a lot better.'

'I think mine will too. Well, I'm going to email Ally and tell her that, if everything goes to schedule, Marilyn, Kate and Gemma will be arriving at Heathrow on Thursday afternoon and I'll ask her to meet them.'

'Tell her not to let Mr and Mrs McTavish know yet, just in case something goes wrong,' said Tom. 'By the way, are you going to tell Allison our plan?'

'Good God no, definitely not. She'd say I've gone completely insane and tell me to come straight home. I'll just say that we're helping Marilyn do a moonlight flit and there's nothing to worry about.'

'Need to know basis then, Philby?'

'Precisely, Burgess.'

'Right, well I'll ring Darren and Laurie while you're emailing. Now that they're an integral part of the plan, I want to make sure they come tomorrow and don't get side-tracked by a couple of bonzer sheilas, or whatever they call women in Australia.'

'Women, I assume.'

'What?'

'Never mind,' I said, 'and afterwards let's go to that restaurant you took me to the first night. Despite the fact that you've consistently warned me against drinking Balinese wine I'm going to try some and that place has it on the menu. I shall splurge and buy a bottle of their best vintage. Probably a '98, I'd say.'

'They don't age wine in Bali,' said Tom. 'They drink it in a hurry before it goes off. It's the exact opposite of European wine. Here, the older it is the worse it is.'

An hour later I ordered a bottle of Balinese rosé wine.

'Make sure it is very, very cold, almost freezing,' Tom told the waitress. 'If it's really cold,' he explained after she'd left, 'it masks the foul taste and you can just about drink it.'

'Is there anything about Bali you actually like?' I asked.

'Of course,' said Tom with a smile, 'and I'll think of it tomorrow and let you know.'

The waitress brought the wine in an ice bucket. It was very cold and quite drinkable.

'This is not too bad,' conceded Tom, 'the other bottle must have been off. Perhaps someone left it in the sun for a few hours and it boiled.'

At nine-thirty we paid the bill and strolled back to the hotel. We paused at the entrance and looked across the bay. The night was unusually still and the air heavy and warm.

'You know,' remarked Tom, 'if it wasn't for this business with Cruyff I'd really enjoy it here.'

'Despite the rubbish everywhere, poor hygiene, hawkers and foul wine?'

'Yes, despite all that,' grinned Tom. 'Goodnight, Geoff.'

CHAPTER TWENTY-FOUR

Wayan Solahto rang at eight-thirty Tuesday morning and spoke to Tom. It was a typically short conversation.

'Will you be at the hotel at eleven?' he asked immediately.

'I'll be here,' Tom answered.

'Good. You will have a visitor. Now, have you thought what to do about the problem individual?'

'Yes, I think we've found a solution, but if there are any complications I'll let you know.'

'Excellent. Good luck.'

'Thank you, Wayan,' Tom said, 'for everything.'

'My pleasure,' replied Wayan and hung up.

Half an hour later Marilyn rang and Tom went over the points we'd discussed yesterday.

'Everything is definitely on for tomorrow night,' he said when he'd finished. 'They've booked a table for four, between seven and seven-thirty. So there won't be a minder with them, at least not in the restaurant.'

'That's good. What else did she say?'

'Well, I didn't tell her what we propose doing with Cruyff while we're waiting for the plane to take off. I just said that we've worked out a good plan to keep him quiet for a few hours until the Fozzine wears off and then we'll let him go, safe and sound.'

'Yes, but in Lombok.'

'Well, she doesn't need to know that. Oh, and I've written down the basic clothes and stuff they need for their luggage, and we'll put in a few souvenirs and odds and ends, as well.' Tom handed me the list.

'Christ, we'll have some fun buying bras and panties in three different sizes. Two bras size 12C. They'd be for Marilyn, I suppose. Yes, I'd say that seems about right.'

'What do you mean? How do you know 12C is about right?'

'I don't, Tom. I meant that the list seems about right and I can't see anything you've missed. I wasn't referring to Marilyn's bra size.' Tom continued to look at me. 'Right, if you can get your mind off Marilyn's breasts for a moment, I suggest that we buy all this stuff tomorrow morning in Candidasa where they don't know us, and Marilyn can have my red backpack. She'll like that.' Several days ago I'd succumbed to a combination of Tom's jibes and the thought of facing British customs again and bought a nondescript replacement.

'All right,' he agreed without enthusiasm, 'but I was hoping I'd seen the last of that, and it's not red, Geoff, it's pink. Well, I'll go and get the rental car. I'll be back before our visitor arrives at eleven.'

Tom had insisted that the second car be hired in his name, so that if anything went wrong the vehicle couldn't be linked to me. He came back with another Suzuki 4x4. Wayan didn't query why we needed two vehicles and told Tom to park it in the hotel compound.

'He's a great guy, Wayan,' said Tom. 'He's been fantastic and never asks any questions.'

'He probably thinks he's better off not knowing.'

'You might have a point,' agreed Tom. 'At some stage, Cruyff or the police will find out I stayed here and they'll connect me to Cruyff's trip, in both senses of the word, to Lombok.'

'But do you honestly think that Cruyff will try to get revenge? He knows there's no way he'll get Marilyn back and when he eventually links you to their escape you'll be out of reach. From what I've heard about him, he'll be more concerned about his image and he'd be a laughing stock if the truth got out. He'll probably tell everyone he got tired of Marilyn and kicked her out.'

'There'll be an awful lot of people who know differently, though,' Tom pointed out.

'True, but once he's over his initial anger he'll be in damage control trying to hush the whole thing up.'

I saw that Tom's attention had wandered and I followed his gaze. A young Balinese woman was talking to Wayan. She was dressed in western clothes and high heels, and carried a small leather briefcase. He nodded in our direction and she came over, walking awkwardly. A lapel badge stated that she represented Java Eco-Tours.

'My name Nyoman. How you do?' She held out her hand. 'What your names, pliss?'

'I'm Tom and this is Geoff.'

'Okay, I have something for you.'

She took several tour brochures from her briefcase and gave them to Tom.

'The rainforest is special tour. You have that one.'

'Fine,' said Tom, 'thank you.'

'We talk five minutes, then I go.'

After she'd gone we went to Tom's room and opened the rainforest brochure. Taped inside was a blister pack of four white tablets, together with a folded note that read, *Use one tablet dissolved in liquid.*

'They look like aspirin,' said Tom.

I read the foil back of the pack. 'Well, they're not. It says Fozzine. I just hope they work.'

Tom split the pack down the middle. 'You look after these, Geoff. If they all get lost we'll be totally stuffed. And don't take them,' he added. 'I know what you pretend avant-garde people are like.'

The Perama bus with Darren and Laurie on board was not due until twelve-thirty. We waited at a beach-side café and watched the hawkers plying their trade.

'Watch out, Tom, here come the *enfants terribles.*'

Six girls, of assorted ages between eight and twelve, approached. They worked as a team selling miniature outrigger boats and postcards of Bali, but their most artful enterprise was the loose-change trick. They were the daughters of the sarong sellers and had already developed formidable sales skills.

The postcards they sold were out of date, extraordinarily unattractive and the edges thick from handling. The remarkable thing was that none depicted Padangbai, but were of other tourist spots in Bali. The first time that the girls showed them to me I joked, 'Go to Padangbai and send home a postcard of Kuta.' They looked at me, unsmiling, still holding out the postcards. 'Right,' I said hastily, 'they won't know the difference in England, so I'll buy these four.'

The model boats, though, were beautifully carved from the local wood and painted brilliant colours. Every time I saw the girls they tried unsuccessfully to sell me one of their boats and I am sure they viewed my refusal to buy one as a challenge to their professional skill.

'In a different country,' commented Tom, 'those kids would all end up millionaires.'

'Yes, but here they'll just scrape an existence. It's a shame, because the loose-change trick is pure genius.'

'Why do you say that?' asked Tom.

'You know they ask all the tourists if they've got any small coins from their own country?' Tom nodded. 'Nearly everyone has and they're no use in Padangbai because the moneychangers only deal with notes and travellers cheques. So, instead of carrying their loose change around and taking it home, they give it to the girls.'

'Yes, I gave them all of mine,' Tom admitted.

'Once they've got more than say, a pound or an Aussie dollar, they go up to a British or Australian tourist and ask, very nicely, if he'll do them a big favour and swap these little coins for a pound or dollar coin. Because, you see, the banks in Klungkung and Amlapura *will* change pound and dollar coins for rupiah. Although he doesn't want a pocket full of small coins, the kindly tourist can't refuse the polite and charming girls. So, in return for the pound or dollar coin, he gets the loose change that they've collected from other tourists. Now comes the brilliant part. A few hours later, or the next day, other members of the group approach the same kindly tourist and ask him if he can spare some small coins from his own country ... *and they get all the loose change back.*'

Tom laughed. 'God, that *is* brilliant. I never really thought about it.'

The girls had reached our table. 'You like massage, Jepp?' They collapsed giggling and Tom guffawed.

'That's Putu's daughter,' he said. 'She must have told everyone about your massage on the beach.'

I laughed with the girls. 'No thanks, they're too stressful, but today I'd like to have a look at your boats.'

The girls laid out the model boats and I sorted through them. 'I think I'll buy a couple of these,' I said to Tom. 'They're great souvenirs of the day we went on the outrigger and you met Marilyn on the rocks. They'll remind me of the fun I had keeping lookout.'

I sensed Tom was about to speak and I looked up and smiled. 'I've decided on these two.' I held them up. 'They're faultlessly proportioned, a perfect pair. Are you feeling all right, Tom, a bit of indigestion, maybe? By the way, I've just had a thought that it will be better if I meet the bus on my own, then you won't be linked to Darren and Laurie. We don't want the four of us seen together in Padangbai, which would straightaway connect us as a group. Perhaps I've caught Wayan Solahto's paranoia, but it seems a sensible precaution.'

'Do you seriously think that people will pay us any attention?'

'Not today, but if things go wrong someone will try to piece things together.'

Tom interrupted me with a nudge. 'Don't look now, but we're being watched.'

I instinctively half turned. 'Exactly, Tom. For all we know those fishermen could be the secret police in disguise.'

'All right, Geoff, anything for a quiet life.'

CHAPTER TWENTY-FIVE

The Perama bus was on time. I waited in the Suzuki and watched Darren and Laurie climb off before I strolled over.

'G'day, Geoffrey,' said Darren. 'Where's Thomas?'

'We're playing cops and robbers at the moment,' I said smiling, 'and we think it's better you're not seen with him in Padangbai. I'll take you to a hotel close to ours and we're meeting Tom for lunch at Waterfall Restaurant in Candidasa, a few minutes up the coast.'

As we strapped the surfboards to the roof bars, Laurie commented, 'So you've got two sets of wheels?'

'Yes, they're part of the highly-secret escape plan. We'll tell you all about it over lunch.'

I sat in the car while Darren and Laurie checked into the hotel. When we arrived in Candidasa, Tom was waiting at the restaurant.

'You'd better tell us the plan before Darren gets too pissed,' said Laurie. 'Otherwise, you'll be repeating the whole thing in the morning.'

'Right,' said Tom, 'tomorrow evening, Marilyn, my two kids and Cruyff are eating at the Puri Sri Restaurant, which is two minutes walk from your hotel. They've booked a table for around seven to seven-thirty and, as far as we know, there will be just the four of them, which means no minder or driver.' Laurie was watching Tom's face, but Darren had half turned and was smiling at two

German girls seated at the next table. 'I have to get Marilyn and the girls to the airport by ten-thirty. It's a maximum two hour drive from Padangbai, probably a bit less, and to be safe we need to set off around eight-thirty.'

'Seems straightforward so far,' said Darren, who was still smiling at the girls.

'Now we come to the tricky part. About half an hour or so after they arrive, Cruyff will feel unwell and need to be helped from the restaurant.'

'How do you know that?' said Laurie.

'Marilyn is going to put something in his drink,' I said.

'What something?'

'Fozzine. It's a locally made date-rape drug.'

'Where the hell are you going to get that?' asked Laurie.

'We've already got it,' said Tom, 'through a friend of our contact in Amed.'

'Now it's getting interesting,' commented Darren. 'I know a girl whose drink was spiked with a date-rape drug while she was in a Perth nightclub. The next day she couldn't remember anything, but apart from that she was okay.'

'She wasn't raped or anything?' I asked.

'No, but she's really ugly and everyone assumes whoever did it put it in the wrong drink. No one in his right mind would waste it on her when all you've got to do is ask her for a shag, not drug her. In fact, you'd be more likely to take it yourself, so you didn't remember her the next day.'

'Let's get back on track,' said Laurie hurriedly. 'Right, when Cruyff comes out of the restaurant he doesn't know which day of the week it is, and Marilyn and the kids get in your car and you drive them to the airport.'

'That's right,' said Tom.

'We're not going to be doing much, then,' said Darren.

'That's not strictly true,' replied Tom. 'I'd like you both in the restaurant to give the Fozzine tablet to Marilyn, and afterwards to help Cruyff from the restaurant and make sure none of the staff come out. We definitely don't want them to witness the getaway.'

'We'll need to create a diversion, so that Marilyn can spike his drink without being seen,' said Darren. 'I'll kick our table over, or trip the waitress up as she's going past with a tray of food.'

'Perhaps if you knocked over your drink it would be enough,' I suggested. 'We don't want to destroy the restaurant.'

'Bugger the restaurant,' said Darren, 'we'll do this properly.'

I looked at Tom, who shrugged and said, 'Anyway, that's not all we want you to do. You see, we have to keep Cruyff quiet until the plane takes off at twelve-thirty. We can't leave him to stumble around Padangbai, drugged and on his own.'

'What happens when they don't go back to Paradise Padang?' said Laurie.

'They won't start to worry until well after midnight, and by the time they send people out to look for them it will be too late. The flight will have left.'

'Sounds like a good plan,' said Darren. 'What do you want us to do with him?'

'Well, we thought that as you're going to Lombok you might like to take him with you.'

Darren and Laurie started to laugh. 'Too easy,' said Darren, 'and we'll teach him to surf while we're over there.'

I was puzzled by their reaction. 'You'll do it, then?'

'Sure,' said Laurie. 'We'll keep him with us on the lower deck with the locals, chooks and derros. No one from first class goes down there. It smells too bad.'

'You've been over before?' I asked.

'Twice. The last time was a couple of years ago. The night crossings can be rough, especially if the wind's blowing, and nobody moves around much except to go somewhere to throw up. If Cruyff acts a bit strange, people will just think he's seasick.'

'You are running a risk, though,' said Tom.

'None that I can see,' replied Darren. 'Anyway, is that all you want us to do?'

'Yes, I think so, thanks,' said Tom.

'No worries,' Darren said. 'Well, if we can go through the details tomorrow, I'd like to invite those frauleins to our table while they're still interested.'

Laurie looked at the ceiling. I looked at the girls and Tom looked at his watch. 'Come on, Geoff, it's time we were going,' he said.

'Why? Oh, right. Okay.'

I tossed my car keys to Darren, who grinned his thanks, and Tom and I went over to the bar and paid the bill. When we turned to leave, the girls were already sitting at our table.

'See you tomorrow,' called Laurie.

'They've got their priorities right,' I commented as we walked to the car.

'They don't give a damn, do they?' said Tom. 'We worry about all the things that could go wrong and the thought of spending ten years in an Indonesian jail, but they're not scared of anything. It's just a bit of fun to them.'

'Were you ever like that, Tom?'

'Not that I can remember. I grew up fearing my dad, authority and poverty, in that order. No one ever explained to me that life was something to be enjoyed.'

'Yes, and as you get older you acquire things along the way, such as a wife, children and a home. And the more you've got to lose, the more scared you become.'

'Can we get off this subject?' said Tom. 'It's starting to depress me.'

'All right. Well, as we're in Candidasa, how about we buy the things for Marilyn and the girls.'

'No, I can't face it now, Geoff. I need a swim. Let's stick to our plan and do it tomorrow morning.'

We swam for half an hour, and while Tom jogged along the beach I went to the internet-café and read Allison's reply to my email. She confirmed she would meet Marilyn and the girls at Heathrow airport on Thursday and wished us all good luck. She said that she had bought a coming-home present for me and thought I'd like a clue to whet my appetite. It's made out of red silk with black lace edging and she will be wearing it when I arrive home on Saturday. And it's not a hat.

'No wild partying tonight, Geoff, we've got a huge day tomorrow.'

'Suits me, Tom. Let's go to the fish restaurant on the beach. We'll be in bed by nine-thirty.'

We arrived at the restaurant early and sat on the terrace. Normally, the hawkers disappear after dark, but tonight I noticed that half a dozen hard-looking men were patrolling the beach road, selling watches, sunglasses and jewellery. They gathered in a group outside the restaurant.

'They're keen,' I said.

Tom turned to look at them. 'I haven't seen that lot before,' he said. 'I don't think they're local. Maybe they're from Java and on their way to Lombok, or perhaps they've come up from Kuta to try their luck in Padangbai.'

The hawkers stared at the customers inside the restaurant for a few moments before they marched in. One of the waitresses spoke to them and they responded sharply, causing her to retreat into the kitchen. A few moments later the chef emerged. He took in the scene, then turned and went back.

'That's odd. What's going on?'

'I'm not sure,' said Tom. 'It's unusual for them to come into a restaurant. Shops, hotels and restaurants are the few places that are sacrosanct, but this lot are breaking the rules.'

The restaurant was half full and the hawkers fanned out with military precision. They initially confronted the more susceptible targets, the solitary diner and the elderly, who were caught with their defences down and were unprepared to counter the surprise invasion. Some quickly bought something in the hope they could continue their meals without further interruption.

'Don't look at them and they'll leave us alone,' I said.

We stared out to sea but, undeterred, a sunglass vendor arrived at our table. 'You like sunglasses?' he asked and opened his case.

We ignored him and he repeated the question.

Tom grunted with annoyance. 'Yes, I like sunglasses,' he replied, 'but I don't want to buy any.'

'What your name?'

'Tom.'

'My name Wayan. Where you from?'

'England. Now, will you leave us alone, *please*. We don't want any sunglasses.'

'They good,' said Wayan and plonked the open case on our table.

'No thank you.'

'Strong and cheap.'

'*No* thank you.'

'See, you try on,' Wayan persisted.

'No.'

'Here, take these.'

'I said, no.'

'For you special price. Only 40,000 rupiah.'

'Are you fucking deaf? Didn't you hear me the first ten times I told you I don't want any of your cheap, shitty sunglasses? What could possibly make you think I'm urgently in need of sunglasses, when I'm sitting under this five-fucking-watt light bulb trying to see what I'm eating? I need a torch, not fucking sunglasses. Do you understand? Now, fuck off!'

'Don't tell me fuck off,' said Wayan. 'This my country. You fuck off.'

Tom stood up and towered over Wayan. He spoke firmly, as though reprimanding a slow child. 'I don't care whose country it is and I want to explain something to you. I am in these private premises eating my meal and enjoying a private conversation with my friend. You and your mates come along, enter the restaurant and intimidate the staff. You then have the gall to barge in uninvited and interrupt customers' meals. You have no respect for people's privacy or personal space; nor have you any manners or concept of reasonable behaviour. Do you seriously think I've come to this restaurant to buy sunglasses, or any of the other rubbish your mates are selling? No, of course I haven't. I've come here to have a meal AND TO ESCAPE FROM ALL YOU FUCKERS,' he suddenly bellowed. 'SO, WILL YOU FUCK OFF AND LEAVE US ALONE.'

There was complete silence. Tom looked around the restaurant. Everyone was motionless staring at him and one woman had paused with her fork mid-way on its journey to her mouth.

'Oh Christ, I'm sorry. It's just that they finally got to me. I'm really terribly sorry, everybody. Please carry on.'

An elderly English lady at the next table broke the silence. She turned her fine features to the hawker at her elbow and spoke in a cultured voice. 'You heard the gentleman. Fuck off.'

The restaurant erupted and, while the customers cheered and clapped, the hawkers withdrew in disarray.

'So much for keeping a low profile while we're here, Tom. If you stay much longer you'll become a cult hero.' I laughed. 'I don't think I've heard that many fucks since I had lunch with an accountant from Dublin.'

'It's my nasty, working-class background, Geoff, poking out of the seams.'

'Well, it fucking worked.'

Tom got up and walked over to the elderly lady. 'Thank you,' he said, 'you saved me then.'

She smiled up at Tom. 'Not at all young man, it is I who should thank you. Those utterly horrible people won't take no for an answer. They remind me of my first husband.'

'Why's that?' Tom asked in surprise.

'He was a man who couldn't understand the word no. He pestered me for years to marry him until finally I gave in and said yes. It was the worst mistake I ever made. You see, I wanted to be an actress.'

'And did you ...?' Tom left the question unfinished.

She smiled. 'Oh yes, on the stage, but that was long after and too late in life to become famous.'

'Well, you haven't lost your sense of timing,' said Tom. 'It was impeccable.'

She laughed. 'My dear man,' she said, 'in life, timing is everything.'

Tom bent and kissed her cheek, and returned to our table.

'Remarkable woman,' he said.

A young Swiss couple came over and gravely shook Tom's hand, and a waitress appeared, carrying two tall glasses. 'We didn't order these,' said Tom.

She put the glasses on the table. '*Arak attack*. Gift from boss.'

The chef was grinning at us from the doorway to the kitchen. Tom smiled and nodded his thanks.

'What's an *arak attack*?' I asked.

'*Arak's* the local spirit they make from palm trees. It tastes like varnish. They mix it with lemonade to make it drinkable for the tourists and call it *arak attack*.'

I took a mouthful and gagged. 'Jesus Christ, I can see why.'

'Come on, it's mostly lemonade. Let's down these and go.'

Tom had emphatically voiced the sentiments of everyone present and that night we were bought many drinks until, much later, we made our way unsteadily back to the hotel.

'It's a bit late now for an early night, Tom,' I said.

CHAPTER TWENTY-SIX

Neither Tom nor I spoke at breakfast and afterwards I walked the hundred yards to Darren and Laurie's hotel. The Suzuki was parked outside, but the doors to their rooms were shut and the curtains closed. I walked slowly back, my head throbbing in the sunlight. Tom had moved a sun-lounger into the shade and was lying on it with his eyes closed.

'Darren and Laurie aren't up yet.'

Tom expelled air through his nostrils.

'Did Marilyn ring?'

He opened one eye. 'What? No, she's going to ring at three or four.'

'What time are we going to Candidasa?'

Tom groaned and sat up. 'Christ, Geoff, later on.'

'Do you remember much about yesterday evening?'

'Not a lot. Why?'

'Well, it's just occurred to me that *arak* must have pretty much the same effect as Fozzine.'

'Go away, Geoff. Don't bother me now.'

An hour later we were shopping in Candidasa. Tom grabbed armfuls of tee shirts, skirts and dresses from a small boutique on the main road.

He dumped them on the counter. 'How much?' he demanded.

'You want all?' asked the owner in amazement.

'Yes. How much?'

The man sorted the clothing and made notes on a pad. 'Special early morning price for you, five million rupiah. Very cheap.'

'Rubbish,' said Tom, 'and I haven't got time to bugger about for hours haggling. I'll give you two million and, if you won't sell the stuff for that, I'll go somewhere else.'

'Not possible,' said the man. 'Best price is four million or I lose money.'

'You weren't listening,' said Tom and walked to the door. 'Cheerio.'

We were ten paces down the road when the shopkeeper caught us up. He was in danger of losing the biggest sale of his life.

'Two and a half million. I sell you for two and a half million.'

Tom looked at him. 'That's a bit better. I tell you what, I'll go up to two million two hundred thousand if you throw in a couple of Bintang tee shirts for my friend and me.'

The man hesitated and Tom started to walk off. 'Okay, you got deal.'

We put the clothes in the back of the Suzuki and went across the road to a fixed-price department store.

'Your bargaining's improved,' I remarked. 'Last week you would have negotiated upwards and bought the stuff for six million.'

'Be quiet, Geoff, you're giving me a headache,' grunted Tom. 'Right, I'll get the backpacks, souvenirs and underwear from here and that's the lot.'

A young female assistant watched us rummaging through the racks in the underwear section. Tom emerged holding up two black bras, like trophies from an orgy.

'Are those big enough for Marilyn?' I queried.

'Leave the bra selection to me. You go and choose the girls' knickers, Geoff. You'll enjoy that.'

The assistant had joined us and she spoke to Tom. 'Are for you?'

'Christ no, of course they're not for me.'

'She means are you buying them, or am I buying them,' I said.

'Oh, I see. They're for me. For my wife, that is.'

'What size wife?'

'Are you going to discuss the size of Marilyn's bust with her, Geoff, or shall I?'

'I think you'd better,' I decided. 'I'll leave you to sort it out while I browse through the knickers, but give me a shout if you need any help.'

Five minutes later I poked my head round the racks of knickers to see how Tom was getting on. He was sitting on a plastic chair with his legs together and his shorts pulled up. He had the cups of a pink brassiere over his large knees and, with rounded hand movements, he was explaining something to the sales assistant, who was listening, straight-faced. It remains one of my fondest memories of Bali.

'Great idea, Tom. Knee warmers for those cold winter mornings while we're waiting on platform two. There is a drawback, though. We won't be able to walk.'

'Don't be a bloody fool, Geoff. I'm showing her the size of Marilyn's bust.'

'Tom, there's a fruit and vegie stall outside. They must have something you could use.'

We arrived back in Padangbai at midday and Tom found a note from Darren and Laurie pushed under his door. They asked us to meet them at the restaurant in Candidasa at one-thirty.

'Damn,' said Tom. 'We've just come from Candidasa. We could have stayed there.'

'It's that close it doesn't matter,' I said. 'Anyway, it gives us time to pack now, rather than leave it to the last minute.'

I put everything in my backpack, apart from what I was wearing that evening, and went to Tom's room. 'I'll help you pack Kate and Gemma's bags and then we can go and settle up with Wayan.'

Tom tossed me the two backpacks he'd bought this morning and I started packing the new clothes.

'I don't know which of the things belongs to Kate and which to Gemma, but it probably doesn't matter. They can sort it out when they get home.'

'Just try to get about half in each,' said Tom. 'It'll look strange if one's full of skirts and underwear and the other one's only got tee shirts.'

'You didn't buy any shoes. Doesn't everyone come back from Bali with dozens of pairs of shoes?'

'It's too hard with the sizes and, anyway, it's not compulsory to buy shoes. They're not going to get arrested because they haven't bought a plane-load of footwear, are they?' pointed out Tom. 'The reason for them having these packs is so they don't arouse suspicion by being the only females in history to visit this shopping paradise without buying anything. In fact, it would be even stranger than that, because they'd be leaving with absolutely nothing; not even what they arrived with. So it's not an issue of shoes, Geoff. It's simply so they have something to check in at the airport. Don't you understand that?'

'Yes, Tom, sorry I mentioned it.' It seemed pointless to remind him that I was the one who had suggested buying the luggage. 'How are you feeling now, hangover nearly gone?'

'Are you trying to say something?'

I looked at his bloodshot eyes. 'Well, you seem a bit liverish today and you've savaged everyone you've come into contact with. I was just wondering how long you're going to keep it up, that's all.'

'How come you're feeling perky, all of a sudden?'

'Simple, I had a Bintang from the bar fridge before I came in to help you pack.'

Tom looked at me, for the first time with the trace of a smile. 'Fancy another one?'

'Now, that's a good idea. I'll pour.'

We paid Wayan for the rooms up until the following day and then drove back to Candidasa, where Darren and Laurie were sitting at the same table in Waterfall Restaurant.

'Jeeze, you two look a bit rough,' said Darren. 'I hope it was worth it.'

'It wasn't,' I said, 'but our appearance belies our good spirits.'

'Yes, it's remarkable how a couple of Bintangs make you feel human again,' said Tom.

'The healing power of Bintang is legendary,' agreed Laurie. 'We know all about it. So, what did you get up to?'

'Tom told a hawker to fuck off, in front of a restaurant full of people, and became an instant hero.' I explained. 'Everyone bought us drinks, hence our delicate condition. Sadly, relations between Britain and Indonesia are now at an all-time low.'

Laurie laughed. 'The hawkers here are shocking. One of them even persuaded Darren to buy a sarong this morning. He told me in London that if he bought a sarong this trip to Bali he'd shout me a carton of Coopers when we get home. So, it was an expensive sarong.'

'A moment of weakness,' admitted Darren, 'and it won't happen again.'

'Who did you buy it from?' Tom asked.

'It was a very good-looking woman,' said Laurie, 'and *that's* Darren's weakness. That and beer, of course.'

Darren grinned. 'Her name's Putu. Do you know her?'

'Geoff does,' said Tom.

I quickly interrupted. 'Look, I think we ought to go through the plan for this evening. We can chat about the sarong sellers later on.' Tom snorted and I carried on. 'Here are two Fozzine tablets. If you each have one, then whoever has the best opportunity can pass it to Marilyn. You must have finished your meal and be ready to leave immediately after the drug takes effect. You help Cruyff down the steps and Tom and I will be waiting at the bottom. Incidentally, Tom's got two tickets for the nine-thirty ferry.' Tom handed them to Laurie.

'Why not three tickets?' said Laurie.

'If we buy three tickets together, the numbers will be in sequence. Should anything go wrong, it will be obvious that the whole thing was planned. So, I'll buy another ticket this evening for Cruyff and give it to you later.'

Laurie nodded. 'Smart thinking.'

'We had a look at the restaurant last night with Hanne and Lotte, the German girls,' said Darren. 'We thought we'd better check it out before tonight.'

'There were about a dozen people there and the road outside was deserted,' said Laurie. 'I guess that's because it's away from the main action.'

'Yeah, it's a good spot to do it,' said Darren. 'Okay, what happens after we get him down to the road?'

'Tom drives off with Marilyn and the girls, and you've got to get Cruyff out of his clothes and into a pair of

Tom's shorts and a tee-shirt. They'll be in the back of the Suzuki with your bags. While you're getting Cruyff changed I'll drive his car up that track to Blue Lagoon, park it out of sight at the top and then walk back down to the Suzuki.'

'Any good at getting a bloke's daks off, Laurie?' Darren asked.

'They're no different from a chick's,' said Laurie, 'so you'll be good at it.'

'Right,' grinned Darren, 'and what shall we do with his clothes?'

'I've bought a backpack to put them in. When you get to Lombok, I suggest you toss the pack in the nearest rubbish bin.'

Laurie started to laugh. 'It really is a double whammy. Not only is he totally out of it with Fozzine, but the bastard wakes up on another island wearing someone else's clothes and he's got no ID. I can see him looking around and saying, "Where the fuck am I?"'

'More likely, "Who the fuck am I?"' said Darren.

We roared with laughter and at that moment there seemed no possibility of failure. Darren and Laurie's attitude was infectious. It was just a game and the good guys would win.

Tom drove back to Padangbai to wait for Marilyn's call, and I stayed with Darren and Laurie and went over the details again.

'That's enough, Geoff, please, no more,' said Laurie. 'We know what we've got to do and we won't stuff up.'

'Sorry,' I said, 'I won't say another word.'

I went and bought three beers and sat back down. 'I was wondering,' I said, 'why you're helping Tom.'

'Why are you?' Darren countered.

'That's different; I'm his friend.'

'But, if you're honest,' said Laurie, 'there's more to it than that, isn't there? There's a reason that's got nothing to do with friendship and more to do with you than Tom. It's a challenge, an adventure that gets you off the treadmill, even if it's only for a couple of weeks. Am I right?'

'Maybe you are,' I admitted. 'I hadn't really thought about it. So my motives are not completely unselfish, then?'

'Perhaps not,' said Laurie, 'but it doesn't matter, you're here and that's what counts.'

'So why are *you* helping?' I asked again.

'Well,' said Laurie, 'we liked the way he just got on a plane and came halfway round the world to find his missus and kids, not even knowing if they'd be here. He sat next to us and talked about it, big and tough, old-fashioned and honest, like a knight setting off on a mission. Search for the Holy Grail sort of thing, with a lot of Monty Python thrown in.' Laurie smiled. 'If it wasn't for his accent, he could've been Australian and we decided that if he needed any help it was a good cause.'

'Also, we haven't done anything exciting for a while,' said Darren, 'and it'll be a great story to tell down the pub.'

'Yes, that as well,' said Laurie.

'Well, it's really nice of you,' I said.

'Being nice,' said Darren, 'is us not mentioning your pommy batsmen.'

I dropped Darren and Laurie at their hotel and arranged to call back at six. Tom had written me a note saying that Marilyn had rung and everything was okay. He was having a siesta and would see me later. I decided to do the same and set my alarm for quarter to six.

When the alarm woke me, I was drenched in sweat and my mouth was parched. For several seconds I lay there disoriented and then, with a groan, I got into the shower and turned the jets on full. After five minutes I felt life return and I knocked on Tom's door.

'Tom, are you awake?'

'Arrgh.'

'Get up and have a shower.'

'Arrgh.'

'I'm going to get Darren and Laurie's gear and I'll see you in a few minutes. If you're not up when I get back, I'll call the whole thing off.'

'Go away.'

Darren and Laurie had everything ready and it took five minutes to load the Suzuki.

'Before you ask us, Geoff,' said Laurie, 'we have the ferry tickets and one Fozzine tablet each.'

'And warm clothes, sensible shoes, condoms and a toothbrush,' added Darren. 'We've showered, combed our hair and our nails are clean.'

'All right, all right,' I said with a smile. 'I'm not that bad, am I?'

'About the same as our mums,' said Darren. 'You're making us homesick.'

I wished them good luck and watched as they strolled along the beach road to the restaurant, unworried and laughing. I drove back to our hotel where Wayan met me at reception.

'Tom get petrol. Back soon.'

'Okay, thanks, Wayan,' I replied. 'We'll be leaving later and I want to thank you for all your help.'

'No worries, Jepp.' The phone rang and he answered it. 'It Ma'lyn for Tom.'

'Okay, I'll take it.' I grabbed the phone. 'Marilyn, it's Geoff. Tom's gone for petrol.'

'Hi, Geoff, nice to talk to you. I trust you're decently attired today?'

'Yes thank you,' I replied, 'and I hope you are too?'

There was a pause. 'You bastard. Tom was right. You were watching.'

'Watching what?'

'Look, I don't have time to play your games. I've only got a couple of minutes while Pieter's getting dressed. Now listen, it's just the four of us and no driver or minder.'

'Fantastic!'

'We're leaving in half an hour and we'll be in a blue BMW.'

'OK, Marilyn, I'll tell Tom. Darren and Laurie are already in the restaurant; they're wearing shorts and Bintang tee shirts. Tom and I will be in the road outside from about quarter to eight.'

Without warning, Marilyn cut the connection and two minutes later Tom pulled into the compound.

At quarter past seven Tom and I sat by the window in his room as we watched the blue BMW nosing its way around the promenading tourists. I glimpsed the outlines of the driver and the front-seat passenger, before it passed beneath us and out of sight. Tom exhaled noisily through his mouth and I realised he'd been holding his breath.

'How are you feeling?'

'Better,' said Tom. 'My family's in that car and in about an hour or so we'll be together for the first time in a while. I just want to get this next part over with and I'm praying nothing goes wrong.'

'Me too,' I said. 'It's now in the laps of the gods.' I felt surprisingly calm. 'Well, I'll shoot down to the port and buy the other ferry ticket, and I'll see you in about fifteen minutes.'

'Okay, Geoff, I'll load up the Suzuki. Are you going to say cheerio to Putu?'

'No, I don't think so, Tom. You know what she's like. She'll sell me another sarong.'

CHAPTER TWENTY-SEVEN

Kate and Gemma ran ahead up the steps to the restaurant. Cruyff followed them and Marilyn climbed slowly, allowing some distance to form between her and Cruyff.

He turned. 'Hurry up, or we'll have finished before you get here.'

'These steps are steep. You carry on, Pieter. See that the girls are all right. I'll catch you up.'

Marilyn spotted Darren and Laurie as soon as she reached the top of the steps. They were seated at a table in the centre of the terrace, directly alongside the walkway to the main restaurant. Cruyff was talking to the manager and Kate and Gemma were leaning against the terrace wall, looking out across the bay. Laurie was facing Marilyn and he smiled slightly when he saw her. She returned the smile and as she walked past their table she allowed her wrap, which she had draped over her arm, to slide to the floor.

She walked several paces before Laurie called out. 'Excuse me. You've dropped this.'

She turned and Laurie was holding out the wrap. She smiled her thanks and took it from him. At the same time, she felt the tablet pressed into her hand.

'That was easy,' Laurie whispered to her. 'It's Darren's turn next. He's the diversion.'

Darren had studied Marilyn with the eye of a connoisseur and, after she left to join Cruyff, he nodded his approval. 'I can see why Tom came.'

'Yes,' agreed Laurie, 'it was careless of him to almost lose her.'

At the far side of the terrace a table was hidden from view by head-high screens. At a signal from Marilyn, the restaurant staff moved the screens round until they formed a straight line behind the table. They were decorated on the inside with balloons and streamers, and a banner that read HAPPY BIRTHDAY GEMMA. There was a brightly-coloured cloth covering the table and wrapped presents piled in the centre.

'Happy birthday, Gemma,' called Marilyn.

The girls laughed and ran over, and Marilyn organised the seating so that she faced Darren and Laurie's table, while Cruyff had his back to them. A waitress brought fruit juices for Kate and Gemma and the manager came to the table carrying a bottle of champagne in a silver ice bucket.

'I didn't see that on the wine list,' muttered Darren.

'He probably had it flown over from France.'

'So, what do you fancy, Laurence old chap, a '78 Bollinger perhaps?'

'Very kind of you Darrence, but I fear all those French bubbles will make me fart. I do believe I'll have a magnum of Bintang this evening.'

'Sound choice, old man,'

They watched the manager fill Marilyn and Cruyff's glasses and then bow and walk away from the table. Laurie caught Marilyn's eye and she gave an almost imperceptible nod.

'Okay, Darren,' said Laurie, 'show time. You're on.'

Darren tilted back his chair until it overbalanced. As he started to go over backwards, he grabbed the edge of the tablecloth in an apparent attempt to stop himself from falling. In slow motion, he rolled onto the floor, dragging with him the tablecloth, complete with beer bottles, glasses, plates and cutlery.

Except for Marilyn, the entire restaurant was focused on the carnage. She popped the tablet out of its blister pack and dropped it into Cruyff's glass of champagne while, amid the uproar, Darren disentangled himself from the debris and climbed slowly to his feet. He brushed a few noodles from his tee shirt before he addressed the restaurant.

'I fell off the chair,' he explained.

'Marilyn,' said Cruyff, turning back to her as waitresses hurried over and began clearing up, 'that is one of the reasons I don't like coming to these places.'

She smiled. 'Forget about it. Don't let it spoil the evening. Just look on it as the entertainment.' Kate and Gemma giggled.

'Perhaps he'll do an encore,' said Kate.

'I'll go over and ask him if you like,' replied Marilyn and the three of them laughed.

'Yes, do that Mum, please,' said Gemma. 'Tell him it's my birthday.'

'I think he knows that already,' said Marilyn, pointing to the banner, 'and now I'd like to propose a toast to Gemma.' They raised their glasses. 'To my darling daughter, happy birthday and have a wonderful year.'

Darren and Laurie had moved to another table and ordered coffee. They watched the four of them drink to the toast.

'So far, so good,' said Laurie. He glanced at his watch. 'It should take about half an hour, so we'll be out of here by quarter past eight.' He saw Darren rubbing his elbow. 'Are you all right?'

'I'm getting too old for that sort of thing. I've damaged my drinking arm.'

'Use the other one.'

'It's not the same.'

'Did you notice how he looked at us, as though we'd crawled out from under a rock?'

'Yeah, I saw that,' said Darren, 'but, of course, he doesn't know we're going to become really good mates in a little while.'

Laurie laughed. 'So good that he'll let you take his daks off.'

Cruyff finished the glass of champagne and poured himself another.

'You're not drinking,' he said to Marilyn.

She noticed a slight thickening of his speech and looked at him dispassionately. 'Cheers,' she said and emptied her glass.

'Mum,' said Gemma, 'when you said it was a birthday surprise, I hoped Dad would be here.'

'That would be a surprise,' said Cruyff and laughed.

'Pieter,' warned Marilyn and turned to Gemma. 'I'm sure Dad remembered your birthday and he'll do something special if he can.'

Cruyff snorted, but the noise sounded wrong. He put down his fork and half stood up, but swayed and sat down again.

'Pieter, are you all right?'

'I don't feel well. It's the food.'

'Right, you just sit there and I'll talk to the manager.' Marilyn nodded to Laurie and spoke to Kate and Gemma. 'Stay here with Pieter while I explain to the manager.'

Laurie watched Marilyn walk over to the manager and then follow him into his office. He got up quickly.

'Pay the bill, Darren. Something's not right. I'm going over to their table.'

A few moments later the manager came out of the office by himself and headed in Cruyff's direction, but Laurie had already reached the table.

'Happy birthday, Gemma, is everything okay?' he asked, smiling.

'Pieter's not very well,' explained Gemma.

Cruyff was slumped in his chair and there were beads of perspiration on his forehead. He stared at Laurie without speaking.

'Sorry to hear that,' said Laurie politely. 'Perhaps we can help.'

'It was your friend who knocked everything off the table,' said Kate.

'Yes, he's good at that. But I'm hoping when he gets older he'll stop doing it.' Kate and Gemma giggled. 'Here comes the manager,' said Laurie. 'Will you let me handle this, please? It's very important.'

'It not the food,' said the manager straightaway. 'Wife say he sick earlier.'

Kate and Gemma exchanged a glance and Cruyff started to say something.

'Better if you don't talk, mate,' said Laurie.

'Gurrgh aarghle.'

'I think he said he's sorry it happened in the restaurant,' said Laurie. 'It can't be good for your business.'

'No,' said the manager, 'bad for business.'

'Urrffer schlopp,' tried Cruyff.

'He's talking Dutch, now,' said Laurie.

'Double Dutch,' contributed Darren, who'd paid for the meal and the breakages.

Marilyn came out of the office and walked over. 'We'll have to take Pieter home,' she said. 'I'm very sorry,

Gemma, but there's nothing we can do about it. I'll make it up to you, I promise.'

'What about my presents?' asked Gemma.

'Well, we're not going to leave them here,' said Marilyn. 'You and Kate carry them down to the car and you can open them later.'

'We'll help you get him down the steps,' offered Laurie. 'We were just leaving, anyway.'

'That's very kind of you,' smiled Marilyn.

'No worries,' said Darren. 'Come on, mate, up you get.'

They stood either side of Cruyff and hauled him to his feet. His earlier animation had subsided and he mumbled softly as they half dragged him from the terrace. The other diners were watching and when the trio reached the top of the steps Darren turned round.

'A word of warning,' he called out, 'don't have the fish.'

CHAPTER TWENTY-EIGHT

As Darren and Laurie supported Cruyff down the steps, they heard the manager explaining that Darren was joking and the customer had been ill before he came to the restaurant.

'What did you say that for?' Laurie asked. 'The poor bugger's had a bad enough time as it is.'

'Just wanted to make sure he didn't come down with us,' grinned Darren. 'He'll spend the next ten minutes going round trying to convince everyone his food's okay, so they don't walk out.'

When Darren and Laurie reached the bottom, they saw the BMW on the far side of the road, with Marilyn and the girls standing beside it. They walked over, with Cruyff swaying and muttering between them. The two Suzukis were parked about forty yards up the hill in the direction of the temple and, after a few seconds, they heard an engine start and the front Suzuki moved slowly towards them, with its lights off.

'What were you doing in the manager's office?' asked Darren. 'That wasn't in the script.'

'He was going to ring Paradise Padang and tell them that Pieter was sick,' Marilyn explained. 'The staff would have sent a car for us, so I told him that I would speak to them.'

'I thought it was something like that,' said Laurie. 'What did you tell them?'

'That we were having a good time and might be back late,' laughed Marilyn.

'Brilliant,' said Laurie.

'It was smart of you to go to our table,' said Marilyn.

'Mum, what are we doing?' interrupted Kate.

'Just wait a minute, darling,' said Marilyn.

The Suzuki drew up beside the group and Tom got out.

'Dad?' said Kate, unsure.

'Daddy,' screamed Gemma, 'you *did* come for my birthday.'

She flung herself at him, and he picked her up and kissed her. Kate had her arms around him and the three of them whirled round in the middle of the road. Marilyn was laughing and Darren and Laurie started clapping.

I watched in horror from the second Suzuki. Tom was meant to stay in the car and they were supposed to drive off immediately, not dance in the road like lunatics. Darren and Laurie should be walking Cruyff up the road to me, but instead they were standing around watching. I drove down the hill and pulled up alongside them.

The laughter and noise appeared to awaken Cruyff from his stupor, or maybe it was simply that the drug had not fully taken effect, because he suddenly straightened and said clearly, 'You are Tom, Marilyn's husband.' There was amazement in his voice.

Tom put Kate and Gemma down. He took four steps, which brought him directly in front of Cruyff, and then, almost casually, hit him. One moment Cruyff was standing erect and the next he was prostrate on the ground.

'My God, he's fallen over,' Laurie said quickly. 'Come on, Darren, help me get him up.'

As I got out of the vehicle, Marilyn was helping the girls into the back of Tom's Suzuki. Darren and Laurie were kneeling beside Cruyff, and Tom was looking down at him, smiling.

'The girls didn't see,' said Laurie.

'Good,' said Tom, 'I didn't want them to.'

'Jesus,' I said, 'I thought you'd hurt your hand and couldn't punch.'

'That's the other hand,' said Tom. 'The one I did the real damage with. This was just a friendly jab.'

'Bloody hell,' said Darren, 'he's out cold.'

'Anyway,' Tom said, 'Can't stand around chatting. Got a plane to catch. Are you going to be all right?'

'Yes,' I said, 'for God's sake, get going.'

Tom shook Darren and Laurie's hands. 'Thanks,' he said, 'I owe you.'

Laurie smiled. 'Don't let them escape again.'

'I won't,' said Tom. 'Believe me, I won't.'

He turned and I walked with him to the car. Tom got in the driver's seat, and Marilyn leant over and they embraced. I stuck my head through the passenger window. 'Hello, Kate. Hello, Gemma. Happy birthday.'

'Hi, Geoff. What are you doing here?' said Kate.

'Short vacation,' I said.

'Are Debra and Josh with you?' asked Gemma. Nothing would have surprised her at that moment.'

'No.' I said, 'I came alone and now I've got to go. Lots of love. See you both soon.'

I kissed Marilyn on the cheek and reached over and shook Tom's hand.

'I'll see you later in Kuta.' I smiled at Marilyn. 'Good luck and safe journey. Hang on to the mobile; you'll need it if the car breaks down, but don't forget to give it to Tom.'

I slapped the roof and Tom pulled away. Cruyff was lying where he had fallen, but he was moving his head from side to side and mumbling.

'Thank God he's alive. I thought Tom had killed him.' I looked up and down the road. It was still deserted. 'Right, let's get him into the Suzuki before someone comes along.'

We carried him across the road to the car, opened the door, and heaved him in. I started to search his pockets. 'I need his keys.'

'I've got them,' said Darren. 'They were clipped to his belt.'

'I'll reverse the Suzuki back up the road,' said Laurie, 'and we'll get him changed while you're moving the BMW.'

They watched me pull on a pair of rubber gloves. 'Forget to do the washing up?' inquired Darren.

'I don't want to leave any dabs in his car,' I said professionally, as though I did this for a living.

'Dabs?' queried Darren.

'It's what pommy crims call fingerprints,' said Laurie. 'Geoff's auditioning for a part in *Midsomer Murders*.'

I got into the BMW and drove fifty yards to the beginning of the track to Blue Lagoon. I checked that no one was about and turned on the headlights. For thirty yards I made good progress, but as the path became steeper and more rutted the underside of the BMW struck the ground with resounding thumps, causing the car to lose traction. I accelerated and the engine roared. The tyres slipped and spat earth and gravel, and the heavy car slewed towards the edge of the path and a drop into the darkness. I wrestled with the steering wheel and overcorrected the BMW, striking the rocky embankment on the other side a glancing blow before continuing up the track. The bend halfway up almost defeated me. The

BMW bucked and bounced, veered sideways, but finally skidded its way round with the engine screaming and the tyres shooting a fusillade of stones into the undergrowth.

I lost count of the times that the chassis smashed against the ground and the wheels spun almost causing me to lose control, but at last the BMW reached the top and, exhausted, I drove across the pasture and parked under the trees. I turned the lights off and waited in the car until my heart stopped hammering. I thought that the sounds of my ascent would have been heard by every person in Padangbai and I expected to hear people shouting as they came running to investigate. But, instead, nothing stirred and I could even hear faint music coming from Puri Sri Restaurant further round the headland.

I got out of the BMW, locked the door and put the keys on the grass under the car. Even though I had Joshua's torch, the walk back in the dark was treacherous and I slipped and fell twice on the loose gravel. Darren and Laurie had driven to the spot where Tom and I had parked earlier and, when I limped up, they were waiting inside the Suzuki with Cruyff.

'You were a long time,' Laurie remarked. 'Did you stop for a beer?'

'Couldn't you have made more noise,' suggested Darren, 'like sound the horn or something?'

'That BMW isn't designed for rough terrain. Tom and I did a trial run in the Suzuki and it was dead easy, but that thing hit all the ruts and I nearly went over the edge.'

'Low ground clearance and too much power,' commented Laurie.

'Yes, they don't make BMWs like they used to,' added Darren.

'They never did,' Laurie said, putting an end to the discussion.

Cruyff was wearing Tom's shorts and tee shirt and was slouched in the back seat. The left side of his jaw was swollen.

'That'll be sore tomorrow,' said Laurie. 'I hope he doesn't remember how he got it.'

'I've generously donated a pair of my thongs,' said Darren. 'His elastic-sided boots looked weird with shorts.'

'It isn't that we thought we'd get busted because of his shoes,' said Laurie. 'It's just that we didn't want to be seen with him dressed like that.'

'We have our standards, old chap,' said Darren in a remarkably good impersonation of my voice.

'Quite,' I said smiling. 'And how is he?'

'He's been awake but he hasn't said anything,' said Laurie. 'Every now and then he slumps over and we have to sit him up, but other than that you wouldn't know there's much wrong.'

'You've done a fantastic job.'

'Not really,' said Laurie. 'We should have brought him straight up to you. It's just that we wanted to see Kate and Gemma after they spotted Tom.'

'It's probably all right,' I said. 'I can't imagine he'll remember very much and, anyway, it was Tom's fault. He was supposed to stay in the car so that Cruyff didn't see him.' I checked my watch. 'It's nearly nine. We'd better get to the ferry.'

'By the way,' Darren mentioned casually, 'Hanne and Lotte are coming with us.'

'What! You're joking. You can't involve them in this.'

'It's okay,' said Laurie, 'they're not involved. They know nothing about it at all and they have no idea that Cruyff will be with us. We're going to tell them the story you made up, that he's drunk or high on something and just tagged along.'

'It makes it more believable,' added Darren. 'I mean, whose going to think that a couple of Aussie surfers and two fraulein backpackers have kidnapped this guy?'

'Anyway, nothing will go wrong,' said Laurie. 'We show our tickets, get on the boat and at the other end we just walk off. On board, it's really laid back and no one's going to bother us.'

'Okay,' I said reluctantly. I didn't want to involve any more people, but it was too late to change the plan.

At the ferry terminal, I sat in the car while Darren untied the surfboards from the roof and Laurie unloaded the packs. Cruyff stood docilely and, except for the swelling to his jaw, appeared normal.

Darren gave me the Fozzine tablet that they hadn't used. 'You're more likely to need this than I am.'

'Not me,' I said, 'I'm married. But, on second thoughts, I will have it. It might come in handy for one of those times Allison tells me she's got a headache.'

Laurie and I shook hands. 'Don't worry,' he said. 'Everything'll be sweet.'

I watched them make their way to the terminal. Darren and Laurie were chatting and laughing, with Cruyff between them swaying slightly. They looked, for all the world, like three happy drunks. When they got to the quay, Hanne and Lotte emerged from the shadow of a shelter and the five of them walked up the ramp and onto the boat.

I waited in the Suzuki until the last vehicle drove on and the ramp was raised. The ferry sounded its horn and, with smoke pouring from the funnel, moved away from its mooring. It was ten minutes to ten.

Tom and I had arranged to meet next to the surfboard stand in Kuta at one in the morning. I had plenty of time and there was little traffic on the roads, but driving in the dark was an entirely different proposition to my short trips during daylight. The road signs, which were almost impossible to spot by day, vanished completely at night. I took a wrong turn near Klungklung and when it finally dawned on me that I shouldn't be corkscrewing up the side of a mountain I had travelled miles out of my way. I backtracked and eventually arrived in Kuta at twelve-thirty.

I searched near Poppies Lane for somewhere to stay and found a small hotel that was still open. I woke up the receptionist who told me they had one vacant room with two single beds. I paid for two nights, parked the car outside and dumped my pack in the room. I arrived at the surfboard stand at five to one.

Tom roared up at twenty-five past and leapt out of the Suzuki. 'We did it, Geoff! They got away.'

We hugged each other.

'Thank God,' I said, 'I was beginning to think something had gone wrong.'

'Flight delayed, that's all. I sat in the car and watched it take off. I wanted to be sure. What about you? Everything all right?'

'Well, you didn't kill Cruyff, in case you were wondering, and Darren and Laurie got him on to the ferry. Like you, I waited until it left.'

'That's terrific,' said Tom. 'Well done, Geoff.'

'Tom, I don't want to dampen your enthusiasm, but I hope to God Cruyff doesn't remember seeing you.'

'I know,' said Tom, 'it was my fault. I should never have got out of the car, but I couldn't help it when I saw them. I just had to.'

'Anyway, it's too late now. Let's just pray the Fozzine works.'

'I already have,' said Tom.

'I've got us a room at a hotel a few minutes away. It was the only one they had and everywhere else was shut, so I didn't have much choice. It's a bit rough, but at least it's got two beds.'

'It sounds fine, Geoff. I was expecting to sleep in the car tonight, so this place will be pure luxury and I've got my earplugs to block out your snoring.'

I yawned. 'You can tell me about your drive to the airport tomorrow, Tom, but right now I am totally and completely shattered and I must go to bed.'

CHAPTER TWENTY-NINE

Tom was out buying bottled water when Laurie rang from Senggigi, Lombok at nine-thirty on Thursday morning.

'It went like clockwork and we left your friend asleep on a bench near the port, but he should be awake by now and feeling like shit. Did Marilyn and the girls leave okay?'

'Yes, same as all the other tourists, absolutely no problems.'

'That's brilliant,' said Laurie.

'And you got rid of Cruyff's clothes?'

'Darren tossed the pack in a garbage bin outside the port. As we got in the taxi we saw two dodgy characters checking it out. Somehow, I don't think there'll be anything left to find now.'

Tom came back a few minutes later and I told him what had happened on Lombok. 'With any luck, we'll be okay,' I said. 'Now, tell me how Kate and Gemma reacted to being taken out of paradise and back to suburbia, before I dash off and do battle with the shops.'

'The drive to the airport was amazing,' said Tom. 'To start off with, we were all talking at once. Kate and Gemma were firing questions one after the other and they wouldn't let me finish a sentence before one of them would ask another question. In the end Marilyn pleaded for everyone to be quiet so that she could tell the story.

She started by saying that recently our marriage had been going through a bad period, and there were a lot of reasons for this, but it didn't mean that we don't love each other any more. Then she'd met Cruyff, this rich and charming man, and she'd foolishly gone off with him. He hadn't wanted her to bring Kate and Gemma, but she loves them too much to leave them behind. However, she soon realised that she'd made a terrible mistake and what she'd done was stupid and irresponsible.'

'It must have been hard for Marilyn to say all that. How did Kate and Gemma take it?'

'I'm sure Kate knew what was going on, so it wasn't a surprise,' said Tom, 'but I don't think Gemma had wanted to believe it, and she'd ignored all the signs and pretended that her world hadn't changed. Anyway, Marilyn said that she was very fortunate I had come looking for them and I'd done some brave and clever things, which thankfully she didn't go into, and now we're going back to live in England and we'll never let this happen again. She also mentioned you, Geoff, and said how lucky we were to have good friends like you and Ally.' He smiled and patted my arm. 'She took all the blame for what had happened, despite me trying to say we were both at fault, and said that nothing had changed and we love Kate and Gemma as much as ever. When she'd finished, the three of them were in tears and, you might not believe this, Geoff, but I was as well.'

'I believe it. I'm nearly in tears myself.'

'So I stopped the car and we all had a big hug. I tell you, Geoff, it's very hard hugging people who are in the back seat of a Suzuki when you're in the front, but we managed it.'

'Couldn't you have all got out? That would have made it easier.'

'Didn't think of it,' confessed Tom. 'Anyway, it was a spur-of-the-moment hug. After we set off again, Kate and Gemma were laughing and joking about what they were going to tell their friends when they got home, and they were really excited. I was relieved, because I'd had an awful feeling they wouldn't want to leave, but I think they'd had enough of it here. And, while the girls were talking and giggling in the back, Marilyn put her arm round me and we chatted quietly.'

'What about?'

'Husband and wife things that aren't any of your business,' said Tom. 'All you need to know is that it was just like the old days.'

'The *good* old days?'

'Yes, those old days, and then we had lots more hugs and kisses when we said goodbye in the airport car park. I wanted to go in with them and it took all my willpower not to rush after them when they walked off.'

'Thank God you didn't. That would have been disastrous. Footage on the surveillance cameras of you walking in with them would prove you were involved.'

'I know,' said Tom, 'but at the time I couldn't have cared less.'

'Well, it's fantastic it's worked out. When you came over, you weren't even sure they were here, let alone that within three weeks they'd be flying back to England.'

'It hasn't sunk in, yet,' said Tom, 'and all we've got to do now is get home ourselves.'

'Well, Wayan Solahto should ring later to let us know if we're in the clear.'

Tom grinned. 'It would be really interesting to see what's going on right now. I wonder if Cruyff's still on Lombok.'

At that moment Cruyff was going berserk in the police headquarters at Denpasar, less than ten miles from where we sat. The Paradise Padang helicopter had brought him back from Lombok, his car had been found, and he had just been told that Marilyn, Kate and Gemma had left Bali.

One hour later I was in a jewellery shop in central Kuta when my phone rang.

'Can you talk?' said Wayan Solahto.

'Just a moment, please.' I smiled at the shop assistant, indicated that I'd be back, and walked outside. 'Now I can talk.'

'Where is Tom?'

'We're both in Kuta. I'm out shopping and he's at the hotel.'

'Go back there straight away and tell him to leave.'

'Why? What's happened?'

'The police have issued a warrant for his arrest. About half an hour ago Cruyff made a formal request for charges to be laid.'

'Oh, Christ!'

'The first thing the police will do is check the hotels, so Tom must get out of there.'

I thought quickly. 'Wayan, the room's in my name. They don't have any record of Tom.'

'That was clever.'

'No, it was pure luck.'

'Well, perhaps it's time that you had some luck. Unfortunately, the Fozzine did not entirely ... *obliterate* his memory and he recalls being hit by Tom outside the restaurant. He must have hit him very hard, by the way, because he broke his jaw,' said Wayan Solahto, with undisguised relish.

'Oh, Christ.'

'He has helped prepare an identikit picture of Tom, but it bears little resemblance to him.'

'That's something, I suppose, but what else does he remember? Does he know that other people were involved?'

'Not according to the offence report. He is unsure how he came to be on Lombok, but he assumes that he was drugged and has given a blood sample to be analysed. Geoff, for the moment you are in the clear, but it is only a matter of time before you are connected.'

'How long have I got … hours, days, weeks?'

'It depends upon the degree of priority that the police give to the complaint. Cruyff is rich and powerful, but he is not well-liked and it is probable that the police will not utilise their full resources. I would … *hypothesise* that you have at least a week before the police link you to the crime. Their primary task will be to arrest Tom.

'Cruyff initially assumed that Tom had left on the same flight as his wife and children and they were all out of Indonesian jurisdiction. However, when they checked the manifesto, they found that he wasn't on the plane. It was then a simple matter to establish the date that he entered Indonesia and the fact that he has not yet departed.'

'So what can we do?' I said. 'Even if he manages to hide until his flight on Tuesday, they'll just arrest him at the airport.'

'Yes, and I am afraid that I cannot stop that. It is a police matter, not internal security, and also it has gone to a high level.'

'So, it's hopeless, then?' I said. 'Tom's going to be arrested and that's that. What are the charges against him?'

'Assault, abduction and, when the results of the blood test are known, administering an illegal substance.'

'Not trivial, then.'

'No,' said Wayan Solahto, 'not trivial.'

'Oh, Christ,' I said for the third time.

There was a slight pause before Wayan Solahto said, 'When is your flight, Geoff?'

'Tomorrow afternoon at four, so I suppose I'll be all right.' I felt relief that I would get away, but the thought of leaving Tom to face the Indonesian criminal system was appalling.

'Geoff, it is of utmost importance that Tom departs on your flight.'

'Why?' I said. 'Surely they'll still pick him up at the airport.'

'You misunderstand me. Tom must travel using your ticket. I believe it is the only way that he will be able to leave Bali. It will require some ... *invention,* but I anticipate that it can be accomplished.'

'What about me? How am I going to get home?'

'It may require a degree of sacrifice on your part. I need to ... *cogitate* over that particular ... *conundrum* and I will ring you again at three.'

'How big a sacrifice?' I wanted to know, but he had gone.

I went back into the shop to collect my daypack. My brain was racing and, like Wayan Solahto, I needed to cogitate.

'You want things you choose?' asked the assistant.

'What? Oh yes, of course.'

I paid for the items and ran back to the hotel. I was out of breath when I arrived, and Tom was sitting on the verandah reading a guidebook.

'Geoff, after you've gone back tomorrow, I've decided to go to Amed for a couple of days to see Murray.'

'Tom, there's a warrant out for your arrest,' I gasped.

'Of course there is,' said Tom. 'Now, what do *you* fancy doing before you leave?'

'I'm not bloody joking. Wayan Solahto rang twenty minutes ago. Cruyff remembers that you were outside the restaurant and hit him. You broke his jaw.'

Tom looked at me closely. 'Jesus, you're serious aren't you?'

I nodded and repeated what Wayan Solahto had told me. Neither of us spoke for a few moments. Tom's euphoria of last night was gone and he sat glumly.

'It's my fault, Geoff. If I'd stuck to the plan and stayed in the car he'd never have seen me.' He shook his head. 'Damn, that was stupid of me.'

'It's irrelevant whose fault it is,' I said, 'and it's pointless thinking like that. What we've got to do is find a way out of this mess.'

'You're right, but it's still my fault. Anyway, at least Darren and Laurie are in the clear and you'll get away before they tie you in with me. *And* Marilyn and the girls are safe. So it could be worse.'

'Not as far as you're concerned.'

'Well, they haven't caught me yet,' pointed out Tom, 'and we've got Wayan Solahto on our side. Perhaps if he bribes enough people it will just fade away. What was he saying about trying to get me on your flight?'

'I'm not sure. He said he had to think about it and then hung up before he'd explained.'

'Well, let's see what he comes up with, but I'm not putting you at risk.'

I hadn't mentioned Wayan Solahto's comment that the plan might involve a sacrifice on my part, and I thought that I would find out what it was before I told Tom.

'And right now I'm hungry,' said Tom, 'so how about we eat at that restaurant round the corner?'

'Tom, in case you weren't listening, half of Indonesia's security forces are out searching for you at this moment. The identikit picture isn't much like you, but nonetheless they'll be looking for a big, ugly, blondish Englishman. So, I think it's a good idea if you sit inside this room with a towel over your head while I go out and get a takeaway, don't you?'

'All right, but not *nasi goreng*. I read somewhere that's all you get in prison here.' He smiled.

I was irritated by his flippancy. 'I think you should bloody well take this seriously.'

'What would you rather I do, Geoff, roll around on the floor and moan? Look, I came out here with a fatalistic attitude. I was either going to succeed, or perish in the attempt sort of thing. I never wanted to put you, Darren or Laurie in any danger and I was opposed to your plan that they take Cruyff with them to Lombok, for that very reason. Now that things have gone wrong I'm prepared to accept the consequences, but that doesn't mean I'm about to turn into a piece of limp lettuce and I'll do my damnedest to get away. The thought of spending ten years in an Indonesian jail terrifies me, Geoff, but it's not going to paralyse me.'

'Fine, we'll fight them on the beaches, then,' I said, 'and in the meantime I'll toddle off and get lunch. Did I hear you say something about wanting lettuce?'

CHAPTER THIRTY

Wayan Solahto rang at five past three. 'I'll pass you over to Tom,' I offered.

'No, what I am about to suggest will need your ... *concurrence*,' he said.

I didn't like the sound of that. 'Right, fire away.'

'In essence, the plan is simple, or perhaps I should say the ... *concept* is simple. Tom assumes your identity and leaves Bali tomorrow afternoon using your plane ticket. In addition, he will need your passport and departure card.'

'I had an awful feeling you were going to suggest something like that.' I said.

Tom looked at me and mouthed, 'What?'

I shook my head at him. 'Okay, Wayan, tell me more.'

'I have arranged that three of the airport officials will be guilty of extraordinary ... *dereliction* of duty and, although Tom is nothing like you in appearance, they will permit him to pass through unchallenged.'

'But what will I do?' I interrupted. Tom raised his eyebrows and stared at me.

'I will come to that in a moment. Please let me finish. As a transit passenger at Singapore Airport, Tom will be required to undergo a security check. However, I have spoken to my Singaporean counterpart and he will ensure that there is no problem. When Tom arrives at Heathrow he will use his own passport, and he will have committed the minor offence of travelling on a ticket that is in someone else's name. Your Vice Consul, Mr. Graham Richardson, will have contacted the British authorities and forewarned them about the irregularities in Tom's documentation. He will receive a ... *salutary* caution, or at worst a token fine.'

'Well, that's wonderful, but what about me?'

Tom attempted to grab the phone, but I pushed him away. 'What's going on?' he demanded.

'Is everything all right?' asked Wayan.

'Yes, it's just Tom. He gets fidgety when grown-ups are talking.'

'Now about you, Geoff,' continued Wayan Solahto, 'you remain out of contact until after Tom has arrived in London, which will be at 2 pm Saturday, our time. You then go to the British Consulate and report the loss of your passport and departure card. You are simply an innocent tourist who has lost his documents. You have not committed an offence by overstaying your thirty-day visa and therefore the fact that you did not leave Bali on the Friday flight is of no concern to the authorities. Mr Graham Richardson will provide you with a temporary passport and our Department of Immigration will supply Mr Richardson with an emergency departure card, which is issued in cases of loss. You will depart on the first available flight to Singapore. You may have to spend a day or two there until you are able to obtain a flight to London, but that is infinitely preferable to the ... *intrinsic* risks of remaining in Bali. At a later date, during its analysis of arrivals and departures, our Department of Immigration will discover that your "lost" passport and departure card were used by an unknown person, presumably Tom, to depart from Bali and the police may suspect you of ... *collusion,* but that will not occur until you are safely back in England.'

'Is that your best offer?'

'Geoff,' said Wayan, 'it is my *only* offer.'

'Oh God. Well, all right; if there's no other way; I suppose so.' I felt sick. 'And you're positive I will get another passport and ticket?'

'Your Vice Consul assures me so.'

'Oh Christ. Well, you'd better explain this to Tom. He needs to hear it from you.'

I passed the phone to Tom and I went out on to the verandah. I heard him raise his voice and I walked out of the hotel and down to the beach. The tide was out and I strode along the hard sand for twenty minutes. When I came back Tom was lying on his bed looking at the ceiling.

'Where did you go?' he asked.

'Down to the beach. I needed to think.'

'I can't let you do this,' said Tom.

'It's too late. I've already decided.'

'I couldn't live with myself if you get into trouble because of me.'

'Then you'll just have to come over again and rescue *me*, instead of Marilyn,' I joked weakly.

'I'm serious. It's very brave of you, but you're not doing it.'

'I've told Wayan I will, so stop going on about it.'

'I'd rather walk into a police station and give myself up than let you take this risk.'

'For Christ's sake, Tom, shut up before I change my mind.'

'That's what I want you to do.' Tom pointed out.

'Yes, well, that's not what I meant and nothing you say is going to make any difference. Now, let's get off the subject. It's our last night together in Bali and, even though we're stuck in this room, let's try to enjoy it.'

Three hours and a lot of alcohol later our predicament seemed less calamitous, and Tom had now accepted that he would use my passport and ticket to escape.

'Believe me, Tom, if there was any alternative I wouldn't be doing this. You see,' I said, 'the situation we are faced with is the certainty that you would be arrested and spend years in an Indonesian jail, against the small inconvenience of me remaining here for another day or two. Ergo, I have no choice. I do it.'

'Ergo?' said Tom. 'Ergo? I tell you, Geoff, the more you talk to Wayan Solahto the more you're starting to sound like him.'

I threw an empty beer bottle, which Tom caught and placed on the bedside table. He stood up and raised his glass, 'I am truly grateful, Geoff, and I believe that your sacrifice will go down in history alongside ...' He paused, unable to think of any suitable candidates.

'Winston Churchill?' I suggested.

'No, I don't think he made your type of sacrifice.'

'How about Charles the First? He sacrificed his head.'

'That was because he was a swine.'

'What about Jesus?'

'That's more like it,' said Tom.

'Well, I hope I don't end up the way he did.'

'You won't,' said Tom, 'I'm sure it's the firing squad over here. Anyway, I will be forever in your debt.'

'Don't mention it.'

'By the way, Geoff, what are you going to tell Allison?'

'I don't know. I emailed her this morning and said that Marilyn and the girls were on their way home and that I'd see her tomorrow.' I thought for a moment. 'I might wait until you're on the plane and then ring her. I'll tell her that you had to leave Bali in a hurry and I let you use my ticket. You can explain about the passport when you see her. I know what her reaction will be and I'd rather you were on the receiving end.'

'Okay,' said Tom. He glanced at his watch. 'Their plane's due to land in about an hour and Marilyn's going to ring from the airport.'

'You definitely won't mention the warrant for your arrest?' I needed to be sure.

'No, there's nothing they can do and they'd be worried sick.'

'Good. Well, give them my love, and if Ally comes on the line tell her I'm in a drunken stupor and you can't wake me up. She's expecting to see me on Saturday and I don't want to lie to her. My reserves are severely depleted at the moment and I'm not up to coping with Ally on full throttle.'

For the first time it struck me that once Tom left tomorrow I would be on my own. With him alongside me nothing had seemed impossible, but I wondered how I would cope without him.

Marilyn rang from Heathrow airport. The flight had been uneventful and they were all exhausted. Allison had gone to fetch the car and they were going straight home to bed. It was good to be back and it was raining.

When we got up on Friday, Tom prepared a list of presents he wanted me to buy for him and I spent the morning shopping in Kuta. There seemed to be more police on the streets than yesterday, but perhaps it was just that I was looking for them. As I walked, I pictured armies of clerks checking hotel records and I knew it was simply a matter of time before they traced Tom Skellam and his friend, Geoff Larkham, to Juniata Beach Hotel in Padangbai. I could almost feel the noose tightening around my neck and I desperately wanted to get out of Bali.

I had left the phone with Tom and when I got back he was talking to Wayan Solahto.

'Geoff's just walked in,' he said. 'I'll pass you over.'

'I've told Tom exactly what he must do at the airport. It is ... *imperative* that he follows my instructions to the letter.'

'Right, and Tom understands all this?' I looked at Tom, who nodded and gave me the thumbs up.

'Yes, we have been over it several times,' said Wayan Solahto. 'Now, I have spoken again to Mr Graham Richardson and he is expecting you to arrive at the British Consulate tomorrow afternoon to report the loss of your passport. He will issue a temporary one on the spot and immediately contact the airlines to get you on a plane to Singapore. Two flights on Saturday evening have vacant seats, so I suggest that you arrive at the consulate fully packed. The first available flight from Singapore to London is on Sunday evening.'

'Wayan, you are a genius. Thank you,' I said.

'To me, it is worth the effort. Stories are already circulating about Cruyff's embarrassing ... *escapade* and how he was made to look ridiculous.' Wayan Solahto chuckled. 'It is a small victory, but it may be the start of something larger. You must understand that now he has lost his aura of ... *invincibility*. Cruyff has been significantly weakened and his rivals and enemies will be ... *snapping at his heels*.'

'Well, I'm pleased that you're getting something out of it.'

'Yes, most definitely,' said Wayan Solahto. 'There is one more thing. Flush the Fozzine tablets that you did not use down the toilet. Good luck, Geoff.'

'And to you,' I said. 'Also Tom and I would like to thank ...' But once more he rang off before I could finish. 'He's made it into an art form, Tom, having the last word in these conversations. I find it very disconcerting that I always end up talking to myself.'

We had an hour before we had to leave for the airport and I gave Tom the presents that I had bought for him earlier. 'I got most of the stuff you wanted. Will you also pack these things I bought yesterday and give them to Allison? The gold chain and diver's watch are for Josh, and the necklaces, bracelets and rings are for Debra and Ally. They can sort them out.' Tom looked at me. 'I know, but it's just in case something goes wrong and I get stuck here. At least they'll know I was thinking of them.'

'Nothing will go wrong and you're only getting me to carry these because you don't want to lug them around yourself. Nonetheless, I will take them back for you, as I do appear to have a small amount of spare room.'

'Very kind of you, Tom. Now, listen. We'll drive to the airport in your Suzuki. I'll stop near the entrance and, assuming there aren't hundreds of police holding up your identikit picture, you get out and go straight into the terminal. If there are any problems, insist that you be allowed to contact the British Consulate.'

Tom nodded. 'I've heard that simple disguises are effective and I've decided to wear this hat and sunglasses.'

I snorted. 'If you wear that hat you'll be arrested straight away for a fashion offence.'

Tom looked at his battered canvas hat. 'Perhaps you're right. Well, in which case, I'll wear my baseball cap.'

On the drive to the airport Tom slouched down in the back and we hardly spoke. I stopped the Suzuki a short distance from the terminal and studied the throng of tourists and taxi drivers outside. It appeared no different to when I arrived ten days ago. There were three policemen standing talking near the entrance. I looked round and saw that Tom was watching them.

'What do you think?' I asked.

'They're always there. Okay, I'm getting out.'

Tom climbed out and heaved the pack onto his back. The policemen glanced briefly in our direction and then looked away. He walked round the front of the Suzuki to the driver's window and we shook hands.

'Good luck,' I said.

'Sure you won't change your mind?' said Tom. 'You can still get on this plane. It's not too late.'

'Christ, Tom, go!'

'All right, Geoff, take care. I'll see you in a couple of days.' Tom reached into his pocket and handed me the polished black shell he had been given by the hawker at Blue Lagoon. 'It is a present. It will bring you good luck.' He smiled and turned away and I watched him walk past the policemen into the terminal.

I drove Tom's Suzuki to the car park, put the keys under the front seat and took a taxi back to Kuta. There was still more than an hour until the plane was due to take off and I sat in a bar near the beach and waited.

At ten minutes past four my phone rang. 'The eagle has flown,' said a woman's voice.

I laughed. 'That's fantastic. Thanks for letting me know.'

'You're welcome,' said the voice.

The risky part for Tom had been getting through the passport and immigration checks at Denpasar airport and the rest of his journey should be relatively straightforward. Tonight would be my last in Bali and it was time to celebrate, but first I had to call Allison and break the bad news that it would be Tom and not me arriving home on Saturday. I wasn't looking forward to this.

'We've had a slight problem here, Ally,' I said casually, 'and Tom has used my ticket to fly back to England. No need to worry, but I'll be over here for another day or two.'

There was a pause. 'What sort of problem?'

'Nothing serious, just a small misunderstanding.'

'I know you, Geoff. What's going on?'

'It's all right, Ally, trust me. The police just want to talk to him, that's all.'

Allison snorted. 'Marilyn told me what you did to Cruyff. Are you both insane?' She became louder. 'If the police are after Tom, it's not going to be over some small misunderstanding, as you euphemistically put it. It's going to be because they want to lock him up.'

'Ally, please, it's all under control.'

There was another pause. 'He can't just use your ticket and, anyway, why won't the police stop him at the airport?'

'The battery is low,' I said. 'I think we'll get cut off at any moment.'

'Don't give me that rubbish. I'm waiting for your answer.'

'Fine, okay then. Well, Tom's used my passport, as well as my ticket, and he's left the country pretending to be me.'

'You bloody fool, have you lost your senses?' Allison yelled and I held the phone away from my ear. '*You've* used this business as an excuse for thuggery, when *you* were supposed to be the moderating influence to keep Tom in check and stop him beating up half of Bali, but Marilyn tells me that *you* planned the whole thing. And now the police are after Tom, but he's escaped and *you're* stuck there without a passport.'

'But only until tomorrow,' I said soothingly. 'The British Consulate is issuing me with a temporary one and I'm getting a flight to Singapore in the evening.'

'Hmmph, and are the police after you as well?'

'No, of course not. Honestly, there's nothing to worry about and, anyway, it was the only way that Tom could get away. Believe me, Ally, I'd much rather it was me on that flight.'

'Well, I still find it unbelievable that two grown men ...'

'Sorry, Ally, the battery really is starting to go. I'll ring you from Singapore. Lots of love, bye.'

Phew! I was glad that was over, but I thought that on the whole it went fairly smoothly. I walked back to the hotel and changed into my beige trousers and peach shirt that Tom sneered at.

That evening, I visited a large number of bars and have a hazy recollection of dancing on a table with a woman from Lancashire, falling over in the street and losing twenty pounds at poker.

CHAPTER THIRTY-ONE

A noise awoke me at eleven the following morning and I found myself lying fully clothed on my bed. I had no idea how I managed to get back to the room and half expected to find the woman from Lancashire in Tom's bed alongside me. My head was twisted at an odd angle against the bed head and I gingerly turned it to check. Apart from my backpack, Tom's bed was empty and the noise that had awoken me was repeated. Christ, someone was hammering on the door.

'All right, all right, I'm coming.'

I staggered to the door and opened it. Two policemen, with guns in holsters, stood on the verandah. The taller was middle-aged, and the other was baby-faced and much too young to be carrying a gun. I stared at them in horror. Something had gone wrong, but why hadn't Wayan Solahto warned me? My brain refused to function and I shook my head and desperately tried to clear it. I couldn't believe that they were after me so soon. But maybe it was nothing to do with Cruyff at all and was in some way connected to my drunken behaviour last night.

I gulped and cleared my throat. 'How can I help you?'

The older one held up an identikit picture of Tom. It looked more like me than him. 'You Thomas James Skellam?'

'No,' I replied, 'you have the wrong person.' I started to close the door but the older one stuck out his foot.

'Passport?' he said.

They thought I was Tom. They weren't after me at all. I started to grin foolishly.

'Where passport?' he said.

'No,' I said, 'wear clothes, not passport. Carry passport.' I laughed.

I knew immediately that I had made a serious mistake. Policemen, the world over, are not renowned for their sense of humour. You don't make fun of them, particularly when they've got guns, and especially not in a foreign country where you are implicated in a crime and don't have the passport they're asking for.

The older one's face tightened and the young one wasn't child-like any more. He pulled out his gun and pointed it at my chest. My legs lost their strength and I back-pedalled out of control until I came up against the bed. I flopped on to it with my legs flailing in the air. They followed me inside and the young one gestured with his gun for me to stand by the wall. I leant against it for support, and I raised my hands and put them on my head. My breath came in short gasps.

'Please don't shoot me.'

'Where passport?' asked the older one.

'I don't know. It's missing. I can't find it.'

He stared at me. 'We look,' he said and I nodded my permission, although it was not a question.

He emptied my packs on to Tom's bed and rummaged through the contents. He checked the drawers of the bedside cupboard and inside the wardrobe, while the child cop kept his gun trained on my chest.

'No passport,' stated the older one. 'Show me pockets.'

I lowered my hands and removed my wallet, some loose change and the car keys. I felt calmer and my breathing was back to normal. I reasoned that if they intended shooting me they would have done it by now. He inspected the contents of my wallet and compared my British driving licence with the International Driving Permit he'd taken from my daypack.

'You Jepprey John Larkham?'

'Yes.'

'You no have passport.'

'I told you, I've lost it, or else it's been stolen. I have to report it to the British Consulate. Please let me ring them.' I pointed to the mobile phone on the bedside cupboard.

The older one shook his head and picked up the car keys. 'You car?' he said, gesturing at the Suzuki parked outside.

'Yes, mine ... rented.'

'I look.'

For five minutes I leant against the wall and tried not to stare at the gun. I couldn't work out where this was leading. As far as they were concerned, my only crime was not to have a passport and that would be rectified this afternoon at the British Consulate. I started to feel more secure.

The older one came back into the room and stood close to me, after making sure that he did not block his colleague's aim. 'No passport in car.'

'No,' I agreed, 'I've already looked.'

'Papers for car,' he said, holding up the rental contract that he'd taken from the glove compartment.

'Yes, that's the agreement.'

He read from it. 'Papers in name Thomas James Skellam, rented Padangbai.'

Oh God! I'd forgotten that the car was in Tom's name. Oh Christ!

'Yes, he let me use it.'

'You friend?'

I nodded.

'Where is he?' demanded the young one, who spoke for the first time.

'I'm sorry. I don't know. He went off.'

The older one looked under the beds and checked the bathroom and wardrobe again. Then he stuffed everything back into the packs.

'You come with us.'

'Please let me ring the British Consulate.'

The older one shook his head and put my mobile phone in his pocket.

'I am a British subject and it is my right to contact the British Consulate.'

The young one shouted at me in Indonesian. He waved his left hand in the direction of the door and pointed his gun in my face. I placed my hands back on my head and again heard the rasp of my breathing.

I walked in front of them to their car. They threw my packs in the boot and drove me to the police headquarters in Denpasar where I was handed over to the duty officer. He recorded my details in a ledger before taking me to a small office where I was photographed and fingerprinted by an unsmiling policewoman. Afterwards, she took me to a small interview room.

I waited there for nearly two hours before the older policeman came in. He was accompanied by a stocky man carrying a manila file. I assumed that the child cop had gone back to school.

'You are Geoffrey John Larkham?' asked the stocky one, without introducing himself.

'Yes, I am.'

'Where is your passport and plane ticket?'

Oh God, they're asking about the ticket. 'I don't know. They're lost or stolen.'

'When did you last have them?'

I thought for a moment. 'About two days ago, I think.'

'Have you reported them missing?'

'Not yet. I was going to today.'

'When did you discover that you did not have them?'

I paused and at that point I began to see the weaknesses in my story. 'Yesterday,' I said.

'What time?'

'I'm not sure.'

'Why didn't you go to the airport yesterday to catch your 4 pm flight?'

I shook my head.

'Because, Mr Larkham, you had already given your ticket and passport to someone else, so that they could get on the plane in your place. That person was your friend, Thomas Skellam, who is wanted by us on serious charges.'

I shook my head again. 'I didn't let anyone use them. I've done nothing wrong and I want to speak to the British Consulate.'

'You are lying,' he said. 'Fifteen minutes ago a charming lady rang your mobile phone with a message. She said that the eagle has landed. I assume that was your friend arriving at Heathrow Airport.'

I stared at him without replying.

'Where is your friend, if he didn't leave on that flight?'

'I don't know. He went off.'

'When did you last see him?'

'I'm not answering any more questions until I talk to the British Consulate.'

He stood up. 'You are in serious trouble, Mr Larkham. It will help you if you cooperate with us. I will give you time to think about it.'

'Please let me ring the British Consulate.'

He ignored me and walked out of the room.

The one who'd arrested me was enjoying himself. 'You in deep shit,' he said. 'Not laugh now.'

'I'm sorry,' I said, 'I didn't mean to laugh earlier.'

'You more sorry soon.'

What were they going to do to me? No one even knew I was here. Oh, shit. Oh God. Oh, Ally, help me.

I was put in a dimly-lit underground cell. There was no furniture and in one corner was a plastic bucket with a tap and a grating alongside. The overpowering stench of rancid sweat and faeces immediately made me retch. Twelve men squatted against the walls of the cell. All were Indonesian. They wore filthy shorts or sarongs and were bare-chested and emaciated. They stared at me before clustering around, but not one of them spoke a word of English. They quickly tired of me and returned to squatting against the walls.

I spent five hours in the cell and listened to men hawk and spit on the floor, urinate and defecate into the bucket, and moan and rant. I refused a bowl of rice and drank once from the tap. Occasionally, I lay on the floor and dozed, but for the most part I squatted against the wall like the other inmates, with my mind turned inwards and everything shut down except my vital functions. At one point I felt someone attempt to undo my watchstrap. I bellowed and a figure crawled away. Later, I discovered that my shoes had been stolen and one of my socks was missing.

CHAPTER THIRTY-TWO

At seven-thirty on Saturday evening two guards came and led me, stumbling, up a single flight of steps to an empty cell. They pushed me inside and closed the door. The walls and floor were bare concrete, and there was a table and two chairs.

Dear God, this is it. I began to shake and my fear was so acute that I vomited down the front of my shirt. My beige trousers and peach shirt were streaked black from the cell floor and the sock on my left foot was vile.

After five minutes, the door opened and Graham Richardson walked in. He stared at me and instinctively took a step back. 'My dear chap, I am so terribly sorry. Are you all right?'

I nodded. I didn't trust myself to speak.

He studied me for several seconds, shaking his head and tutting. 'I will get you moved immediately. Are you sure you're all right?'

I nodded again. 'Yes, I'm okay.'

'Good.' He went to the door. 'Just wait a moment.'

'I don't think I'll be going anywhere,' I mumbled.

Graham Richardson turned round and smiled. 'That's the spirit,' he said. 'Sorry, it was a silly thing to say.'

He went outside and there was a short conversation in Indonesian. I heard footsteps retreat down the passage and after ten minutes they returned. Graham Richardson came back into the cell.

'Geoff, I have arranged for you to be taken somewhere more salubrious where you can clean up and get changed. There will be antibiotics there and I strongly advise you to take them. I will come and see you later this evening, but first I have some calls to make.'

'What about the interrogation?' I asked.

'There won't be an interrogation and no one will even talk to you unless I am present.'

'Thank you, Graham. That's what I was worried about.'

I was not surprised that he didn't offer his hand. Mine were caked with filth and streaked with drying vomit.

Half an hour later, two guards escorted me to the rear of the building and into the back of a closed van. They drove me to what I now know is a low-security prison on the outskirts of Denpasar. I was taken to a small room that was furnished with a single bed, two chairs and a table, and there was a tiny bathroom leading from it. It was uncannily similar to the hotel room in Kuta.

I washed my hair twice and stood in the shower scrubbing my body for ten minutes before I was able to remove all traces of the cell. The horrors of the day started to recede.

Graham Richardson knocked on the door and came in. He looked at both the room and me approvingly. 'That's better,' he said. 'You shouldn't have been in that cell. I can't understand why they put you there.'

I knew why. I pictured the look on the policeman's face when he said that I would be sorry for laughing at him. 'This is a thousand times better, Graham. I don't know how to thank you.'

'My dear boy, don't mention it. When you didn't contact the consulate this afternoon I started making inquiries. I came as soon as I found out from Wayan Solahto that you'd been arrested.'

'I'm so very glad you did, Graham. I would have died if I'd spent any longer in there.'

'Just think of it as a bad dream.' He looked around the room. 'It's not bugged, so we can talk. Incidentally, you'll be staying here until we can get you back to England. It's not too awful and it costs about the same as the hotels in Kuta.'

'I have to pay to stay in prison?' I asked.

'There is the alternative.'

'Right,' I said hastily, 'I'll pay.'

'And, if you've got money, the guards will bring in little extras like beer and cigarettes, so you'll live quite well. Also, you are classed as a low-risk prisoner, which means that you will be able to use their public phone at designated times, but, of course, you can't go outside. It'll be like staying at an English bed and breakfast on a wet weekend. In fact, better, because you won't have to look at floral wallpaper and eat greasy sausages.'

I smiled for the first time in a long time. 'So you think I might not want to leave?'

'No, you'll get tired of rice and yearn for roast lamb,' said Graham Richardson. 'By the way, Tom arrived safely and I've spoken to your wife.'

'What did you tell Allison,' I asked, 'and how did she take it?'

'I said that the police are holding you while they conduct further inquiries, and that you are safe and well and there is no cause for worry. She took it very calmly and said that she would come out on the first flight.'

I felt a lump in my throat. Oh Ally, how much I love you.

'However,' continued Graham Richardson, 'I told her that there was no point in coming over at this early stage and I was optimistic that the matter could be resolved fairly quickly.'

The thought of Allison being here had lifted my spirits and now I felt deflated. 'How quickly?' I asked.

'It depends on a lot of factors and I will tell you what I have found out in the last couple of hours. I have spoken with Made Tokarno, the police officer in charge of your case, and I have subsequently obtained an opinion from our legal advisers. There are two separate areas of inquiry being conducted by Made Tokarno. The first relates to the fact that Tom left Indonesia illegally using your flight ticket and passport. If the police can prove that you knowingly allowed him to use your documents, then you will be charged with collusion in a criminal act. The corollary to this is that you aided and abetted a person who is wanted by the police to escape capture, and you will also be charged with that offence.'

'They sound serious.'

'Yes, but they are difficult to prove,' replied Graham Richardson. 'Your story is that you and Tom had a row and he went off in a huff. You discovered later that your ticket and passport were missing and you strongly suspected he had taken them. You didn't want to get Tom into trouble, so you didn't report the loss and, anyway, you assumed he would return them to you. Because you wanted to extend your stay in Bali, the loss of your ticket didn't really bother you. It would involve you in the additional expense of purchasing another ticket, but that was not a major issue. You had no reason to believe that Tom had taken your passport and ticket for any purpose other than to play a nasty trick, and you had absolutely no idea that he would use them illegally.'

'You've got me convinced,' I said.

Graham Richardson smiled. 'Now, the charge of aiding and abetting Tom to escape presupposes that Tom knew a warrant had been issued for his arrest and that he conveyed this information to you. Of course, he should have been completely unaware that he was a wanted man and the police will never find out that he received the information from Wayan Solahto. So, any police action against you would probably fail due to the absence of proof that you knew there was a warrant for Tom's arrest. Even if the prosecutors were to consider that there is enough circumstantial evidence to justify proceeding with either matter, I am sure the judiciary would give you the option of paying a hefty fine out of court rather than risk the expense of going to trial, due to the uncertainty of obtaining a conviction.'

'So, I should get out of here quite soon?'

'If it were just those two issues then I'd say yes, but there is the drugging, assault and kidnapping of Pieter Cruyff to contend with. He is incensed that Tom appears to have escaped with your assistance and he assumes that you also helped Tom with his abduction. The police have discovered that you stayed in the same hotel and you both vacated your rooms that night. This, combined with the fact that Tom used your ticket and passport to leave Bali, strongly indicates that you are involved.'

'What happens now?'

'Under Indonesian law you can be held for a maximum of sixty days without charge while the police conduct their investigation and try to build a case against you. The police don't believe that Tom could have carried out the operation to get his wife away without help from the locals, both inside and outside Paradise Padang. Therefore, they'll be interviewing a lot of people around Padangbai and that could take weeks.'

I thought of Wayan at the hotel, his brother Nyoman with the outrigger, and Kadek and Made inside Paradise Padang.

Graham Richardson saw the expression on my face. 'It's not too bad here, Geoff. You can do lots of reading and write your memoirs or something.'

'No, it's not that, Graham. I was thinking about the people who helped us and the trouble they'll get into.'

'I wouldn't worry too much, Geoff. The local police are sure to be on their side and won't try very hard.'

'I hope so, but if they really start digging they'll find a trail the size of a motorway. They can trace the calls on my mobile phone and there's a piece of paper in my wallet with lots of suspicious phone numbers on it.' I groaned. 'They'll link me to Wayan Solahto and he'll be involved.'

'Have you ever rung Wayan?'

I thought for a moment. 'No, he's always called us.'

'They will never trace those,' said Graham Richardson. 'What other phone calls could be embarrassing?'

I reeled off what I could think of. 'Murray in Amed, Marilyn's airline, Laurie rang me from Lombok, Marilyn had my phone and rang Tom at the hotel.' I stopped and considered the implications. 'But, of course, all of those could have a perfectly innocent explanation.'

'Exactly,' he agreed, 'and what about the phone numbers you wrote down?'

'Well, there's Murray's, and an incomplete number to contact Wayan Solahto, and your card, of course. There's the hotel in Kuta where Darren and Laurie were staying, and that's about it.'

'Once again, they don't mean very much,' said Graham Richardson. 'Now, as I see it, there is a wealth of circumstantial evidence against you. However, unless a witness comes forward and gives the police firm evidence of your involvement, I don't think that there will be enough to formally charge you. Your mug shots were emailed to Cruyff, but fortunately he wasn't able to identify you. In fact, he appears to have confused you with an Australian fellow, but he doesn't have much recollection of events after Tom walloped him.'

I started to tell him what happened, but he stopped me. 'No, I'd rather not know, Geoff. I fear that I know too much already.'

'Sorry, I forgot I was talking to the British Vice Consul.'

He smiled. 'Your greatest threat is that Cruyff might be able to persuade someone to talk. He is conducting his own inquiries, and if he throws enough money around and gives assurances of immunity then a witness may be found.'

I wondered whether Wayan at the hotel would give evidence against me if Cruyff offered enough money. If so, I would be spending a long time in a Balinese jail.

'What do you think his chances are?' I asked.

He shrugged. 'I don't know. Money talks in Bali, particularly the large amounts that Cruyff has. But your good friend, Wayan Solahto, is running interference for you, and at this moment he is busy pulling strings. He's taken a liking to you, Geoff. He calls you the reluctant hero.'

'Reluctant is right, but I don't know about hero. I have never been so scared in all my life as I was in the police cells. By the way, Graham,' I said, 'I meant to ask you how the police got on to us at the hotel in Kuta.'

'Good luck, mainly. They couldn't find a record of Tom at any hotel, so they checked all new registrations for Wednesday and Thursday and yours stood out because it was done in the middle of the night. The policemen were just following up the lead, and if you'd been able to show them your passport they would probably have gone away happy. But once they started searching and found the car-hire agreement in Tom's name, then you were in trouble. Incidentally, why was it in his name?'

'Tom did it so that if things went wrong I wouldn't be implicated. But, in the end, it had the opposite effect. It's always the little things that trip you up.'

'Yes, that's true with most situations in life. Well, I must go now,' said Graham Richardson, 'but I'll call in tomorrow to keep you posted. Oh, I nearly forgot, I've brought you a packet of biscuits.'

'Are they chocolate digestive, by any chance?' I asked.

'Yes, as a matter of fact they are. How on earth did you guess?'

'Oh, just that they're my favourites.'

'Mine too,' said Graham Richardson and his lips twitched.

CHAPTER THIRTY-THREE

At 10.30am on Sunday, back in England, Tom, Marilyn and Allison sat around the dining-room table at our home, while Debra, Josh, Kate and Gemma watched a DVD in the lounge.

'It's not your fault,' said Allison, 'so stop blaming yourself. Geoff made the decision and he knew the risks.'

'But it should be *me* in jail,' said Tom.

'Well it isn't and we're wasting time talking about it. Now, what can we do to help him?'

'Tom and I can't go back,' said Marilyn. 'You've got to go and we'll look after Debra and Josh. They can stay with us as long as you want.'

'Thanks,' said Allison, 'I'm thinking about going, but Graham Richardson says there's absolutely nothing I can do in Bali, and he and your friend, Wayan Solahto, are already trying everything possible to have Geoff released. So, realistically, all I could do is give Geoff moral support and that won't get him out of jail.'

'Then, what did you mean?' asked Marilyn.

'Well, when I spoke to Graham Richardson yesterday he said that the police haven't got enough evidence at this stage to lay charges, but Cruyff is carrying out his own investigation and is offering money and immunity for witnesses to come forward.'

'If Cruyff is making enquiries locally, then he's bound to discover the link between Wayan at our hotel and

Kadek and Made inside Paradise Padang,' said Tom. 'I wonder how much money it would take for one of them to talk.'

'So it's only a question of time before someone comes forward?' Allison said.

'Probably, and if Cruyff pokes around for long enough he'll find evidence to connect Darren and Laurie.'

'Right,' interrupted Marilyn, 'so what *does* it need for the charges to be dropped?'

'The only thing I can think of,' said Tom, 'is if Cruyff withdraws his complaint.'

'But why would he do that?' asked Allison.

'I could go over there and give myself up in exchange for them letting Geoff go.'

No one said anything for a few moments. Then Allison shook her head. 'Let's try and think of something else.' She looked at Marilyn. 'I know you're not going to like this, but could you ring him up and simply ask him if he'll drop the complaint? Appeal to his better nature or something.'

'He doesn't have one, Ally, and also he'll be feeling very vindictive towards me at the moment.'

'Yes, but getting Geoff locked up isn't going to bring you back and Geoff's not a major player in this, just Tom's friend who got involved.'

'Well,' said Marilyn, 'I could try, but I think that he badly wants someone to pay for what happened and Geoff is the only one he can get his hands on.'

'All right,' said Tom, 'if you ring him up and he says no, what do we do then? Marilyn, what did you learn about him when you were there? Is there any way that we can force him to drop the complaint? There must be something we can threaten him with.'

'Blackmail, in other words,' said Marilyn with a smile. 'Now you're going to add that to your long list of crimes.'

'Well,' said Tom, 'having gone this far it seems a shame to stop. I mean, after you've drugged, assaulted and abducted someone, what's a trivial thing like blackmail?'

'So, what nasty secrets did you find out while you were there, Marilyn?' asked Allison.

'That he's involved with drug syndicates and money laundering.'

'Is that true?'

'Yes, but everyone knows that already, according to Wayan Solahto and Graham Richardson,' Tom pointed out. 'So, unless you've got some proof, that's not likely to help much.'

'Perhaps you're right,' agreed Marilyn, 'but one evening a couple of drug barons and their entourage came on board the yacht and we had cocktails at sunset, and that was supposed to be top secret.'

'You were there,' asked Allison, 'on the yacht?'

'Yes, I was one of the ornaments.'

'So, you could tell the police about him entertaining drug barons?' suggested Allison.

'Even if they believed her,' said Tom, 'what does it prove? Only that he doesn't choose his friends very wisely.'

'They'd have to believe me,' said Marilyn, 'because I've got photographs of them.'

Tom and Allison stared at her.

'How did you get those?' asked Tom.

'I took them with the camera Pieter gave me. Everyone was up the front of the boat speaking Indonesian and I got bored, so I sat at the back of the boat and shot off a few photos. They're mostly of the coastline and the sunset but the people on the boat are in some of them. I'm pretty sure Pieter didn't know I took those.'

'I bet he didn't,' said Tom. 'Where are the photos?'

'In the camera,' said Marilyn, 'I'll go home and get it.'

Fifteen minutes later Marilyn came back with the camera and Tom looked at the pictures.

'That's Cruyff,' he said, 'on the left. Who's the guy with his arm round him?'

'Nyoman something or another,' said Marilyn. 'He's supposed to be the top drug man in Bali, and the one next to him is his boss. He comes from Jakarta and runs all of Indonesia. The other one is his bodyguard.'

Tom changed to the next picture. 'Who are the girls?'

'I don't know. They were hired for the trip.'

He zoomed in. 'One of them hasn't got any clothes on.'

'Yes,' said Marilyn, 'they all ended up like that. And before either of you ask,' she added, 'I didn't.'

There were four photographs that clearly showed Cruyff with the drug chiefs and their associates. Tom passed the camera to Allison.

'He might not want these pictures to get around,' she said after she'd looked at them, 'but what do they really show?'

'Well, they might not prove he's a criminal,' conceded Tom, 'but you're right when you say he wouldn't want them to get around. You see, according to Graham Richardson, Cruyff is a social climber who gets invited to embassy functions and high-society garden parties and suchlike. Graham has met him a couple of times.'

'Why does he get invited if he's known to have links with organised crime?' asked Allison.

'Because nothing has ever been proven, Ally,' said Marilyn. 'It's just one of those delicious rumours that makes him exciting and a bit dangerous.'

'Well, that would all change if these pictures were published in the *Jakarta Times*,' Tom said. 'It would no longer be a delicious rumour, but a hard fact. Cruyff's reputation would be totally shot to pieces and I think his drug buddies would be very, very pissed off with him that he's allowed photos to be taken while they were on his yacht, especially the one where they're cavorting with a naked woman. You don't do that sort of thing in Muslim countries, or at least you don't get caught on camera doing it.'

'Then, these pictures could be crucial,' said Allison, 'but how do we use them?'

'We email them to Wayan Solahto and he'll know exactly what to do with them,' said Tom. 'We need his address from Graham Richardson.'

'I'll talk to Geoff first,' said Allison. 'He should ring around lunchtime and he might know something we don't.'

I rang Allison at 7 pm Bali time. It was the first time we'd spoken since my arrest.

'Are you all right, Geoff? How are they treating you? Are you eating okay?'

'Everything's fine, Ally,' I assured her. 'Honestly, I've stayed in worse hotels in England. The food's reasonable but you don't get much variety. It's either rice with a few vegies mixed in, or noodles with a few vegies mixed in, and it all tastes the same. When I get home don't make a stir-fry for a few months, will you?'

'All right, I promise. Now listen, I need to talk to you about something important.'

'Right, I'm listening, but I don't know how secure this line is, so you'd better be ... *circumspect.*' Circumspect? God, Tom was right. I am starting to sound like Wayan Solahto.

'I'll talk in riddles.'

'Don't do that. I won't understand what you're on about.'

Allison paused for a moment. 'Marilyn has some holiday snaps of our mutual friend with his pharmaceutical colleagues, not quite but almost *in flagrante delicto*. Are you with me so far?'

'I think so.'

'Good. Well, if these snaps were to get into the right hands they would be powerful leverage.'

'Ah ... I see. Exactly how much leverage, do you think?'

'A great deal,' said Allison.

'That could be very useful.'

'Yes, especially if our friend could find it in himself to drop the completely false allegations against you. I'll repeat that for the tape, *completely false allegations against you.*'

'For God's sake, Ally, don't make jokes. They get you into terrible trouble over here.'

'All right, no more jokes,' Allison said. 'Geoff, you sounded really odd then. Are you sure you're okay?'

'Yes, it's just that the Balinese police don't have a great sense of humour.'

'Right, I'll bear that in mind. Now, Graham Richardson thinks that the police charges relating to the passport and plane ticket won't proceed due to lack of evidence, or alternatively can be disposed of by paying a fine.'

'That's what he told me.'

'Are you sure he knows what he's doing? Half the time he sounds like Bertie Wooster.'

'Don't be fooled by that, Ally. There's no one I'd rather have on my side right now.'

'All right, Geoff, you know him. Well, I need to email these holiday snaps to the person who can make best use of them.'

'Send them to Graham Richardson. He'll get them to the right person, and you need to move fast before our friend finds some witnesses.'

'I'll email them right now.'

'Love you,' I said, 'and Allison ...'

'Yes?'

'You're very clever.'

'I know,' she acknowledged, 'although it was Tom who saw the implications. And, Geoff, I do think that if I'd gone over to help Tom, instead of you, it wouldn't be such a mess.'

There was no answer to that.

I rang Graham Richardson and told him that Allison was emailing him some pictures that could prove interesting, and I would like to talk to him once he'd looked at them.

Graham Richardson arrived an hour later. He straightaway closed the door and handed me an envelope from his briefcase. I pulled out Marilyn's photographs and looked at them eagerly. 'They don't seem very much,' I said, 'just a naughty romp on Cruyff's boat.'

'That's because you don't know who the people are,' said Graham Richardson. 'These photographs are dynamite, because they show conclusively that Cruyff is associated with a major drug cartel which operates out of Indonesia. That man,' he pointed at the top picture, 'is the head of the organisation and the one next to him runs the Bali operation. If these were printed, it would be disastrous for Cruyff's reputation and the authorities would be compelled to investigate his business dealings. He'd receive a huge amount of unwanted attention and, worse, his drug partners would be extremely upset with him. I'd say that Cruyff will do just about anything to suppress these pictures.'

I looked up and closed my eyes. 'Thank you, God,' I murmured.

'I always thought that God was on your side,' Graham said smiling, 'but, even so, it was very careless of Cruyff to let Tom's wife take these photographs.'

'Very,' I agreed, 'but then he wasn't expecting her to run off and use them against him.'

'True. But, still, he must be getting soft.'

'Well, he didn't seem very tough when I met him, although he was a bit under the weather.' We smiled. 'Graham, I assume that Wayan Solahto is the best person to make use of these?'

'Yes, he will know exactly what to do. I have already spoken to Wayan and, with your permission, I will email them to him.'

'Thanks, Graham, and as soon as possible please, before Cruyff finds a witness to take his money. It's not too bad in here, but I'm starting to miss my family.'

From that moment, events moved swiftly. Late on Monday afternoon Cruyff formally withdrew all allegations against Tom and me. The police were prepared to believe that I hadn't given Tom permission to use my passport and plane ticket and they weren't going to proceed with any charges. I later learnt that I had Wayan Solahto to thank for this. He had pulled some of his many strings and I was now a free man.

Graham Richardson supplied me with a temporary passport and, as a result of some high-level diplomacy, I was allocated Tom's seat on the 12.30 am Tuesday flight. Murray rang as I was packing.

'Graham and Wayan gave me daily bulletins,' he said, 'but I wish I could have been more involved, instead of stuck up here in Amed.'

'Your help was crucial, Murray. Without your two friends we wouldn't have got anywhere.'

'Well, it's the most exciting thing that's happened round here for years, and I'm pleased you won't be spending the next five years in Denpasar jail.'

'Not as pleased as I am.'

'I'm coming to London for a couple of weeks in September, so how about we have dinner and you and Tom can tell me the whole story?'

'I'll really look forward to that,' I said.

At 9.30 pm I said goodbye to Graham Richardson outside the British Consulate.

'Graham,' I said, 'you saved my life on Saturday and I'll never forget it.'

'It was my pleasure. It's nice to do something other than bail out lager louts. I felt I was being useful for a change.' He looked at me shrewdly. 'You never did tell me why you ended up in that filthy holding cell and not the place they put the tourists.'

'I made a joke,' I said, 'a bad joke.'

'Ah well, they can be taken the wrong way sometimes. My mother used to say that it was best not to make a joke until you'd known the person at least ten years. Jolly sound advice as well.'

'I'll remember it,' I said.

He walked with me to the taxi; I thanked him again and we shook hands. The driver put my pack in the boot and, as I climbed in the back, it occurred to me that he looked familiar.

'Geoff,' said Wayan Solahto from the front seat, 'what a happy coincidence.'

'Wayan,' I cried, 'I thought you'd disappeared into your shadowy world, and I wouldn't see you to say goodbye and thank you for everything you've done for us.'

He smiled. 'It turned out to be a very profitable ... *collaboration* for me as well. The photographs spell the demise of Pieter Cruyff in Indonesia and his empire will disintegrate rapidly. I am contemplating how to use them to best effect, but there is no immediate rush. Their ... *efficacy* will not diminish in the short term. For the moment, though, all I have asked Cruyff to do is officially withdraw his complaints against you both and to deliver Tom's family's possessions to the British Consulate.'

'I'd forgotten about the things they left behind. That was very thoughtful of you, Wayan.' I pictured the jumbled collection that Tom and I had bought in Candidasa. 'They'll be delighted to get their stuff back.'

'However, there is one outstanding matter,' said Wayan Solahto, 'and that is the charge against Tom for departing illegally using your passport and ticket. Of course, in the overall scheme of things, it is a relatively minor offence and unimportant so long as he does not visit Indonesia again. However, I am using some influence to have the matter dismissed, as it would be nice for him to visit Bali simply as a tourist and not as someone embarking on general ... *mayhem.*'

'Yes, he's got a knack for mayhem,' I agreed and we laughed. 'Wayan, I'd like to know just how close the police and Cruyff got to proving a case against me?'

'Close enough,' replied Wayan. 'The clerk at the port confirmed that you bought a ticket for the 9.30 pm. ferry. You obviously didn't use it because you checked into the hotel in Kuta at 12.30 am. Cruyff and two men with surfboards were seen getting out of the Suzuki at the port, but the witness didn't see the driver and was unable to identify you. Forensic officers spent hours trying to get your fingerprints from Cruyff's BMW, but were unsuccessful. You did drive it, didn't you?'

I recalled the traumatic drive up the track to Blue Lagoon. 'Yes, but I wore rubber gloves so that I didn't leave any dabs.'

'*Dabs*,' said Wayan Solahto. 'What an interesting word.'

I expected him to write it down, but he didn't.

He carried on. 'Your friend at the hotel, and the other people who helped you, did not ... *succumb* to Cruyff's offer of a reward, but if he'd increased it enough someone may have been tempted. Most of the evidence against you was circumstantial, but it might still have been sufficient to obtain a conviction, and in any event you would have ... *languished* in prison for weeks while the investigation continued.'

'Thank God for those photographs,' I said. 'By the way, Wayan, did anything happen to the check-in and immigration people who let Tom through at the airport?'

'They fall within the jurisdiction of my department,' said Wayan with a smile, 'and they were severely reprimanded for such remarkable laxness. Within twelve months they will be forgiven and receive promotions.'

I smiled. 'I'm glad you were with us and not against us, Wayan.'

'So am I,' he said.

We had reached the airport and Wayan's driver, Gede, got out to fetch my pack from the boot.

'Is there any chance that you will come again to Bali?' Wayan asked.

'Definitely. It's a tremendous place and I'll bring my family.'

'Excellent,' said Wayan, 'I am glad that you have not been put off by the discomfort you ... *endured* while you were incarcerated. And when you do come again I would like you to meet my family. They are very interested in the two crazy Englishmen.' He laughed. 'I must go. Good luck, Geoff.'

I started to reply, but the taxi pulled away and again I was talking to myself. I watched the tail lights recede and grinned. Wayan Solahto, my friend, the next time we meet I'll be ready and definitely have the last word.

CHAPTER THIRTY-FOUR

It seemed like the whole world had come to meet me at Heathrow Airport. Allison, Joshua and Debra; Marilyn, Tom, Kate and Gemma; my parents had come from the golf course; and Mr and Mrs McTavish were there, with Rory at the front of the group, dressed in a kilt.

I was engulfed with hugs, kisses and handshakes which I returned indiscriminately. I kissed my mother's elbow, Tom's ear and Marilyn's nose. My hand was pulverised by Rory McTavish while I kissed Allison over his shoulder, and I held Debra and Josh in a one-handed embrace as Marilyn left lipstick on my shirt. Tom's customary bear hug made me sag at the knees and my father's slap on the back nearly knocked me to the floor. It was wonderful to be back.

Then came the moment I was dreading. Rory McTavish stood squarely in front of me. 'Yer wee noo abracken skoll arsering, Geoffrey.' His spittle flew at my face and I jerked my head back. 'Aye yon sproggen anoo fok grinner knobwrench. Och bonnie rectum and spunk goblin, mon.'

'Would you mind saying that again?' I asked and looked desperately at Marilyn and Tom, who had covered their mouths with their hands.

Rory McTavish repeated the sounds, which were accompanied by globules of spit projected in short explosive bursts and punctuated by loud thwacks from his false teeth. I remembered Tom had said that when Rory McTavish became agitated and his teeth were clacking and there was spit flying around, he was either talking about the British government or David Beckham. It seemed unlikely he'd be discussing Beckham now, so I assumed he was probably commenting on the help I'd had from the British Consulate. Oh well, here goes.

'Yes,' I said gamely, 'after paying my taxes all these years it's good to get something in return.'

His eyes narrowed and he curled his upper lip, as though I had just confirmed an earlier opinion. 'Aye, sphincter strakken and anal infarction yer grit gosvomit,' he spat.

Out of the corner of my eye, I saw Marilyn and Tom holding onto each other and weeping with laughter.

'That's the last time I risk my life to save you two,' I hissed.

I pleaded tiredness after the long flight and finally was allowed to leave with Allison, Debra and Josh. I was keen to be alone with them and later discover Allison's red and lacy surprise that she had promised she would be wearing. She caught me looking at the front of her blouse and smiled.

'Roast lamb,' I said, pushing away my plate. 'You have no idea how wonderful that tasted.'

'Graham Richardson made me promise to cook it this evening. He said you would really appreciate it after the prison diet of rice and noodles.'

'Were you honestly in jail, Dad?' asked Josh.

'Yes, but not for long and I was never charged, I was just helping the police with their enquiries.'

'That's what they all say,' said Josh.

'Was it horrible?' asked Debra.

'It wasn't too bad on the whole,' I said. 'The worst thing about it was that I wasn't free to go outside and my only view of the world was a small square of sky through a high-up window. When Oscar Wilde was in prison, he referred to it as a little tent of blue that prisoners call the sky.'

Debra thought about it. 'I suppose it would seem like that,' she said, 'but why *is* the sky always blue?'

'Perhaps because it's unhappy,' suggested Allison, 'and when it rains it's crying.'

'Ha ha,' said Debra, 'very funny, Mum. But really, why is it blue?'

'It's not always blue,' I pointed out. 'Sunsets turn it red and at night it's black.'

'During the day it's blue, though,' said Debra.

'It's something to do with tiny particles in the atmosphere that make the sky look blue.'

Josh decided to join in. 'But why blue? Why not brown?'

'Well,' I said, 'it's just the way it's worked out. That combination of particles makes the colour blue.'

'But why?'

I picked an orange out of the bowl on the table. 'That's like asking why this is called an orange. It's called an orange because that's its name.'

'An orange is called an orange because it is orange,' said Josh. 'If it was pink, it wouldn't be called an orange.'

'Good point,' I said and saw that Allison was laughing into her serviette. God, I was out of practice. Two weeks away and Josh was running rings round me.

Debra and Josh had gone to bed and I was sitting in the lounge feeling mellow and very happy to be home. Allison went to the sideboard and poured two glasses of port.

'Well, I've got a bit of jet lag, so I think I'll have an early night.' I yawned theatrically and looked pointedly at Allison.

'Good idea,' she said. 'I'll stay up and do some ironing.'

'No you won't,' I said. 'I've been waiting patiently all evening to see the present you're wearing.'

'Present, what present?'

'Come on, Ally, I've just got out of prison.'

'Oh, you must mean these,' she said softly and began to unbutton her blouse. She eased it from her shoulders and let it fall to the floor behind her.

I groaned.

Allison smiled faintly and stepped out of her skirt. 'The silk is Italian, the lace is French and the colour is cerise. When I turn round, you will see that the panties are a G-string.' Allison revolved slowly.

'Oh God!' I moaned.

'Is there anything else you want to know about your present?'

'No, not at the moment thanks, Ally, but will you do me a favour?'

'Yes, I should think so. What is it?'

'Darling, will you take your bra off and crawl towards me on all fours? Then, when you reach me, stick your finger in my mouth.'

'Your mouth?'

'Yes, darling. I'll explain as we go along.'

I decided to go to work in the morning to check my desk. I had been due back on Monday, but when the Balinese police arrested me Allison rang the office and told them that I would be away for another week.

Summer had retreated and the morning was cool. I hoped it was somewhere distant, regrouping, and that

August would be hot. I had come to enjoy the heat of Bali.

I arrived at Oakover junction and Tom was waiting for me. 'I thought you might go in today,' he said.

'Only for the morning, and just to see if anything urgent needs doing, otherwise I'll spend the rest of the week thinking about it. Anyway, what are you doing here? I thought you weren't going in until Monday.'

'I wasn't, but I need to talk to Simon about my future with the company, and I wanted to see you to find out what happened after I left Bali.'

As we walked to the station, I told Tom how I was arrested in the hotel room and about the time I spent in jail.

'It was really rough, then?' he said when I'd finished.

'The first few hours in jail were the worst of my life and something I never ever want to go through again.'

'I probably won't be able to repay you,' said Tom, 'but I'll be eternally grateful.'

'Not grateful enough to save me from Rory McTavish yesterday,' I pointed out.

'He hasn't got any easier to understand, has he?' grinned Tom. 'But I thought you handled it pretty well.'

'Jesus, Tom, you know full well I didn't have a clue what he was talking about and just took a wild guess. But Marilyn must understand him. I mean, she's his daughter, after all. What did he say, do you know?'

'He welcomed you home and thanked you for helping Marilyn, or words to that effect.'

'So, my reply about getting some benefit from my income tax didn't make much sense?'

'Not a lot,' agreed Tom.

'And what did he say after that?'

'You're better off not knowing.'

'Fine, it suits me.' I changed the subject. 'I know it's early days, Tom, but how are things between you and Marilyn? Everything still okay?'

'Great,' said Tom, 'it's been really good. But she experienced something pretty exotic when she was in Bali and I wonder if she'll stay happy with the routine of suburban life.'

'They say that once you've tasted caviar you're never again content with lumpfish.'

'Are you calling me a lumpfish?'

'Of course not, Tom. I was talking figuratively, by comparing caviar to the roe of the lumpfish.'

'I think you could have chosen your metaphor better.'

'No offence intended, Tom.'

'Hmm. Well, I was going to say that she and Ally have been working on some business project and it's giving them a real buzz.'

'I don't know anything about that.'

'I don't know much either. They're pretty secretive about it and, as Wayan Solahto would say, it's in the ... *embryonic* stage.'

We laughed and rounded the corner. The station building loomed in front of us. The brickwork was cracked and the once-white paintwork grimy with dust and traffic fumes. We became silent and our pace slowed until, finally, we stopped at the foot of the steps. I stared up at the building with a gradually dawning knowledge and I looked at Tom in horror.

'I can't do this any more.'

'I never could,' said Tom. 'What are we going to do?'

'I don't know, but we'll think of something,' I said and we turned around.

THE END